# CALLIE'S HONOR

## KATHLEEN LAWLESS

ISBN print: 978-1-989873-32-8

**Praise for Kathleen Lawless**

*ANORA'S PRIDE*: "Four stars!"
~ *Heartland Critiques*

"*CALLIE'S HONOR* is a great western romance."
~ *S. Wurman, Night Owl Reviews (4.5 Stars)*

*CALLIE'S HONOR*: "Chemistry...steadily simmers until it finally boils over. If you have not been introduced to the works of Kathleen Lawless, this is an excellent place to start... You will not regret it."
~ *C. Bell, Long and Short Romance Reviews (4 Books)*

*MADDY'S FUGITIVE* "has it all—romance, action, mystery, and solid characters and plot. Tension between Jud and Maddy as well as the mystery surrounding Jud's innocence grabbed my attention and held on tight."
~ *Jen, Romancing the Book (4 Roses)*

"I liked it way too much. Lol!"
~ *Dee, Shameless Romance Reviews (4 Stars)*

*MADDY'S FUGITIVE* "was a fun, passionate, engaging whodunit with a strong, stubborn heroine. I was quickly drawn in ... an interesting, worthwhile story."
~ *Josie, Night Owl Reviews (4.5 Stars)*

"A fast-paced book that hooks the reader from the very first page."
~ *Anne Black, RT (4 Stars)*

∾

Sign up for Kathleen's VIP Reader Newsletter to be updated on new releases or when her books go on a special fan pricing for her readers. http://eepurl.com/bVosb1

## Dedication

In memory of my mother,
Lois Bernadette Lawless Shandley (1931-1972),
who taught me the invaluable lesson,
"It's better to be looked over than overlooked."

# PROLOGUE

*Oregon, 1868*

Rafe straightened from the unmarked grave and turned to the Shoshoni brave next to him. "I won't forget this."

"You go after them? The white men who did this?"

"Honor demands it."

His blood brother's face remained sober, although his black eyes danced with teasing. "You chase honor only when it suits you, Brother."

"You're a fine one to talk." Rafe clasped the other man's hand. The difference in the color of their skin in no way lessened the bond he felt deep in his heart. "I won't forget this."

"If you wish it, I would accompany you."

"I know. But it's best I go alone."

"Be careful. It is your face, also, that other men will be on the lookout for."

Rafe ran a hand along his clean-shaven jaw. "Always had a hankering to wear a beard."

Wounded Bear clasped his forearm. "You know even if you find these men it will not return your brother to his life."

Rafe pressed his lips together. "No, it won't. But I aim to see to it that the Denzell boys have killed for the last time."

"And the father?"

"I'll think of something fitting. Lord knows there's plenty of blood on the old man's hands, even if his sons did the killing."

# CHAPTER 1

Callie heard the approaching rider long before his image appeared on the horizon. She tossed the last of the scraps to the chickens and headed back to the cabin, steadfastly refusing to quicken her pace. If she was going to live alone in the wilds of Oregon, she had to learn not to run for cover anytime a stranger blew across her path. Besides, her shotgun stood just inside the cabin's front door, within easy reach. Chances were good her lone visitor was just someone on his way to town, maybe stopping in to ask directions.

Still, Callie picked up her gun and felt its reassuring weight. So far, anytime a man trespassed onto her territory it had boded ill, and she wasn't about to be taking any chances.

Narrowing her eyes against the sun's glare, she raised the shotgun and waited. The stranger was not making very good time, due to the fact he was hauling a brown-and-white calf along behind him at the end of a dusty rope. The calf bawled its protest at being dragged along this way.

Man and horse pulled up abruptly, less than a stone's

throw from her front steps. "Good day to you, ma'am." The man's voice was pleasant enough as he touched the brim of his hat, although he didn't remove it the way Callie expected a real gentleman would. He seemed to be deliberately leaving his hat in place, as well as his face in shadow, making it impossible for Callie to tell whether or not she'd seen him around these parts before.

"Good enough day," Callie said tightly, her hold on the shotgun unwavering. The man before her sat his saddle with the ease of one born to it. It was difficult to judge which was the more splendid creature, the man whose face remained hidden or the ebony horse beneath him.

The man tugged on the rope, eliciting a fresh complaint from the cow. "I was wondering if this animal might belong to you. Happened upon her wandering across the road a ways back. Noticed a hole in the fence when I passed by earlier. Thought she might have got away on you."

"I daresay she's mine, all right," Callie said, her suspicions lessening ever so slightly. "I expect fetching her back slowed your journey some."

"Not in any particular hurry," he drawled, as he dismounted in one fluid movement. He approached Callie and passed her the rope. "I'd feel right more comfortable, though, if you'd put that shotgun down. Firearms have a habit of sometimes going off unexpectedly."

"Not in my hands." Callie replied. Cautiously she accepted the rope, warm from his touch.

"You've got a nice spread here," the man continued, glancing at the cozy log cabin and nearby barn. Smoke drifted lazily from the chimney and was soon lost in the blue of the tireless September sky.

When he tipped his hat back she saw that his eyes were an identical blue. Broad of shoulder, lean of hip, the stranger was even more impressive on foot than astride his mount. He had to be nearabouts the tallest man she'd ever seen. A full, dark mustache rode his upper lip above a jaw shadowed with several days' whisker growth. He looked hard, Callie thought. The way a body needed to be in order to survive in this raw, untamed land.

Yet she found she wasn't fearful, having already learned the hard way that fear rendered a body weak. Marriage to Bert had taught her that, and a few more things besides.

"Mind if I water my horse while I'm here?"

"Help yourself," Callie said. "Best water in the state."

She made no effort to still the note of pride that crept into her voice. And why should she? She'd practically broken her back for what little she had. Her homestead. Her livestock. Her independence. An independence that had only truly become hers when she'd buried Bert last May.

"Don't mind if I do." Spurs jangled as man and horse moved to the well. Callie stood on the porch, cradling her shotgun in one arm and hanging onto the rope with her other hand. "You'll need to be mending that hole in your fence, lest you lose the rest of your livestock," he added.

"It's too late to go out now," Callie said. "I'll see to it first light."

"Yep. Sun'll be down soon." Having watered his horse and drunk his fill, the stranger refilled his canteen. As he turned to face her, Callie had difficulty looking away from the silvered water droplets beading on his mustache. When she finally did it was too late; his horse had cropped the colorful head off every nasturtium she had so carefully started from seed and lovingly transplanted.

"Can't you control your animal!" Callie exclaimed as she stomped down the steps.

"Well, ma'am, I—" He pushed his hat toward the back of

5

his head and glanced down at the spoiled flowerbed. Then he shrugged. "What's done is done. I'm truly sorry. I guess old Marshall here was just plumb sick and tired of hay and oats."

"Nothing for it." Callie turned away, feeling the hot dryness behind her eyelids. She knew it wasn't reasonable to feel this way over a handful of flowers that would die anyway, come first frost. It was just so damned unfair. Bert was dead and buried, and still she wrestled with feelings of not being allowed to have one single thing that was hers and hers alone.

She was mistress of her own domain, free to plant a hundred more nasturtiums next spring if she wanted to. And no begging for a few miserable pennies to buy seed, the way she'd been forced to do in the past. She truly was free!

"Ma'am?" The stranger was facing her. "Did you hear what I said?"

Feeling suddenly reckless, Callie stood the shotgun on the ground alongside her. No need protecting herself and all that was hers; obviously she was in no danger from this man. "Did you say something? I'm afraid I was woolgathering."

"Yes'm. I said I was of a mind to see to mending the fence for you. My way of putting things to rights between you and Marshall here." He gave his horse an affectionate pat on his satiny nose.

"You needn't bother," Callie said. "You did me the service of returning my property. Besides, flowers are an unnecessary indulgence out here."

"I thought they lent the place a right homey air."

"Did you, indeed?" Callie started to bestow a smile on the man but stopped just in time, reminding herself she didn't care what he or any other man might think. "Well. I'd best be seeing to my chores. Thank you again."

"Pleasure."

She was halfway to the cabin when the deep rumble of his voice halted her. "I was wondering, ma'am. Would your husband object if Marshall and me was to take shelter in your barn for the night? It'd be a sight more pleasant than sleeping out in the open. I could stop and fix your fence on my way out in the morning, by way of payment."

Instinctively Callie opened her mouth to refuse, then paused. Didn't the scripture verses clearly state, "I was hungry and you gave me to eat. I was cold and you gave me shelter. I was thirsty and you gave me to drink"? To say nothing of the fact that the man had ridden miles out of his way to return her lost cow. It would be wrong of her to refuse.

"Very well, you have yourself a night's shelter, mister. And I will take you up on your offer of mending the fence. I can't afford to lose any more livestock."

"Much obliged. Mrs.—"

"Lambert." She hesitated before adding, "Mrs. Callie Lambert."

"Name's Millar. Rafe to my friends."

"Pleased to make your acquaintance, Mr. Millar. You'll find plenty of fresh hay in the barn."

Inside the barn Rafe stripped the saddle and blanket from his mount's back. "Well done, Marshall, old boy," he murmured as he added an extra measure of oats to the horse's feed. "Couldn't have done better myself." For although Rafe had arrived with every intention of stopping over at the Lambert homestead, he'd wanted to make his presence seem as casual as possible rather than the purely calculated move of a man who knew exactly what he wanted and didn't allow anything or anyone to stand in his way.

Callie Lambert wasn't in his way any, but her spread was conveniently close to old man Denzell and his two murdering sons. And even though Rafe had deliberately sabotaged the good widow's fence, he'd put things back to rights tomorrow. He took a considerable amount of pride in putting things to rights.

After searching out a clean stall, Rafe kicked a pile of hay into some semblance of a mattress and spread his bedroll atop it. Truth be told, he was a sight more comfortable sleeping under the stars than with any sort of roof stretched over him. A roof had a way of making a man feel confined. Pinned down. Not to mention making a man soft. He needed to keep the elements at bay. Rafe propped his shotgun in the hay alongside his bedroll. He had no intention of letting himself get soft, or of staying inside for an unnecessary second when he could be out getting the lay of the land.

The silence had about the same way of making a man feel hemmed in as a roof did, Rafe mused as he took in the big-sky picture, from the lush valley cradling Callie's homestead to parts south. Parts that included his primary target, the Double D ranch, Denzell's spread.

Dark green stands of spruce, pine, and fir hugged the undulating slope on the far side of the creek. Timber rights alone must be worth a pretty penny.

He pursed his lips thoughtfully. Word was Callie Lambert had been widowed four months. How long till some of the locals came courting, he wondered. A pretty young widow with a spread like this would be quite desirable.

"Mr. Millar."

At first he thought he'd only imagined her voice. But when he swung around she was real enough, a soft breeze pushing at her skirts and outlining the slender limbs beneath. Her face was shiny and he guessed she'd been standing over a hot stove. His gaze dropped to the covered plate in her hands.

"You weren't in the barn," Callie said. "I fixed you a plate. Didn't want it to grow cold."

Three long strides closed the distance between them.

He took the plate from her, noticing for the first time how the green of her eyes matched the green hillside behind her. She looked younger in the softer light. More vulnerable. Or maybe it was just the absence of her rifle.

"You didn't have to do that."

"I know."

The words came at him, as simple and direct as her gaze, unlike the city belles with their highfalutin' airs, stylish gowns, and coy speech and mannerisms. Powdered and coifed and smelling so sweet a man's gut ached, most females were intent on one thing and one thing only: snagging themselves a husband. Making the poor bastard's life hell. He wondered how much the late Mr. Lambert had suffered before going to his final resting place. He also wondered if her wealthy neighbor to the south might be the widow's next target.

"Would you care to join me?" He indicated a couple of sawed-off tree stumps.

"I don't think so, thank you."

"Suit yourself." Rafe sat and lifted the towel covering his meal, releasing the homey scent of fresh meat and vegetables in a rich stew broth. "Mind if I ask why?"

Callie brushed her forehead where strands of gentle

brown hair had escaped the confining topknot. It was a futile gesture. "Not one to set idle, I guess."

Rafe nodded and dug into his stew, as if unconcerned. "Oh, I almost forgot." From the pocket of her apron she pulled out a chunk of fresh bread. "I didn't want it to get sogged up on the plate."

"'Preciate that." Rafe ate in silence for several moments, while Callie watched.

When some comment seemed required, he asked, "You bake this bread, Mrs. Lambert?"

Callie nodded. Rafe noticed how she worried her bottom lip. Something was sure enough on her mind. He took another bite. Best to let her come about it in her own way.

"Sure you won't have a seat?" he asked, after several more minutes had passed in silence.

To his surprise she sat, looking at him in a rather disconcerting fashion. He knew his beard was starting to fill in. He also knew it was likely posters of Luke had been plastered up around town. He understood, though, that she wasn't much of one for going to town.

"Where you from, Mr. Millar?"

Rafe managed a careless shrug. "Here and there. No place in particular."

"Grew up in Wyoming, myself."

Rafe nodded. Waited for her to say more.

"Got married out there. Mr. Lambert was on his way west when he heard about the Land Act. Husband and wife got twice as much land as a single gent."

Rafe bit back a smile and practiced the potent charm that was his trademark. "If you don't mind my saying so, ma'am, I sincerely doubt that's the only reason Mr. Lambert popped the question."

Callie frowned. Maybe she didn't recognize a compliment when it came right at her. He tried again. "What I meant was, you're a very attractive woman. Not to mention one hell of a cook. Mr. Lambert is one lucky man."

"He's dead." She issued the words with a suddenness that startled him. Not so much the words themselves but the way she announced the fact.

"I'm sorry," he said.

"I'm not. He wasn't a very nice man. But I wanted to explain."

"Explain?"

"If folks in town were to hear about you stopping here overnight... Well, it wouldn't be seemly."

"You'd prefer I not mention this in town, that it?"

Callie's face cleared like the skies after a thunderstorm.

"Exactly. Not that I especially care what that mealymouthed bunch of busybodies happens to think, but..."

"I understand. Your reputation is safe with me."

Callie rose. "I appreciate that."

"Has to be a hard life out here, for a woman alone."

Callie opened her mouth as if to speak, then seemed to think better of it. She glanced around her, an expression of satisfied pride on her face. "Nothing's too hard when you're fixed on something you want."

Rafe thought briefly of the Denzells, of other times, things he'd wanted in days past. The lady had herself a point. He stood, not quite sure of what to do with his empty plate. "I couldn't agree with you more."

When Callie started toward the cabin it seemed only natural to fall into step beside her. "You never wanted to settle down someplace?" she asked. "Work the land, put down roots?"

Rafe laughed. "I'm afraid we Millars are a rootless

bunch. Hardly remember my ma or my pa. My brother and me raised ourselves."

"How terrible."

"I've seen folks grow up worse off."

"Whereabouts have you been?"

"You name it, I've seen it. Riverboats down south. Gold-fields in California. Trapping up north. Boston. New York. New Orleans. Mexico."

"I was so happy to finally get here, I don't expect a body'd ever get me to move again."

"Rough trip?" Rafe asked.

A shadow crossed Callie's face. "You could say that."

Abruptly she changed the subject. "I got a pot of coffee on the stove. You like some? Or there's more stew."

"Coffee sounds like just the ticket." He paused at the bottom of the steps. "You want I should wait for you out here?"

He saw the hesitation march across her features. She scanned the skyline where the sun dropped low on the hori-zon. Then she said, "I guess there's no harm in you coming inside. "

Following her in, Rafe took a seat at the scrubbed pine table. The smell of freshly perked coffee permeated the air above the cooking odors. The cabin was neat, if sparsely furnished. He took note of the many homey touches, from drying flowers and herbs above the ugly black stove to the cheerful red-and-white gingham at the window above the sink. Amazing, really, that she kept the place going inside and out. She must be a tireless worker. Obviously her home meant everything to her. Rafe couldn't imagine feeling that way about anything. Maybe he had once, but...

Across the table, Callie wondered what sudden thoughts brought the frown to his face and the shadow to his eyes.

She filled two mugs and pushed one in front of Rafe, then placed the milk jug and sugar bowl within easy reach, wishing she'd taken the time earlier to make an apple brown betty, like she'd planned. But she'd been busy putting up preserves before Rafe—Mr. Millar, she corrected herself quickly—arrived.

They sipped their coffee in companionable silence for several minutes before he spoke. "You get on all right with your neighbors hereabouts?"

Callie, intently stirring her coffee, jerked so abruptly that the hot liquid sloshed down the sides of the mug and onto the table. She jumped up and grabbed a rag, glad of an excuse to delay her answer. Not that she was duty-bound to say anything, but she preferred talk to the thoughtful silence between them.

"Neighbors, you say. Let me think." She busied herself rinsing the rag and hanging it on a line strung above the stove. "There's a big homestead to the south. Family by the name of Denzell. Matter of fact, the Denzells are my only neighbors. He's bought out near everybody else."

"That a fact. Wonder why?"

Callie searched his face for hidden motives behind his question, finding none. But she kept her guard firmly in place. For all she knew, Mr. Millar could have been sent here by Denzell to feel her out, him not being the type to take kindly to the word "no."

"Land-hungry, I suspect. He came by right after Bert died and offered to buy me out, too. I suppose he thought I might be glad of an excuse to move on."

"I take it he was wrong."

"Yup."

"How'd he take it? Your refusing his offer?"

"Mind if I ask why you're so interested?"

"Sounds like the man I'll wind up talking to about a job, if I stay. Pays to know who you're talking to."

Callie nodded. "Denzell wasn't too worried. Said one winter out here alone ought to be enough to change my mind."

Rafe's blue eyes settled on her in a disconcerting way. Suddenly Callie found the room uncomfortably warm.

"Sounds almost like a threat."

She jumped up. "I don't think he meant it that way. More coffee?"

Rafe took the hint and rose to his feet. "No, thank you, ma'am."

Up close, Callie realized she'd never been face to face with a man who emanated such power. She felt positively tiny alongside him, even after she straightened her back and rose slightly onto her toes.

"There's warm water for washing on the stove, if you've a mind," she said. "Can I get you anything else? A blanket or a pillow or anything?"

"Marshall and me'll make out just fine. Thanks again for letting us stop over."

Callie watched him depart with a comfortable roll to his step. He seemed like a man who knew himself well and rested easy with that knowledge.

So why did something about his presence make her feel skittish? Maybe because he didn't suit the role of a drifter so much as that of a man with a purpose. A purpose to what end? Callie wondered. Then she told herself it really didn't matter. Come tomorrow he'd be gone.

# CHAPTER 2

*"Callie girl!"*

*She froze at the look on Bert's leering, bloated face as he slowly un-threaded his belt and approached. He was drunk again. A mean drunk. just like her pa and her older brother. She squeezed her eyes shut, steeling herself for the bite of the leather. Bad as Bert's beatings might be, they were nothing compared to how excited he got. And what happened next...*

Callie bolted upright in bed, bathed in sweat, her night-gown twisted in a knot about her hips. She pushed the damp hair back from her face and stifled a groan. The glimpse of daylight behind the curtains meant she'd over-slept. She tumbled from bed and splashed cold water onto her flushed face, wishing it was half so easy to sluice off the memories. Bert was dead. He would never hurt her again. Why did she allow him to violate her dreams the way he'd violated her life for six miserable years?

Twisting her hair into its customary topknot, Callie winced as she gave the pin an unnecessarily hard jab that dug into her scalp. Time and again Bert had threatened that she needed breaking, just like a wild filly. He'd died without succeeding in breaking her. And she'd stood dry-eyed at his grave, vowing no man would ever put his hands on her again.

Out in the kitchen she grabbed her apron from its hook near the sink, then paused. Something wasn't right. The room was warm. The stove was lit. That was when she remembered Rafe Millar.

He'd spent the night in the barn. He must have come inside this morning and lit the stove while she slept. And much as she disliked the idea of a stranger in her cabin, she had to admit having the stove already lit was a rare treat. She'd fix a home-cooked breakfast, her way of thanking him.

En route to the henhouse she stuck her head in the barn but saw no sign of the man or his mount. He must have gone out to fix the fence. Even as she wondered if he'd be back, she caught sight of his bedroll neatly stacked atop one of the stall doors. He would be back. And breakfast would be waiting.

Callie hummed a speeded-up version of "Onward Christian Soldiers" as she collected the warm eggs. She was still humming as she headed back to the cabin when, over the squawking of the chickens, she heard sounds of a horse and rider.

The approaching horse was an impressive gray, but the heavy-jowled man astride was less impressive. She'd disliked and distrusted Denzell from their very first meeting, unlike Bert, who'd been taken in by the man's swagger and boasting.

"Mornin', Callie."

"Mr. Denzell," she said, not breaking her stride. "What brings you out this way?"

"Nice day for a ride," he said.

"I thought it looked like rain, myself." She watched with satisfaction as Denzell flushed.

"Hope you don't mind my dropping in like this. But just last night me and the boys was sitting around wondering how you was doin'. Thought to see if maybe you had a change of heart about my offer."

Callie felt herself tense. Her steps slowed. "Nothing has changed, Mr. Denzell. Particularly the way I feel about this place."

"You expect old Den to believe you're so attached to this miserable patch of sod and its rundown cabin that you couldn't possibly bear to part with it?" His eyes glittered knowingly, and Callie felt herself freeze inside. "'Specially when it carries such warm and wonderful memories of your life here with Bert."

Like an animal scenting danger she detected something amiss with Denzell's words, coupled with the way he looked at her. Almost as if he knew firsthand what a hell Bert had made her life. How could he possibly know? Her gaze slid in the direction of the cabin and her shotgun. Why did she feel the sudden need for protection, just because Denzell sat there, twin six-shooters strapped to his sides, his shotgun laid across his saddle?

He gave her a hard look. "What if I were to sweeten the pot? Make it worth your while to move someplace else. Maybe someplace like California. I hear the sun shines there every day."

Callie swallowed her feelings of unease and managed a sweet smile. "Why, Mr. Denzell. I don't want you to go having pity on me now, just 'cause I'm a widow. If I ever did decide to sell, I wouldn't dream of accepting one penny more than fair market value."

Denzell's face reddened. "Just how you planning to

survive? Bet you don't got enough pluck to buy seed for next spring's planting."

"I thought I might sell some of my timber."

Denzell threw back his head and laughed uproariously.

"Little lady, you got one hell of a lot to learn. Starting with who owns the only mill in these parts."

"You don't own the only mill in the state," she retorted with more bravado than she felt.

"Give me time, Callie. Give me time." With that, Denzell turned his horse. The big gray pawed the ground and reared slightly. "Time'll come when I own the whole damn state, lock, stock, and barrel, including this place."

"Over my dead body," Callie murmured under her breath. Only when Denzell was out of sight did she turn and climb the steps to the cabin.

Once he heard the cabin door slam, Rafe sauntered around the corner of the barn and stared in the direction of the dust stirred up by Callie's departing visitor. "The early bird does indeed catch the worm," he mused aloud. One thing was for sure. Denzell wanted Callie's homestead bad. Had to be some powerful important reason for that. Be up to him to ferret out the whys and wherefores. He believed in knowing everything there was to know about the enemy.

Nonchalantly he crossed the yard to the well, pulled up a bucket of water, and stripped off his shirt. He allowed his thoughts free rein as he splashed water over his chest and arms. Now that he'd mended Callie's fence it was time to plot his next strategy, make himself indispensable around here for a while longer. As he dried himself with his shirt, he scanned the darkening sky and gave a satisfied nod. Thought he smelled a storm brewing. It could prove to be just the thing!

Callie stepped onto the front porch and froze. Rafe

Millar stood near the well, stripped naked to the waist. Angling through the clouds, a single shaft of sunlight touched his deeply tanned, glistening wet skin. As if aware of her watching him, he slowly turned. Their gazes locked across the yard.

Callie swallowed thickly and opened her mouth to tell him breakfast was ready, but her voice refused to work. The sight of Bert with no shirt, his graying middle-aged chest and saggy stomach, had never rendered her more than repulsed.

Rafe Millar was something else. He was lean as a whipcord, and his every movement emphasized the powerful pull of muscles visible beneath smooth, golden skin. His chest was sprinkled with a generous dusting of curly dark hair that thinned across a flat belly and arrowed into his pants.

He tossed back his wet hair and shoved his arms into his shirtsleeves but didn't bother to fasten the buttons as he strode toward her. Each step raised a fine plume of dust. To her mortification Callie found her vocal cords still frozen.

Reaching the steps, he propped one booted foot on the first runner and leaned across his bent knee, peering up at her. "Did I hear company come and go already this morning?"

Callie's tongue moistened her dry lips. "Mr.... Mr....Denzell."

"Your neighbor?"

Callie nodded. Swallowed again.

"Little early to come calling, isn't it?"

Callie flushed, certain that he referred to her rising so late. She shifted her weight from one foot to the other. "Depends."

Rafe cocked his head to the side and flashed her an

engaging grin. "Got your fence fixed right as rain. Speaking of which..." He glanced skyward.

As if by prearranged signal the first drops of rain fell, round dark splotches clearly visible on the dusty dry earth.

"We need the rain." Callie wiped her hands on her apron. "Come in. I fixed some ham and eggs and fresh biscuits."

Rafe's grin widened. "Best offer I had all day. 'Cept I'm afraid you're going to spoil me with this home cooking. Make it mighty difficult to leave."

"I take it you're fixing to stay in the area then?"

"For a spell."

"What kind of work are you looking for?"

"Pretty much anything."

"Denzell might be able to use you at his mill."

Rafe nodded as he took the seat she indicated. "'Course, what I like best is working the land."

In the midst of dishing up a mound of potatoes, Callie paused and gave him a measured look. "Strange choice for a man with wanderlust in his veins."

"Not forever, mind," Rafe said, tipping his chair back so the front legs were lifted clean off the floor. "Just a short time. Don't suppose you'd be looking to take on a hand to help you around here a spell?"

Callie plunked the plate in front of him. "Managing just fine on my own."

"I thought that's what you'd say." Rafe set his chair to rights and dug into the plate of food.

Nothing wrong with the man's appetite, that was for sure. Callie watched the way Rafe consumed four eggs, a mountain of fried potatoes, a slab of ham, and half a dozen biscuits with butter. Truth was, it would be a real treat to hire an extra set of hands for a while, battening everything down in readiness for the approaching winter. But Denzell had unwittingly spoken the truth. Miserly Bert had died without revealing where he'd stashed his money sock, and it had taken all but Callie's last dime to pay for his casket. Bert didn't cotton to banks, so Callie knew in her bones the money had to be someplace on the ranch. She'd wasted many a valuable hour in the past four months trying to locate it, but to no avail. And while selling her timber was one option, Denzell's was the only local mill. He'd made it twice over plain he wasn't about to help her gain her independence.

"I didn't thank you proper for lighting the stove this morning."

"My pleasure. Your neighbors tend to drop in on you very often?"

Callie shook her head. Staring down at the table, she traced the pattern of wood grain with the handle of her spoon, her thoughts a million miles away, lulled by the rhythmic sound of the rain on the roof. A sound that rose to a near-deafening crescendo. She jumped when an angry burst of wind lashed hail against the window.

"Looks like we're in for a pretty good storm," she finally said.

Rafe tipped his chair back on its hind legs. "It does, indeed. You won't take it amiss, I hope, if me and Marshall sit it out where it's dry?"

Callie realized she could hardly order him off her property in the middle of a hailstorm. As her gaze circled the kitchen she noticed his hat and jacket, pegged on the back of the door as if they belonged there. Fighting down a sudden rush of resentment at the way he'd made himself at home, she rose and went to the window. The sky looked as if someone had drawn a black curtain across it. Hailstones the size of robin eggs were bouncing across the yard. Callie hugged herself, clasping her elbows tight. "Good thing I brought in the last of the pumpkins yesterday."

"It's gonna be quite a show of thunder and lightning, unless I miss my guess."

She hadn't heard him move. Yet he stood directly behind her, his words warm against the back of her neck. The hair there stood on end, prickling a warning, and she felt—or imagined she felt—the heat from his body all the way down her spine. She felt trapped. Swallowing hard, she refused to give in to the rising sense of panic.

Instead she forced herself to turn, to meet him face to face. His lids were half lowered, his expression unreadable. Callie was reminded of a coyote she'd seen one night on the trip west. The animal had been hurt bad. One foot half chewed off, it must have been crazy with pain, circling their wagons and their fire. The menfolk had been unable to drive it off. Eventually one of them had put the creature out of his misery.

Rafe was that coyote in his prime. Alone. Fearless. Determined.

A force to be reckoned with.

Let someone else do the reckoning, she thought.

A fork of lightning ripped through the sky, its sudden brightness reflected in his eyes. Eyes filled with a purpose she couldn't begin to guess at. The light dimmed. The resonant march of thunder echoed through the cabin's walls, underscored by the clatter of hailstones on the roof.

"You have to go," Callie said abruptly.

Rafe didn't say a word, just eyed her for one long minute before he moved to the door, shrugged into his jacket, and put on his hat.

"I didn't mean right this minute," she amended. "I mean, you might as well wait until it lets up."

Rafe gave her another dark, measuring look. "I'll check on the animals."

Once he'd left, Callie added another log to the stove and put on a pan of water to heat before she started clearing the dishes. As she worked, her thoughts were a jumble. After Bert died she'd thought things couldn't help but get better. Instead, it seemed they were getting worse. Alone out here she felt like some sort of target. First Denzell and his persistence to take over her land.

Now Rafe. Something about him spoke of elements of danger. He had the steely look of a man with a mission. A man whom nothing would sway from what he'd come to do.

First and foremost, though, was the shaky state of her financial affairs. She had to find Bert's money sock. Fast. And Lord help her if she didn't, 'cause come spring she'd have no choice but to give up. To let go of the only thing she truly cared about. Her home. Callie vowed she'd die first.

Her thoughts were shattered by a terrible, ear-splintering sound of devastation and destruction.

Rafe!

# CHAPTER 3

Callie flung open the door and rushed onto the porch. Slippery hailstones sent her feet sliding out from beneath her. The breath was knocked from her lungs as she bumped down the front steps and landed in the mud.

"Are you all right?"

Rafe's voice penetrated her consciousness as she stirred, unsure how long she'd lain there unable to move or catch her breath. It could have been seconds or several long minutes. Overhead, the drone of thunder had receded in the distance. The sky no longer lit up with lightning forks. The rain hadn't lessened any, though, and besides being thoroughly soaked from her scalp to her toes she grew aware of a dull throb in her right ankle.

"Don't move."

As if she could, Callie thought crossly. She felt his hands making a swift yet thorough examination of her limbs, beginning at her shoulders and running down her arms, past her waist and hips to her legs. Callie might have panicked if his touch hadn't been as impersonal as any doctor's. When he probed her right ankle, she moaned slightly.

"Hurt anywhere else?"

Everywhere, she thought as she shook her head. Not that she'd admit it to him. Besides, she'd been bruised up before. She'd heal.

Rafe leaned over her. "Put your arm around my neck." Stubbornly Callie ignored him and tried to hoist herself to her feet. She failed miserably and landed in a crumpled heap.

Rafe glared down at her, hands on hips, rainwater dripping off the brim of his hat. "Now, shall we try it my way? Or do you enjoy lying here catching your death?"

Callie pressed her lips together, glanced up at him from beneath sodden strands of hair, then nodded. If she had to, she could crawl inside on her hands and knees, but it wasn't something she felt like doing in front of him.

"That's better."

Bending down, he lifted her into his arms as if she weighed no more than a hunk of firewood.

"The porch is slippery," she murmured against the warm skin of his neck. Closing her eyes, she inhaled an interesting combination of scents that included leather, horses, and clean, musky male skin.

"So I noticed." He managed the few stairs effortlessly, kicked open the door, and crossed the room to deposit her unceremoniously on the settee near the stove.

Callie gritted her teeth at the stab of pain that radiated up her right leg to the knee. "What in tarnation was that noise I heard? Sounded like the roof was being ripped right off from overhead."

"You know that big tree near the henhouse?"

"That beautiful old pine?"

"It's now on top of what used to be the henhouse."

"Oh, no!"

"Henhouse isn't much more than a pile of kindling," Rafe added as he drew off his gloves, shrugged out of his sheepskin jacket, and shook the worst of the rainwater off his hat. He hunkered down alongside her. "Take off your stocking."

"I will not!" Callie managed an indignant look and sat back, arms folded tight across her chest.

"Have it your way." Without the slightest trace of embarrassment Rafe pushed her skirt up past her knees and located the top of her cotton stocking. Despite Callie's outraged squeal he had both stocking and shoe removed in a trice. Removed so smoothly, so effortlessly, that Callie had a notion it was hardly the first time he'd separated a woman from her undergarments. The thought was outrageous, and she blushed, rightly ashamed of herself.

She tugged her sodden skirts back down into some semblance of modesty, a movement that brought a slow, knowing smile to Rafe's lips. "I need to see if you broke your ankle, Callie." It was the first time he'd used her Christian name, and somehow, coming from him, it sounded completely natural. For her part, she'd been thinking of him as Rafe almost from the first.

"It doesn't feel broken," she muttered, aware of the pressure of his cool fingers against her skin. He cradled her heel in one large callused palm, but when he tried to rotate the joint she sucked in her breath.

He glanced up at her. "Doesn't feel too good, though, does it? Take off your other stocking."

"What for?" She flashed him a suspicious glance. "The other ankle's just fine."

"I want to compare. See how badly swollen this one is."

"Oh." Self-consciously, she reached up under her skirt and unhooked the second stocking, slowly rolling it over her knee and down her calf. Rafe unfastened her shoe and tossed it alongside its mate. His eyes fastened on hers as he peeled the second stocking from her foot. Callie felt the slow flush of physical awareness lick up the backside of her legs. Although she was modestly covered, her senses registered the unaccustomed intimacy of their pose, aware of the way she felt flushed from more than just the fire.

"I thought so."

She bit her lip when his thumbnail grazed the arch of her foot. The resulting sensation was funny, almost ticklish. Reflexively she jerked her foot away. "You thought so what?"

"Bad sprain," Rafe said, pushing himself to a standing position. "I expect it'll be a week before you can put much weight on it."

"A week?" Callie sputtered. "I can't be laid up a week. I've got chores to see to. Animals to feed."

Rafe ignored her. "Got any bandages?"

"What for?"

"Need something to bind that ankle."

"You're making a big fuss about nothing, Mr. Millar. Why, already I feel nearabouts good as new." As she spoke, Callie swung her legs over the edge of the settee and tried to stand. Her right ankle collapsed and she would have fallen had Rafe not been there. He caught her and swung her up in his arms. She could feel the beat of his heart, the banded strength in his arms cradling her against him, the way his belt buckle dug into her hip.

The heat of his body crept through her wet dress and warmed her intimately. She was embarrassed to feel her nipples harden and see their pointed peaks through her clothing. She squirmed slightly, hoping he didn't feel it too.

"What's that you were saying?"

"There's some bandages in the far drawer in the bedroom."

"Let's just mosey in and get them, shall we?"

He shouldered open the bedroom door and ducked his head beneath the door frame. She kept her eyes on his face. This close she could see each individual whisker, the sensual line of his lips beneath his thick dark mustache. Not until he placed her on the pristine white bed covering did she realize he wasn't wearing a belt. She felt herself blush as hotly as any virgin, belatedly aware what part of his anatomy had been jabbing into her hip.

Trying to recover from her embarrassment, Callie folded her hands primly in her lap as he rummaged in the drawer she indicated. She had herself well in hand by the time he turned back to her.

"Tell me if this hurts. I'll be gentle as I can."

Callie nodded and forced herself to concentrate on the crown of his head as he ministered to her injury. He had wonderful thick dark hair that fell near the collar of his shirt in a natural wave. She wondered if his hair felt as silky as it looked, and locked her fingers together more tightly.

"There you go." He stood and surveyed his handiwork.

"Soon as the storm quits I'll find you a stout walking stick. You'll be hobbling around here before you know it."

"I appreciate your help, Mr. Millar," Callie said. "I just want to make one thing clear."

"And what would that be?"

"I don't want you altering your plans because of..." She paused. "Because of me" would sound awfully presumptuous, easy for him to misinterpret. "Because of the storm or me being hurt."

"All due respect, Callie. But I have no intention of it."

"Fine," Callie said. "I just wanted to make that perfectly clear."

"More bad news, I'm afraid," Rafe said, entering the cabin a short while later.

Callie looked up from the stocking she was mending.

"What's that?"

"More'n half the roof blew off your barn in the storm. I herded the animals down to the one end that's dry. Found a hunk of old canvas in the shed and tacked it up so's to keep the hay from getting wet. You'd best see to getting it fixed proper as soon as possible. You'll need to rebuild your henhouse, too. I don't know where your chickens flew off to, but they'll likely head back once they figure it's safe."

Callie laid her mending aside. "Thank you for everything, Mr. Millar."

"Wish I could do more, but..." He shrugged.

Callie nodded. A walking stick was propped against the end of the settee. She'd be fine, she told herself, not willing to admit that Rafe's leaving gave her a funny feeling.

"Good luck," Callie said.

"And to you."

"Stop in if you pass by this way again..." Callie bit off her impulsive words, embarrassed. She sounded as if she was pining for his company, which was hardly the case. "If you're of a mind," she finished lamely.

"Never know which way the wind might blow me," Rafe said as he pulled on his gloves and touched his fingers to the brim of his hat. A second later the front door closed behind him.

Callie listened to the retreating sound of man and horse and told herself she was glad. She didn't want or need a man lumbering around the place.

She glanced around the cabin, looking over the peeled

logs, the heavy beams supporting the roof. She'd been over every inch of the cabin and the barn, to no avail. But she must have missed someplace. Damn Bert, anyway. Where could that miserly husband of hers have hidden their money?

She didn't know exactly how much he'd hoarded away. He never doled out more than a few dollars at a time, barely enough to pay for a handful of groceries on the rare occasion they went into town for supplies. He didn't believe money matters were anything for women to be concerned about. Still, that didn't stop him from boasting whenever he came home from a poker game with big winnings in his pocket.

Just before he died he'd been hinting about another windfall coming his way. He'd never told her more than that, and she'd heard it too often to discount it as the wistful ramblings of a hard drunk. Right now she needed his cache to buy a few staples to see her through the winter, along with the seed she'd be needing come spring.

Callie yawned. Rafe had stoked the fire up before he left. He'd packed in enough wood to last her several days, too, as if he knew managing a walking stick and an armload of firewood would be tricky. Through the window she could see that the rain had stopped and the sky was lighting up. She really should try to hobble out and see how bad the barn was leaking. She'd venture out soon, she promised herself as she drifted off...

Some time later Callie jerked awake. She took a deep breath, aware she was no longer alone in the cabin. Behind her she heard a rustling sound signaling stealthy movement. Feigning sleep, she tried to remember if her shotgun was still alongside the door. She opened her eyes slightly. It was. But the distance between her and the door was great.

Suddenly a long thin shadow appeared in front of her, grotesquely out of proportion against the cabin's log walls as the intruder stood directly behind her. Callie fumbled for her walking stick, grasped it firmly in both hands and swung around in her seat—only to see Rafe.

Her shoulders slumped. The stick clattered to the floor.

"Didn't mean to startle you none," he said as he stooped to pick up her stick and place it within easy reach.

"Well, you did." Callie kept a wary eye on him. "I heard you head out a while ago. What are you doing back here?"

Rafe ducked his head as if in agreement. "Got as far as the river, only to find the bridge is washed away. Water's up too high to cross, from the rains. Marshall just gave me one of his looks and turned around and trotted back here, sweet as you please."

"Indeed," Callie said. "Thought I'd take you in again, did you?"

Rafe shrugged. "Didn't feel too good about leaving you here, laid up and all. Figured I could make myself useful straightening out a few things. Rebuilding the henhouse. Fixing the barn roof."

"I can't pay you," she said flatly.

"We'll work something out."

"I don't want you here."

Rafe met her gaze steadily. "Can't say as I blame you. Strikes me you're a lady who values her privacy. But for the time being I don't see as how you've got much choice. You can tell me to get, but you can't make me."

Callie's gaze slid sideways to her gun.

"I know what you're thinking," Rafe said, "but I kind of doubt you could make yourself pull the trigger, even if you managed to get hold of that big old shotgun and point it my way."

Rafe watched the play of emotions across her face. He had the upper hand, and well she knew it. She just didn't happen to like it. He wondered what made her so wary, then realized she was a woman alone out here in the wilderness. It was smart of her not to trust him any farther than she could throw him.

Which left it up to him to make himself so indispensable that any more talk of him leaving was forgotten—at least until he'd done what he came here to do. And his wasn't a mission to be rushed. Had to take his time. Get the lay of the land. Strike the Denzells' exposed flank when they least expected it.

He gave Callie his most coaxing, irresistible smile.

"You look like a lady who could use a cup of tea about now. Am I right?"

He heard her soft sigh of surrender. "I suppose you might as well make yourself useful."

"Don't you fret any on that score." He had every intention of making himself very useful.

Leaving Callie to sip her tea in front of the fire, Rafe sauntered outside, located the double-bladed ax inside the woodshed, and started chopping away at the fallen pine. He chopped and stacked the wood steadily, not too fast. Wouldn't do to run out of things for him to do around here. Callie's sprained ankle was a nice piece of luck, but no more lucky than what he'd come to expect. Too bad brother Luke's luck had run dry so fast.

Once the rain stopped, Rafe slipped out of his jacket and mopped his brow with his shirtsleeve. He still hadn't got used to the feeling of Luke being gone, even though he knew it was so. Had known it for a fact even before Wounded Bear had rounded him up and broke the news. Funny thing, being a twin. As if a part of you was always with the other one. A chunk of Rafe was buried out on the prairie with Luke, while another part wouldn't rest until justice was served.

First he had to get near Denzell, find out all he could about the man. Because if Denzell had killed Lambert and framed Luke for the murder, as Rafe believed, why would he have had his boys kill Luke out on the prairie? Luke must have had something on Denzell. Something that made Denzell want him silenced permanently. Something that added up to make Denzell one dangerous man.

Denzell was like a cornered wolf: You never knew where he'd strike next. Since wild animals prey on those who are weaker, Rafe had a hunch Denzell's next target would be Callie.

And whether she realized it or not, she was damned vulnerable. Any woman who looked like that wasn't safe. Those haunted green eyes. That way she had of looking at a body with a hint of reproach, as if somewhere down the line life hadn't treated her too kind. Callie Lambert wasn't his concern, he reminded himself harshly. She sure had felt good trussed up against him today, though. She weighed no more than a youngster, yet her body had spoken to his like a full-grown woman. Got him harder than a monk in a whorehouse. Even now, his body reacted to the memory.

Gripping the ax in both hands high over his head, he split the log in one swoop. She wasn't any kind of woman for the likes of him, he reminded himself. He'd tried settling down once. It hadn't lasted. And Callie had to be the most settling-down kind of woman he'd ever run across. All cool moves and unflappable temper. Come hell or high water, she'd manage. But he was afraid she might not come out ahead where Denzell was concerned. The man was the worst type of viper.

In the distance Rafe heard the sound of someone riding hard this way. Now what? he wondered as he tossed down the ax and made his way to the barn where he'd left his gun.

With his Winchester in hand, he returned to the wood-pile and squinted in the direction of the approaching rider. Male. Alone. Not Denzell senior. Could be one of the boys, but he doubted it. From what he'd been told, they went every place together. Even the bed of their favorite whore.

# CHAPTER 4

Horse and rider drew abreast of Rafe and stopped. The burly, black-frocked man raised a large wooden crucifix high over his head. "Repent, ye sinner."

For one brief second Rafe wondered if maybe the devil himself had come down to punish him for his lustful thoughts. But the man before him was much too ordinary to be Satan or his henchman, and Rafe had an idea that when his time came he'd warrant more than some overstuffed missionary come to deliver his come- uppance.

"Good day to you, Reverend. What brings you here-abouts?" Rafe kept easy hold of his rifle as he watched the older man's awkward dismount.

"Reverend Bligh, good sir," the other man huffed, short of breath. "I don't believe we've had the pleasure."

"New to these here parts, myself." Could be his imagination playing tricks on him, but it struck Rafe that the reverend wasn't exactly overjoyed to see him here. Did the churchman have courting in mind? Was four months considered a decent mourning period by Oregon Territory standards?

The reverend adjusted his collar and dusted the cuffs of his black frock coat, all the while eyeing Rafe in a furtive manner. "What brings you to the Lambert spread? You were acquainted with old Bert, perhaps?"

"Never had that opportunity," Rafe said. "Mrs. Lambert, though, she had herself a slight mishap. I expect I'll be sticking around till she gets back on her feet."

The churchman's eyes widened. "A mishap? Is she all right?"

"Why'n't ya go up, see for yourself?"

"I believe I'll do just that."

Rafe watched the reverend lumber toward the cabin, Bible tucked under one arm, crucifix clutched in his stubby fist. Rafe estimated the man had seen forty come and go, some years back, making him more than twenty years Callie's senior.

Turning, he focused his attention on the churchman's mount. Nice-looking animal. Very nice! Rafe ran his hand over the horse's flanks. Interesting, too, seeing as how it had the Double D brand from Denzell's ranch.

Upon hearing the new arrival, Callie had hobbled to the cabin's doorway in time to witness from afar the exchange between the two men. How she wished she could read lips. Rafe's territorial stance and the reverend's response made it appear an interesting conversation indeed. Now the reverend paused at the bottom of the steps, glanced up, and removed his hat. "Good day to you, Mrs. Lambert."

"Reverend Bligh. Seeking out the lost members of the fold, are you? Or could it be the collection plate is missing Bert's weekly contribution?"

"Callie, Callie." Slowly he mounted the steps to the porch, his tone chiding. "I noticed you haven't been attending Sunday services since Bert..." He lowered his eyes and made a hasty sign of the cross before looking up to her once more. "Figured you be doing your grieving in private, and that you might be in need of a sympathetic ear."

"Not at all," Callie said, leaning on her stick as she turned and led the way inside. "I've been busy. I have a ranch to run."

"Truly, my entire congregation has been busy, my dear. Yet in the four months since you buried your husband not one of us has seen you in town. Folks have expressed their concern." He cocked his head in Rafe's direction. "Perhaps, if we'd known you'd hired yourself a hand, folks wouldn't have been so worried that you were alone."

"Who's so all-fired worried?" Callie asked bluntly as she took a seat near the fire. "Don't recall a huge crowd at Bert's burial, myself."

Bligh paused, then seemed to recover. "Why Mr. Denzell, for one. Him being your closest neighbor and all—"

"Mr. Denzell is plain put out that I don't just up and sell my place to him."

The preacher lowered himself heavily into a chair across from her. "I truly believe your neighbor to the south has your best interests at heart, Callie. The good Lord knows this is a difficult life out here for a woman alone."

Callie refused to be lulled into a false sense of trust by either his singsong voice or concerned frown. "So Mr. Denzell keeps telling me. Truth be told, I find it an easier row to hoe than the life I knew with my husband."

Bligh sucked in his breath and crossed himself, as if to ward off evil incantations. "Mrs. Lambert, I fear I must caution you against speaking ill of those who have departed this life before us."

"Just stating a fact." Callie noted his reluctance to meet

her gaze. Did all husbands flail their wives with their belts on Saturday, then show up at the Lord's house on Sunday, the image of a concerned and loving spouse?

Reverend Bligh stared pointedly to where the bandages cradling her injured ankle were just visible beneath the hem of her skirt. "Some folks might say you're not having much luck on your own, with the henhouse broke and a hole in the barn roof you could shoot a cannon through."

Callie straightened. "Folks have a need to mind their own business."

"Am I to take it, then, you're not of a mind to sell?"

"I'll tell you the same thing I told Mr. Denzell last time he was by this way. I'm of a mind to stay put. With or without the blessing of the churchgoing townsfolk."

"What all do you know about yonder hired hand?"

"Not much," Callie admitted. "Mostly he's passing through."

"Is it wise having him here? You know, a woman alone can't be too careful these days."

"One thing I know is how to mind for myself," Callie said. Her words were punctuated by a loud knock on the door. She glanced over to see Rafe poke his head inside.

"I'm all done chopping that wood, Mrs. Lambert. Is there anything else you'd like me to attend directly?"

She waved him in. "Come in, Mr. Millar. I believe you've met the Reverend Bligh? Reverend, this here is Mr. Millar. He's giving me a hand around here for a spell. Helping me put things to rights after the storm."

Bligh narrowed his gaze to a squint as Rafe joined them. "Whereabouts did you say you were from, Millar?"

"I didn't say, Reverend."

Bligh harrumphed and reddened, tugging at his collar as if he suddenly found it too tight. "Not trying to mind a man's right to privacy, you ken. It's just that with Mrs. Lambert here being newly widowed and all, I kind of feel responsible and—"

"Responsible for her widowhood?" Rafe drawled.

Callie hid her smile. Rafe was obviously enjoying himself.

"No. No, not at all. What I meant is, responsible for her well-being."

"Seems like you and Mr. Denzell have something in common there."

The reverend's color continued to rise. "Only natural, really. Mr. Denzell being her closest neighbor and all."

"And no doubt a generous supporter of your church, I'll wager. He make you a gift of that horse you rode in on?"

"Not at all. In fact, I have the bill of sale about me someplace."

Callie watched the interaction between the two men.

Rate's words held a definite underlying edge. As for the reverend, he looked as if he might well choke on his collar. The silence between them deepened until eventually Bligh rose.

"I hope to see you at services soon, Mrs. Lambert. You too, Millar, if you're in town long enough. The Lord's house has a way of soothing our hurt and helping the pain of loss to heal."

"Leaving so soon?" Callie inquired sweetly.

"Indeed it was quite a ride out here. I'd best be getting back to town before dark."

"You just ride out here now?" She shot Rafe a sharp glance. "Isn't the bridge washed out?"

"The bridge washed out? Where would you get an idea like that?"

"What with all the rain and all..."

"No, indeed. Believe me, the crossing was rough but quite safe."

No sooner had Bligh departed than Callie turned on Rafe.

He met her gaze directly. "You thinking what I'm thinking?"

"And what would that be, Mr. Millar?"

"Wondering why the good father there would lie about how he got here with the river too high to cross."

"Why should he lie?"

"Exactly what I'm wondering."

Callie took a deep breath and heaved herself to her feet. "All I know for sure is that one of you is lying. Who should I believe? A drifter I never set eyes on before yesterday? Or the pastor of the local church?"

Callie stood at the window as night slowly stole over the land. The setting sun bled red into mauve and turned the sky deepest purple. Stars winked visible one at a time and soon littered the sky. She'd seen it hundreds of times before, yet tonight, somehow, things looked different. As if she were viewing it for the first time, from a new perspective. Had she done the right thing in not sending Rafe away earlier? Sure as shooting, he was lying to her. It followed that a man who'd lie about one thing would lie about any old thing that served his purpose. Was she asking for trouble?

She tensed, hearing the clatter of crockery hitting silverware. At the sink behind her Rafe was washing the dishes. One more sight that was new to her. First he'd whipped up a more than passable pot of chili and insisted on serving her. Next he scooted her away while he did the washing up. Callie'd never known a man to cook or clean, and certainly wouldn't have taken Rafe for a man with any domestic leanings. Yet he appeared to have the situation well in hand.

Rafe put away the last plate and hung the drying cloth on the line strung above the stove. He straightened to face her. Their gazes met and locked. Callie felt a shiver run down her spine. Walking stick in hand, she hobbled to the hearth and reached toward the fire, feeling its heat. Needing its warmth. So much of her life to this point had been lived in ice and silence.

"You cold?" Rafe asked.

"Some," Callie admitted. "Not used to just setting around. Being waited on."

"May as well enjoy it while it lasts," Rafe said. "You want I should heat some water so you can take a bath?"

The idea of a hot bath sounded this side of heaven.

"No," Callie said brusquely. She didn't want to be beholden to him, or to any man. After Bligh left, Rafe had gone down to the creek. He'd come back with his hair damp, looking and smelling all fresh and squeaky clean. If she could get herself down to the creek, that's where she'd bathe.

Silently he came up behind her and draped a shawl about her. His hands lingered on her shoulders as he lifted her hair out of the way and snugged the shawl up around her neck. "That better?" he asked huskily, his warm breath fanning the side of her neck and bringing a rush of pinpricks to her skin.

Callie whirled. "No, damn you!" Even she was surprised by the vehemence in her voice. "If I want a shawl, I'll get it myself. I don't know who you are or what you want, Rafe Millar, but I'll see you in hell before you come sneaking around here, acting so all-fired nice, trying to make believe you're someone I can trust. I trust no one. You hear me? No one."

Rafe backed away, cursing his own stupidity. The last

thing he wanted to do was raise her suspicions. But it seemed he'd done exactly that. He gave her a sheepish grin. "Forgot myself for a minute there. It won't happen again." He hunkered down and tossed another log on the fire. Callie didn't trust him and he didn't trust her, which made them just about squared even in his eyes. He didn't understand or trust any woman who had Callie's cool, unflappable facade, yet whose eyes shone with fiery passion the way Callie's did. The woman had a secret or two of her own, he'd bet on that. Secrets he didn't care to find out.

"What do you think brought the good reverend out this way?"

Callie shrugged and tightened the shawl across her shoulders. "Wondered why I wasn't going to Sunday service, I expect. He probably misses Bert's contributions to the collection plate."

"Were the two of you regular churchgoers, before..." He let his words trail away.

"Before he died? Bert would have turned over his own mother to the devil before he missed the chance to make an appearance every Sunday. Spit and polished, all pious and holy, singing in that deep baritone of his like he was the angel Gabriel himself."

Rafe could hear in her tone everything she wasn't saying. That Bert had had nothing to feel pious about. That Callie had hated being there with him, party to his lies. No wonder she kept her guard up the way she did. For Rafe's part, he wasn't about to win any medals restoring her faith in humanity. Matter of fact, if she should find out just why he'd planted himself here on her spread it would only serve to reinforce what she already knew. Rafe Millar was no man to be trusted.

His thoughts shifted abruptly to Nishu. She had gifted

him with her trust and her love, and it had all ended in tragedy. Resolutely he shook off the past, forcing himself to concentrate on the mission at hand.

"Somehow I can't help but wonder," he said.

"Wonder what?"

Those passionate eyes were blazing on him, hot enough to fry his soul in hell if she knew what he was about. "If maybe old Denzell didn't recruit the reverend to make a plea on his behalf. Enlist the good father's voice to help convince you to sell. Ever think of that?"

He watched Callie ponder his words, turn them over and examine them from all angles before she shook her head. He admired that about her. She wasn't one to fly back with a quick response, but took her time. Thought things through careful-like.

"Why would he? Doesn't make one lick of sense to me."

"Whatever you say." As he'd suspected, Callie Lambert had a habit of taking folks at face value. The reverend, being a man of the cloth, couldn't possibly be up to no good. Denzell, by the same token, wasn't suspect, just doing the neighborly thing. As for himself, that was another matter. Callie was smart not to trust the likes of him.

*Callie, you got a rough lesson ahead. You need someone looking after you.* And he felt an unexpected wrench, knowing that he wasn't about to be that someone.

Callie observed the play of emotions across Rafe's face.

The second his eye caught hers all hint of expression vanished, so quickly she wondered if she might have imagined it. Personally, Callie bet that Rafe Millar was one heck of a poker player. "I'll be going to bed now," she said abruptly, even though she didn't feel tired. She just knew she couldn't spend any more time in Rate's company today. Tomorrow she'd worry about when it came, and not one moment sooner. She paused on the threshold of her room. Rafe stood near the fire, one side of his face clearly illuminated in the light, the other side in deepest shadow.

Showing his true colors, she realized. A man who allowed the world to see one side of him, while keeping the other side hidden. Right now she had need of his strength and abilities. But not if it meant sacrificing her independence.

"Whereabouts are you fixing to sleep?" she asked. "The barn won't be near dried out enough yet."

"Where would you like me to sleep?"

Callie flinched from the bold intimacy in his tone and told herself she imagined it. "The front porch is covered and dry," she said.

"The front porch is just what I was thinking."

"There's a hammock under the steps. You could string it up, if you were of a mind."

Inside her room Callie closed the door, aghast to see how her hands were shaking. Damn and blast! Rafe Millar was making her some kind of skittish. She had a fair idea of the kind of woman he chose to spend his free time with. The kind of woman found in a saloon wearing face paint and not much more than her underthings. Callie managed to strip off her clothing and wrestle into her flannel nightgown, all the while cursing her injured ankle, which made her movements slow and awkward. She freed her hair and was brushing it smooth, getting ready to braid it for the night, when she slipped and knocked over her stick, which flew into her nightstand and sent the jug of water flying across the room.

"Callie! You okay?"

Rafe stood framed in the doorway, shirtless, the top of his breeches unfastened.

"Just clumsy," she said, sinking onto the bed.

Without bothering to ask permission Rafe entered her room and picked up her walking stick and the water jug. Callie tensed. This was her room. Hers.

"I'll just wipe up this water so you don't slip in it."

"I can manage."

He gave her a hard look and left. She'd just struggled to her feet when he returned with a rag and crouched to wipe up the water, which had left a trail from the nightstand clear across to the door.

"I said I'd do it."

"Yeah, but I said it first."

Callie realized she didn't have the energy to argue. In spite of herself she found her eyes drawn to the pull of muscles through his shoulders and arms as he worked, the way the lamplight lent a golden glow to his skin.

She tried to distract herself by braiding her hair, but her fingers refused to cooperate, working the strands into unmanageable tangles that defied her efforts with the brush.

Before she knew how it happened, Rafe had straightened and removed the brush from her hand, taking over the task of unsnarling the stubborn strands. His hands were gentle and sure as he first smoothed her hair, then divided it into sections for braiding. Callie held her breath, feeling the faint pressure of his fingertips, cool against her scalp.

"I used to braid my wife's hair."

His words were so low she almost believed she imagined them, yet his hands moved deftly and competently, lending credence to his claim. Callie was afraid to move. Afraid to speak. Afraid to break the spell that entwined them.

"Got something to tie this with?"

Wordlessly she passed him a faded satin ribbon. A

moment later the mattress shifted as he stood up. Slowly she pivoted around to face him.

"I didn't know you had a wife."

Poker player or not, Rafe couldn't hide the flash of emotion that jumped to his eyes. "She's dead. Anything I can get you?"

She shook her head.

"Good night, then."

"Good night." Wonderingly she reached up to touch the braid that fell across one shoulder. She heard Rafe's booted feet cross the cabin floor, followed by the firm closure of the front door behind him.

He was being too kind. He must want something.

Didn't all men want something?

Her heart started to beat so rapidly she found breathing difficult as she slid under the covers and lay there wide-eyed in the darkness. What if someone suspected what had really happened the day Bert died? What if Rafe had been sent to discover the truth?

# CHAPTER 5

The cold light of dawn brought Callie little relief from her suspicions concerning Rafe's presence on the ranch. He was too slick. Too pat. Flexing that potent charm of his, catching her off guard with his unexpected gentleness.

Well, she wouldn't be caught off guard again. And with that thought firmly in mind she stepped into the shadowy recesses of the barn. The air inside smelled damp, moist, and earthy, underscored by the sweetness of clean hay from the loft above.

She'd spent the morning going through every nook and cranny of the cabin one more time. Bert's money sock definitely wasn't there. With Rafe out rounding up some boards to start rebuilding the henhouse, she'd take advantage of his absence and search the barn.

Weeks earlier she'd scouted the land near the cabin, looking for telltale signs of recently disturbed earth, someplace where Bert might have buried his stash. To no avail. Yet she knew wherever he'd secreted it had to be easy to get to so he'd have a stake each time he went off to play cards.

She had to find that money!

If she failed, it meant Bert was laughing up his sleeve at her from wherever he was, having left her stuck here penniless, her independence so close yet not within her grasp.

Callie started, hearing an unfamiliar sound from overhead. Glancing up, she realized it was only the wind flapping the makeshift canvas tarp. She released her breath as slivers of sunlight crept in and danced on the far wall of the barn.

Knowing Bert and his sneaky ways, Callie had a notion the money sock had been stashed somewhere, if not exactly in plain sight, then the next best thing. As she picked her way through the straw she paused to tap each post that divided the barn's interior into individual stalls. Surely a hollow post would sound different from the others. She also looked for one that wasn't anchored the same as the rest, one that a man of Bert's size and strength could easily shift aside to reach his cache in the hollow below.

She worked her way from stall to stall, post by post.

Intent on her efforts she barely felt the sliver that became embedded deeply in her thumb or the perspiration that dewed her hairline and upper lip.

The final post in the last stall was as fixed and unmoving as all the rest. Frustrated, she grabbed the railing and gave it an agitated shake. Rafe's saddlebags, slung carelessly overtop, fell to the ground, spewing forth their contents.

Callie fought the surge of panic that rose instinctively to the surface. Bert was dead, and not about to come along and backhand her for her carelessness. She dropped to her knees and began stuffing the contents back into the leather pouches. A box of shotgun shells. A well-thumbed copy of Moby Dick. A bandanna. Matches. Callie's horse whinnied in her nearby stall. Overhead the canvas seemed to flap louder, almost a warning, as she fumbled with Rafe's things.

Hurry. Hurry.

Guiltily Callie glanced over her shoulder. What might Rafe think if he happened along now...

Haste made her careless. The thick sheaf of papers she was gathering together slid from her grasp, fanning handwritten notes and yellowed newspaper clippings across the brittle straw. Callie fumbled as she tried to collect them.

Suddenly she heard a step.

She gasped.

Rafe stood over her, his face in shadow, his stance menacing.

"Here. Let me." He knelt alongside her and in less than a minute had reorganized the papers, after which he stood and reached down to help Callie to her feet. "I guess you didn't hear me call."

She glanced to where he retained hold of her hand and thought of a small, pale bird caught in a strong wooden trap. In spite of herself she started to tremble and knew he could feel it. Callie despised her show of weakness and the man who was ultimately responsible. Even though he was dead, it was Bert's fault she felt this way.

"I wasn't meaning to pry. I was just passing by and somehow your saddlebags fell and—"

"No harm done," Rafe said easily, releasing her hand. "I've got nothing to hide. I came to tell you that I found that pile of sawn boards down by the creek, right where you said. Should be plenty to rebuild the chicken coop. Maybe even enough left over to sheet the roof." He pointed to the canvas overhead. "Can't vouch for how long that'll stay put."

"Fine." Callie preceded him from the barn and started back to the cabin. But her voice was flat and there was a dejected slump to her shoulders as she walked favoring her good ankle. He stared after her for a moment, then set off in the opposite direction to unload the wagon.

It sure was something, the way she'd flinched from him when he reached down to help her to her feet back there. He'd seen a similar reaction from whipped dogs and whipped men alike. As if she half expected him to haul off and flatten her just because he found her going through his stuff. And, damn it all, he'd had to fight the urge to pull her against him, to reassure her and chase away the nightmares. He might be every bit a scoundrel, but he'd never raised a hand against a woman. And couldn't abide those men who did.

Besides which, he'd seen her grasp the stall rail and shake it. Had watched his saddlebags hit the ground and seen the way she scooped everything back into them. Callie Lambert might have been looking for something out in the barn, but she didn't have a snoopy bone in her body. Which was a lot more than he could say for most people he met.

Like the Denzells. One reason he'd been so long fetching the boards was because he'd angled close to the Double D ranch where a copse of trees straddled the property line between the two homesteads. Besides sheltering him from prying eyes, the woods afforded a clear view of the Double D's comings and goings. One of those goings included the good Reverend Bligh, who had not made his way back to town yesterday the way he'd said. Instead, he'd reported back to Denzell. As far as the Denzells went, Rafe smelled bad things all around.

It didn't take long to unload the boards he'd fetched.

What would take some doing was scraping away the splintered mess in order to start over again in the same spot—if, indeed, Callie wanted the henhouse there. It occurred to him that the new coop would be more sheltered if it was built on the far side of the yard. After getting a rake from the barn, he got started clearing up the debris.

"You should be resting that ankle," Rafe said as he entered the cabin. "Near as I can tell you've been shuffling around most of the day."

"I made some lemonade." Callie offered him a glass. Rafe crossed the room and accepted the drink.

"Sounds good," he said. "But your ankle won't mend if you force it to carry your weight too soon."

"I can't just sit idle," Callie said, "not when there's so much needs doing."

Rafe took a long drink and backhanded his mouth and mustache. "Tell me what needs doing, and I'll see to it."

Turning away. Callie forced an awkward laugh. "I might get used to that. Then where would I be when..." When he left.

The words hung between them unsaid, yet understood. Callie prized her independence. Her home. Rafe was just passing through. He couldn't get caught up in the widow's problems. He needed his wits sharp and his energies high to accomplish what he'd come here for. Playing ranch hand had gotten him this close to the Denzells. To him, it was all part of the game. A game Callie didn't know anything about and wasn't about to be understanding. Deliberately he stepped back to the role of hired hand.

"You should set a spell. But first, there's something I want to ask you."

Callie followed him out near the remains of the wrecked henhouse and listened to Rafe voice his reasons for recommending the new site. She kicked at the pile of rubble. "What about this mess?"

"Might as well set a match to it," Rafe said. "Can't see it's good for much else."

"I guess," Callie agreed. Suddenly she dropped to her knees and started scrabbling frantically through the ruined mess.

Rafe watched in stunned silence for a full half-minute.

"Callie. What on earth are you looking for?"

"Don't mind me," she said. "Just go on with what you were doing." As she spoke she pushed aside a pile of boards, crawled over them and started on a second stack.

Seconds later Rafe scooped her to her feet, despite her outraged squeal of, "What do you think you're doing?"

"You tell me." Deliberately he kept her close, elbows pinned to her sides so she couldn't flail out at him. He had a hunch she could flail up a storm. She twisted from side to side in his arms. His grip tightened reflexively.

"Let me go."

"I just want to ask you something first, if you'd stay still long enough. Okay?" Eyes on hers he reached into his inside shirt pocket, pulled out a dirty gray sock and dangled it in front of her. "This wouldn't happen to be what you're looking for, would it?"

Callie gasped and snatched the sock from his grasp. As she delved through the contents, it sounded to Rafe as if the entire countryside had suddenly gone quiet. Her gaze met his, distrust clearly written across her face.

"Where did you get this?"

"Found it in the rubble this morning when I started to clear up."

"Why didn't you tell me before?"

"I forgot."

"You forgot? Or were you planning to keep it for yourself?"

Rafe released her then, so suddenly she stumbled before regaining her footing. She winced when her full weight landed on her injured ankle.

"If I was planning on keeping it for myself, I would have rode out of here this morning and kept on going."

She seemed to be mentally weighing his words as she glanced from the money sock to him, then back to the sock. He held his breath. If she ordered him off the ranch this minute, everything he'd accomplished so far would have been for naught.

"I suppose that's true enough," Callie conceded. "It's just that I've been looking for this for months now. I knew it had to be here someplace, but I didn't know where Bert..." Her words trailed away, her eyes on the distant horizon. "It figures. The henhouse is the one place I didn't think to look. Bert always claimed he couldn't abide the smell of chickens."

"Is that what you were looking for in the barn earlier?"

Callie nodded.

"This mostly all the money you got?"

She nodded again.

"Is it enough to keep Denzell from forcing you off the ranch?"

"For now it's enough to buy winter supplies and seed for the spring planting. The rest is up to the Almighty."

Rafe returned his attention to the ruins. "Okay if I burn this mess now?"

"More than okay." She paused and Rafe could see there was something more she was of a mind to say, but he knew better than to rush her. "I don't have much to spare, but I'll be able to pay you a little something for your troubles."

"I told you before, I don't want to be paid."

He could tell she didn't believe him. "Everyone wants to be paid."

"Not me."

"And if I insist?"

Rafe blew out a long, impatient breath. He didn't want her money, but he did want to ease her suspicions. "Are all women from Wyoming as ornery as you?"

"I never knew any other women. Except for the nuns. They weren't ornery."

"I guess not. Well, I met a few Wyoming gals in my day. And I swear I never met anyone who had quite so many quills sticking out of her spine as you do."

"I'm sure you've known a great many women, Mr. Millar. And I'm not surprised to hear that they were meek and mild-mannered. But hear this: if you insist on staying on and working my homestead, you'll be paid for your efforts. The decision whether to stay rests with you."

That said, Callie turned and made her way back to the cabin, Bert's money sock grasped tight in one fist. Her back was rigid as a flagpole, yet he saw the way she favored her good ankle, all the while trying not to.

Callie was shaking from head to toe by the time she reached the cabin's front steps. She told herself it was the excitement of having finally found the money, and nothing whatsoever to do with the sensations she'd felt at being held tight in Rafe Millar's arms. He was a bully same as all men, flexing his strength, strong-arming her into submission. Well, no more! Not now that she was a woman of means.

Taking a deep breath, Callie tipped the sock upside down over the table, shaking loose every last coin and paper bill. Then she lined them up, counting slowly, savoring the powerful feeling that came with having money of her own. The final tally fell short of her expectations, although it was a darn sight better than nothing. She pulled out a sheet of paper, her pen, and the bottle of ink. Best to start keeping an accounts ledger. See how far she could make her small cache stretch.

Next, she made a quick scan of the cabin, seeking the perfect hiding spot for her wealth. Money brought with it a certain responsibility, and she wasn't about to take any chances. In what she considered a stroke of cleverness she opened the hem in her warm winter cloak, stitched the money securely in place, and closed up the hem.

Only as she tied the final knot and clipped the final thread did she think back to the episode earlier in the barn and Rafe's saddlebags. Something niggled in the back of her mind. Something important that she ought to be aware of.

The sensation continued as she brewed a cup of tea, increasing in intensity until she couldn't stand it. With a quick glance to where a new chicken coop was rapidly taking shape thanks to Rafe's skills with a hammer, she stole back out to the barn. His saddlebags were just where he'd left them, complete with the collection of tattered notes and newspaper pages.

Squelching her feelings of guilt she unfastened the flap and withdrew the packet. She unfolded the most recent-looking pages and started to read. Involuntarily she gasped. The story was from *The Oregonian,* dated four months earlier, detailing the account of Bert's murder. Follow-up articles recounted the story of the man believed responsible, and his escape.

Callie's hand shook as she refolded the pages. Who was Rafe Millar? A man who roamed the countryside, preying on widows and orphans and other poor unfortunates? Or a man sent here by persons unknown to discover the true events of that day, contrary to those she'd told the sheriff?

To think that she'd invited Rafe Millar into her home. Eaten at the same table with him. Lulled herself into feeling safe when he was around.

"Twice in one day's kind of stretching the odds of coincidence, wouldn't you say?"

Callie whirled, the damning proof clutched in one hand. She shook the paper at him. "Who are you? Why have you come here?"

He sauntered right up to her, cocky as you please, and retrieved his belongings, including the newspaper stories, which he stuffed back inside his bag. "I told you before, I have nothing to hide. If you wanted to go through my things, you ought to have asked me first."

"How do you explain this?"

"The fact that I knew what happened to your husband before you told me?"

"You came here deliberately."

"That's true enough. I thought you might be interested in selling. But before I could even ask about it, you made it plain as the nose on your face that nothing and nobody was going to see you budge. So I moved on. Or set out to. Not my fault I couldn't make it across the damn river."

To her dismay. Callie found herself wanting to believe him. Wishing it was possible to trust another human being. "Reverend Bligh didn't seem to have any trouble."

He grabbed her arm and she felt the steely strength of his fingers biting into her flesh. "Your churchman is a liar. I saw him this morning setting off from Denzell's place. You might ask yourself what the two of them are cooking up that brought him calling yesterday, all sweet and pious and concerned for your well-being."

Callie stared at his hand on her forearm until he released her. "What were you doing near the Double D?"

"Got turned around, looking for those boards is all."

"Why should I believe you?"

"Why would I lie?"

"I don't know. But you're up to something no good, that much is for sure. And I won't be party to it. I want you off my property. Now!"

"'Fraid I can't do that, Callie,"

"What do you mean you can't do that? I'm ordering you off my land. I'll fetch the sheriff here, if I have a need to."

"I make it a point never to leave a job half done. Which includes your henhouse."

"I don't believe you. No more than I believe your trumped-up excuse for being here in the first place."

"Believe what you want. I'll finish up tomorrow, then I'll go. Peaceable-like." He stabbed her shoulder with his index finger. "But don't say I didn't try and warn you. Your neighbor and that reverend are up to no good, and you're sitting plumb in the middle of it. I can smell it."

"Only thing I smell around here is a liar, Mr. Millar. You can soak in the river till your skin shrivels and your hair falls out. Won't do nothing to erase the stink."

"Is that a fact? Well, speaking of baths, it wouldn't hurt you any to have one yourself."

With that he flung his saddlebags over his shoulder and left her fuming that he'd gotten in the final word.

## CHAPTER 6

Anger ripped through her, the force of it carrying her to the flowerbed despoiled by Rafe's horse. Her limbs trembled with fury as she knelt and plunged her hands into the moist soil, plucking out every last nasturtium. Seedlings that she'd coddled and transplanted with such loving care months earlier were ripped from their nest and tossed into a haphazard pile.

After emptying the flowerbed, she sat back on her heels and wiped her sweaty forehead with the back of her wrist. Damn Rafe Millar and his arrogant cocksure ways! How dare he talk to her like some soiled dove he came across in a saloon or house of ill repute?

Far worse than that, how dare he insinuate himself here on her homestead, pretending to care about her home and her animals. For all she knew, he'd engineered that whole episode with the lost cow. It was just the kind of stunt a selfish, black-hearted vagrant would pull. Unless...

Rising, she told herself she didn't dare consider any unlesses. She'd take to her grave the truth about Bert's death and the man deemed responsible.

Her gaze traveled south, in the direction of the Double D ranch. It also appeared Rafe Millar had an uncommon interest in the doings of her neighbors. She'd called him on it, more than once, in fact, and he'd always responded with a quick, pat answer. But something about the whole setup didn't ring true.

No more than Rafe's sounding truly sincere when he'd warned her about Denzell and Bligh being up to no good. As if he was genuinely concerned about her. More likely his concern was all part of an act designed to throw her off guard. And successfully, at that, for she'd been feeling off guard more often than not lately.

Damn Rafe Millar to hell and back! The man had the most ingratiating attitude. Needed taking down a peg or two, is what he needed. Callie was a respectable lady. A property owner. A woman of means. She smoothed back her hair, then glanced down at her shapeless black skirt, its hem mired in dust. Atop the skirt was a dingy gray blouse she'd washed so many times a body could nearabouts see clear through it.

She held her hands out in front of her, nails and fingertips crusted with dirt. It had been a long time since she'd dressed like a lady—or smelled like a lady, for that matter. She heaved a sigh for all the losses in her life, big and small, vowing then and there to replace them with accomplishments. She'd take her place in society if it was the last thing she did. Command the kind of respect she deserved.

And come tomorrow she'd take herself and her newfound wealth into town. While she might still be in mourning, that didn't mean she had to dress as though she didn't have two bits to rub together, did it?

Inside the cabin Callie dragged the washtub out from under her bed and heated the big black kettle of water. The hot water reached to midcalf level once she squashed herself into the tub with her knees bent up near her chest. She unwrapped a tiny sliver of the scented soap she'd made herself until Bert put an end to it, claiming soap was an unnecessary indulgence. Bert's favorite boast was that there weren't nothing wrong with the good honest scent of a body's sweat. Any odors that didn't wash off with creek water alone, the good Lord must have meant to be there.

Raising the soap to her nose, Callie inhaled the delicate lavender fragrance. Come spring, she'd grow masses of lavender. Enough to make sachets and pomanders for every drawer and closet in the house. And no man would tell her it was a waste to grow something a body couldn't eat. She became positively giddy at the thought.

The giddy feeling persisted as she dried herself and laid out clean clothes. Dressed in a dark green skirt and an ivory blouse with a panel of lace at the throat, she stood in front of the cheval looking glass and frowned at her reflection as she attempted to coax her dead straight hair into something a little more elegant than her usual topknot or braid.

She was sorely out of practice with feminine skills, and the resultant French roll was more than a trifle off-kilter. She had spent too many years trying to make herself as unattractive as possible, in hopes Bert would find her physically repugnant. He'd complained long and often about her fine, limp hair, the way her cheekbones stuck out of her face, the way she didn't put any meat on her bones. No more shape than a boy, Bert used to say.

Turning sideways and dabbing a little rosewater behind her ears, Callie conceded he was right. She was unfashionably thin. And pale. Leaning close to the glass, she pinched her cheeks in an effort to put some color in them. Then she went to check on dinner.

Once the roast was nicely browned, she pulled out her best cloth napkins and lit two candles on the table. No more saving her nice things for "one day" that might never come, Callie decided. Out of the hazy memory of her childhood came a picture of a small bottle of scent that her mother had never opened. Callie didn't know where Ma had gotten the scent from, only that it was her most prized possession. How much more satisfying if Ma had splashed herself generously with it each day, enjoying that one small luxury. That way she would have died leaving an empty bottle behind instead of a full one.

The sun had long gone down and the roast had been fetched from the oven when Callie rose and wandered to the window. She could make out the silhouette of the new henhouse in the rapidly approaching dusk. Stepping onto the porch she took a deep breath of the clear, sweet evening air, which held just the faintest hint of fall. Overhead, the first few stars were making themselves visible. A body would never know there'd been such a storm of late.

Closer by, the homestead was peaceful and serene. She heard the occasional muted cluck of the hens as they checked out their new lodgings. Grasping the post that spanned the porch from floor to roof, she rested her forehead against the rough wood and surveyed her land, hers as far as the eye could see. It was a good feeling.

The good feeling was ruined by a shadowy movement over near the barn, reminding her that she wasn't alone. Soon, she promised herself. Soon this land would be exclusively hers. With a sudden about-face she returned to the cabin and slammed the door behind her.

The smell of fresh herbs and cooked meat wafted up as she sank her carving knife into the roast. Her stomach responded with a most unladylike noise. She'd just carried her plate to the table and hadn't yet said grace or taken a bite when she heard the sound of footsteps on the porch stairs , followed by a knock at the door.

Dash it.

The knock was repeated. "Come in." The door opened to reveal Rafe, who hovered uncertainly in the shadow of the threshold. "I didn't mean to disturb your meal," he said. "I just wanted to say the henhouse is finished. I'll be on my way at first light."

Abruptly Callie's appetite faded. Across the room their gazes met, but at too great a distance for her to glean any understanding of Rafe's expression.

"Well," she said finally. "Are you coming in? Or just planning to stand there and invite in every bug in the state?"

She sensed his hesitation before he stepped inside and closed the door behind him. As he crossed the room she noticed that, like herself, he had recently bathed. His still-damp hair gleamed darkly in the lamplight, combed straight back from his distinctively broad forehead. He was wearing clean buckskin trousers, every bit as tight-fitting as the last pair, and a clean leather jerkin.

"It'd be easier for a body to thank you if you'd take a seat." There was something almost primal about the way he looked, standing in her kitchen. As if he had little in common with the trappings of polite society. He appeared edgy, like he couldn't wait to get back outside, out under the open sky with the stars for his roof and the coyotes for company. Amazing, really, that he'd stayed this long.

"I didn't expect you'd cotton to sharing a table with someone you called a liar to his face."

Finding the right words had never come easy to Callie, and today proved no exception. She glanced down to where her hands lay, folded primly in her lap. It appeared she'd wounded his masculine pride and he'd taken exception to her attack on his character. "I may have spoke too heated, and I apologize. For certain I appreciate all you've done around here."

Rafe turned the chair around and straddled it, arms resting along the curved back, eyeing her closely. "Your food's getting cold."

She pushed her untouched plate to one side. "I don't feel quite so hungry as I thought."

Rafe tapped the chair back with maddening precision, a thoughtful look on his face.

"Well," Callie said finally. "Are you going to accept my apology or not?"

"I'm thinking on it."

With an impatient expletive she pushed her chair back and made to leave the table. Slick as silk Rafe reached across the table and manacled her wrist, arresting her movements. She froze, feeling the deadly pressure as those lean brown fingers tightened their grip.

"You've got an annoying habit of flouncing off anytime the discussion isn't going exactly your way."

"I apologized," she said ungraciously. "What more do you want?"

"You could wait and see whether or not I decide to accept it."

As he spoke he turned her hand over in his and traced the lines that crisscrossed her suddenly sensitive palm. She tried to pull away, but he didn't let her. He'd spotted the sliver stuck deep in her thumb and frowned at it. "See, I've been called a great many things in my life. Some of them were true. Some of them weren't. But a liar...?" Looking her way once more, he shook his head slowly from side to side.

"If there's one thing I pride myself on, it's speaking the truth."

His grip tightened, stopping at a point just short of pain. "Fetch me a pin and I'll get this sliver out for you."

"It doesn't hurt." She sucked in her breath and closed her eyes when he pressed near the injured area.

"It's your right hand, Callie. Barn wood. Sure to get infected if you don't get it out."

"Oh, very well." She pulled free of him and got out her sewing basket.

He frowned at the needle she passed him, lost from sight against his large, sun-browned fingers. "Can't hardly see this one, let alone hang onto it."

Compressing her lips she passed him a darning needle.

"I said you needn't bother."

He slanted her his trademark wolfish grin. "Miss the chance to watch you squirm? I wouldn't hear of it."

Callie settled in her seat, crossed her ankles, and tucked her left hand under the table, out of Rafe's sight. Reluctantly she extended her other hand across the table.

"Can't work like that," he said, getting up and moving his chair alongside hers. Reaching around her in a position that felt almost like an embrace, he positioned her hand in his.

Callie jumped when he brushed the side of her breast as he reached across the table and moved the candle closer. "That's better."

Not to her it wasn't.

It was worse, much worse than anything she'd imagined, being held that way and wishing, Lord help her...Callie didn't know what she wished.

She was conscious of his shoulder brushing hers, the steady rise and fall of his chest, the way his breath warmed the side of her neck.

Other parts of her body grew warm in reaction, as well.

Most notably, a spreading warmth low in her belly that seemed to be flooding her limbs, especially where his leg rubbed against hers.

"You okay?"

Callie nodded jerkily. She wasn't, but she'd die before she admitted it to him. Her thumb had started to throb hours ago, and watching Rafe probe it with a sharp needle, she sucked in her breath and squeezed the inside of her leg under the table. Shut her eyes and squeezed hard.

Not for anything would she let him see just how much she hurt.

"Just about there...Damn. It broke off," he said in husky tones that feathered the hollow curve between shoulder and neck and distracted her most pleasantly from his probing.

"Hold steady now."

Callie bit her lip till she tasted blood, eyes closed against the sudden hot sting of tears.

"Got it!"

She let out her breath in a rush.

"You can let go now."

Only then did Callie realize with something akin to horror that it had been his leg she was squeezing under the table. She felt herself flush. How on earth had that happened?

Gently Rafe pried her fingers from his buckskin-clad thigh. "You've got yourself quite a grip. I'm sorry if that smarted some."

Callie fought to regain control. "I'm sure it'll start to feel better any minute now."

Rafe angled her chair around till they faced each other and he had one knee on either side of her. "You don't trust me, Callie. Now, just why exactly is that?"

Callie averted her gaze.

His free hand snaked between them. Thumb and fore-finger pinched her chin, turning her face back around to his. "I expect an honest answer, now."

Eyes steely, chin thrust forward, Callie met his gaze.

Her skin burned every place Rafe held her. "I don't trust any man."

She expected him to release her like a hot rock.

Instead, he took his time about it. Slowly his fingers uncurled from around her wrist. Slower yet the fingers imprisoning her face gentled, till their touch bordered on a caress. "Why's that?"

Feeling her hands tremble slightly, she reknotted them in her lap, away from his gaze. "Never met a man yet who gave me any reason to trust him. Including my pa and my older brother."

"I see." Rafe sat back in his chair and crossed his arms over his chest. "In that case, apology accepted." He extended his right hand toward her, leaving Callie little choice but to slide her hand inside his. She was conscious of the warmth of his skin, the callused, leathery feel of his palm and finger-tips. The sensations chased clear up her arm in the most unsettling of ways.

He didn't let her go right away. Instead, he raised her hand to his lips and pressed a kiss on the spot where he'd removed the sliver. Then he did something that caught Callie totally off guard. He guided her wounded thumb slowly to outline the contour of his lips, bottom and top.

Callie felt as if melted wax spilled through her limbs in a heated rush. His lips were indescribably soft, contrasted by the bristles of his mustache. Opening his lips he pulled her thumb just inside the hot moist cavity of his mouth and gave a slow gentle suck that she felt clear down to her toes. Then, ever so slowly, he returned her hand to its mate in her lap.

"I see you had a bath."

Callie bit back a self-conscious smile. "You too."

"I like your hair that way."

Callie felt her blush deepen. She didn't want him to think she'd taken special pains solely for his benefit. "If you want, I could give you a shave before you go."

Rafe fingered the dark growth stubbling his jaw. "I'm getting kind of used to it. You don't like it?"

Callie tried for a careless shrug. "It doesn't matter to me one way or the other."

His eyes held undisguised laughter as they met hers, silently challenging her words. Callie's gaze slid from his, lighting with sudden fascination on the pie safe.

"You smell real good."

Her blush intensified. The cabin felt stifling. She jumped to her feet and fumbled in her skirt pocket. "Since you're leaving early, I wanted to pay you." She placed a handful of coins on the table before him. "Is that a fair amount for your labors?"

Rafe nodded, but didn't take the money, which lay between them, winking in the candlelight. Callie all but held her breath as he lazily made his way to his feet. Once again she was aware of the way he dwarfed the small cabin. Not just his physical size and strength, but something harder to define. Something linked to the air of power and control he managed to exude. He was a man in charge of every situation. Capable of meeting and mastering whatever life flung at him.

It was that same sense of control that Callie felt keenly lacking in her life. Something she needed to reclaim for herself, especially with Rafe Millar catching her off guard ever since he'd shown up at her doorstep.

Even now, days later, her scalp tingled at the memory of him braiding her hair. Her limbs went weak when she recalled the way he'd stripped off her stockings and bandaged her sprained ankle. In a few short days he'd made a tremendous impact on her life. Come tomorrow she'd be glad to see the back of him. More than glad.

As if reading her mind, he took a step toward her.

Followed by a second.

Callie's heart rate increased as they stood chest to chest, belly to belly, with scarcely an inch between them.

"Since you don't trust me, anyway," Rafe said, his breath touching her forehead like steam rising from hot water. "I guess it won't make much difference if I kiss you."

"Don't." The word barely escaped from the tightened muscles of her throat.

With one finger beneath her chin he tilted her face up toward his. "Any woman smells this good, she needs kissing, if only as a thank you from the lucky man close enough to notice."

Callie trembled clear down inside her boots as he lowered his head to hers.

# CHAPTER 7

R afe had intended the merest brush of his lips across hers. Just enough intimate contact to shatter her cool composure. To try to force her to toughen up. 'Cause inside, Callie was as soft and untried as goose down. And vulnerable as all get out. Unfortunately for him, her insides weren't the only thing he discovered to be underbelly soft.

First off, there was her skin. And despite his best intentions, his hold on her chin gentled to a lingering caress as he slid his hand across her cheek to her temples, burrowing through her silky hair before seeking out the vulnerable nape of her neck. Her lips, too. Soft as velvet. Sweet as just-tapped maple syrup.

He felt himself moving against her, deepening the kiss.

He parted his lips. Flicked the seam of hers invitingly with his tongue. When she didn't respond, his tongue got busy, boldly tracing the outline of her lips. After which he sucked ever so gently on her lower lip, coaxing it to join his.

Callie stood in his arms, wooden as any fencepost. If he didn't know better, he'd think she was a woman who'd never been kissed, let alone known the marriage bed. Then again, maybe she just hadn't been kissed with any sort of expertise, something Rafe Millar was about to change forever.

He pressed his free hand against her back, fingers splayed, outlining the curve of her spine, then moving lower, past her waist to the rounded curve of her hips. Insinuating himself closer, he could feel her breasts flatten against his chest, accompanied by the frantic flurry of her heartbeat.

Raising his head he drew a breath, looked long and purposefully into her glazed, disbelieving eyes, and kissed her again. This time he caught her off guard, her lips parted ever so slightly, and his tongue slid inside, coaxed her mouth open wider, and kissed her proper.

With bold, sure moves he explored the sweetness of her, inhaled her subtle feminine scent. The telltale stirring in his loins gave him pause to slow things down. For despite her sweet and feminine softness, Callie wasn't the type of woman he'd ever take a tumble with. So he'd best be stopping before things got out of hand.

Damn, if she didn't feel good pressed against him. He took one last deep breath, inhaling her fragrance, then gently, carefully, he released her. First her lips, followed by a slow and reluctant peeling of his body's length from hers. Callie was breathing hard, chest rising and falling with agitation, eyes sparking with something that could be either anger or passion. Something that made Rafe wonder if he was about to get his face slapped.

He stepped back, just in case, and tried to gauge her reaction. Twin dots of color dimpled her cheeks. With her hair mussed and her eyes on fire, she looked wild and untamed. And damned desirable. A far cry from her usual pale, poised, and controlled self. So his kiss had accomplished one thing, at least. Had shook her up good. Shown her how vulnerable she really was. His body's automatic response had seen to that.

"I hope you're not waiting on an apology," he said at last, when it appeared she wasn't about to speak or strike out. "I never apologize for kissing a woman who needs to be kissed."

His words seemed to bring her around. She dragged the back of her sleeve across her mouth. "That was disgusting!"

Rafe couldn't help himself. He rocked back on his heels and laughed. Softly at first, then with growing gusto. Callie looked suitably affronted. "I don't see the humor in the situation."

"Here you are," he said, "all slicked up. Mad 'cause I kissed you. You would have been madder still if I didn't."

"I am not slicked up," Callie informed him. "And if you knew anything about decent folk, you'd know no one kisses in such a vulgar way." She punctuated her words with a shudder.

"You're wrong on both counts, Callie," Rafe said. "I know slicked up when I see it. As for the kissing part..." He gave her his most damning grin. "I barely got started."

She refused to meet his teasing gaze. "I want you off my ranch at first light."

"Not to worry," Rafe said. "I'll be gone long before then."

Back in the barn, Rafe gnawed his beef jerky, his thoughts still with the woman he had recently kissed. If that husband of hers had never taken the time to kiss her good and proper, he could hardly imagine what might have followed in the intimacies between man and wife. No wonder Callie didn't trust anyone in pants. Seemed not a one had ever done anything right by her. Even him.

Especially him.

He felt a mild twinge at his earlier outright lie. His bold

claim to always speak the truth. He preferred the truth to lies, sure enough, but life threw out more than a handful of special circumstances. Times when a lie was a gentler, kinder way to go. And times when a lie was a matter of life or death.

Lying back on his bedroll, hands stacked beneath his head, he stared at the makeshift canvas tarp above him and deliberately pushed his thoughts away from Callie, back in the direction of Luke and his murderers, the Denzell brothers. Rafe was allowing himself to get distracted from his true mission in these parts. It was damned unfortunate Callie Lambert seemed to have got herself tangled up in the middle of things, but it was none of his affair. Lighting out of here in the morning was for the best. There had to be other, less complicated ways to attack Denzell's exposed rear flank. It was simply a matter of biding his time and coming up with a workable plan.

Callie barely slept a wink. First there was the incessant drum of autumn rains on the cabin roof all night long. Second there was the even more unsettling memory of Rafe Millar's open mouth against hers, the hot invasive feel of his tongue teasing hers, and—the Almighty forgive her! Callie quickly crossed herself for good measure—the fact that she desperately longed to kiss him back. Had to hold herself rigidly in check so as not to melt like softened wax against the contours of his masculine strength. Given half a chance, he'd turn that strength of his against her, the same way all men eventually did.

Closing her eyes, she called to mind the clean, creek-washed fragrance of his skin and hair. The feel of his whiskers rasping her chin, his unexpectedly soft mustache brushing her upper lip. The bold way he made no effort to disguise the feel of his aroused manhood pressing against her. Callie felt a fresh flood of scalding sensations at the memory. Restlessly she moved against the sheets. No decent woman felt this way. Did she?

She tried to imagine a different life from the one she knew. A life where her husband's embrace kindled the same kind of shivery sensations as Rafe's did. Where a wife welcomed her husband's attentions rather than submitted to his brutality and harshness.

The rain let up 'round about the time Callie finished her breakfast, and she decided to follow through with her plans for a trip to town. There was no sign or sound from Rafe Millar, and since he claimed so stalwartly to be a man of his word, she assumed he'd made good on his promise to leave before first light. And good riddance.

After seeing to the most urgent of her chores, Callie hitched two horses to her rattletrap buckboard and headed in the direction of town. As she crossed the river, she noticed the bridge showed signs of recent repair work, new wooden boards standing out in golden sharp contrast to their more gray and weathered counterparts. As recent as the other day? Or just new enough that Rafe noticed and stretched the facts to suit his purposes?

Midday was approaching by the time Callie reached the tidy town of Springfield, tucked into the valley formed by the fertile plains of the McKenzie and Willamette rivers. The story went that the first settler built his house in "the field near a spring," which eventually gave the town its name.

Driving down Main Street, she noticed that several new shops had opened since her last visit here, including a milliner's and a dry goods. Bert had accompanied her last time and wouldn't have sat still for her poking through any new shops, even if she'd had the urge. Callie was struck anew by the realization that she now had no one to answer to, no one's needs to consider save her own. A heady feeling, indeed.

Pulling the buckboard to the side of the road, she tucked her basket over her arm and stepped carefully up onto the wooden boardwalk. The roadway itself resembled one large oozing mud puddle after last night's rain. Which reminded her she still needed to hire someone to fix her barn roof. She wondered how much the repairs might cost, envisioning her meager stash of funds shrinking far too rapidly for her peace of mind.

Perhaps the purchase of a length of yard goods to sew herself a new gown was an unnecessary expenditure after all. It would be best to content herself with a few staple food items. A measure of cocoa with her purchases would be enough of an indulgence, unless she saw something else that caught her eye instead.

Passing the church, she reached the corner housing the general store. Outside the barber shop several old-timers sat on a crude wooden bench. She tensed, hearing Bert's name muttered between them. Would folks never leave things be? Was the scandal of Bert's shooting something she'd be confronted with every time she set foot off the ranch? Her first trip to town as an independent woman was something to be savored, not dreaded. And already she felt the isolation that had gripped her on each previous trip. She was an outsider. Something of a curiosity. She had never really fit in here and never truly would.

Telling herself she didn't care, she reached for the door to the general store. A woman stepped out, head turned as she spoke to someone behind her, and walked smack into Callie. As they stepped apart, Callie recognized the older woman from Sunday services and was about to exchange pleasantries, but the words froze in her throat at the expression on the other woman's face.

The woman straightened, pulled her skirt aside as if Callie might soil her, and said sharply, "Mind where you go!"

Callie recoiled in like fashion, spine rigid. "You, ma'am, walked straight into me."

The woman looked her over. "Impertinent chit. No wonder you couldn't keep your husband at home." With that, she turned her back and left Callie staring, open-mouthed. The old-timers were suddenly abuzz with conversation among themselves, and Callie knew that word of the encounter would be all over town in a flash. She'd always felt the townsfolk didn't much care for her, but did they blame her for Bert's drunken and disorderly conduct?

She received an equally cool reception in the milliner's, where the shopkeeper seemed disinclined to wait on her, and Callie left without making a purchase. Entering the general store, she was well aware of the way all conversation ceased. As she paid for her items she felt all eyes upon her, and she heard the talk start up again as soon as she set foot outside. She heard, or imagined she heard, snickers among the inaudible comments. Having grown up the daughter of the town drunk, she'd hoped to leave such things behind when she came west to start over.

With a light basket and a heavy heart, she made her way to the lumber mill at the far end of town. With any luck the manager would know someone who'd be willing to come out and fix her barn roof.

En route to the mill she passed directly by the dry goods store. Her feet halted in front of it, as if they had a mind of their own. Through the window the subdued daylight reflected on a bolt of cloth. The material shimmered in greenish-blue tones, a rich, jewel-like taffeta. She inched closer, imagining how a gown fashioned from such a fabric would look either green or blue by turns as a body moved about in it and the light danced across its tucks and creases. Her fingers tightened on her reticule, conscious of the weight of the coins inside. A heavy longing, like a brick, seemed to sit on her chest as she gazed wistfully at the cloth.

Finally she proceeded to the mill, only to be informed by a rather blunt and bad-smelling man that posting a notice on the tack board inside the general store was her best bet.

She was mentally composing the notice, wondering if it ought to contain a mention of wages, when she glanced across the street to where her wagon sat and realized it was axle-deep in the mud.

"You ought to have stayed home, Callie Lambert," she told herself. Holding her skirts up out of the mud, she picked her way cautiously across the slippery street, placed her basket onto the wagon floor, and bent to survey the full extent of the damage. It appeared as if she'd need to be pulled free. Surely the livery would be able to help. She had just started in that direction when a familiar figure stepped in front of her, blocking her path.

"Now if this isn't some unexpected pleasure." Denzell raised his hat in greeting and leered openly.

Callie refrained from scowling. It wouldn't surprise her to find out he'd engineered the whole thing, mud and all. At the very least, he must have seen her wagon stuck and decided to hang around and ingratiate his way into her life.

"It's been some spell since we've had the pleasure of your pretty face in town."

"You know how much work is involved in keeping a ranch," she said politely.

"Don't I just." As if by prearranged signal, Denzell was joined by his two sons, one on each side. Callie didn't even know their given names. They'd always been "the Denzell boys," and probably would continue to be "boys" well into their twilight years. One was tall and skinny, with a scar across one cheek. The other was stockier, with rusty red hair. All three Denzells had the same squinty, mean eyes.

"I was just telling the boys here how I noticed your barn roof was half off, last time I was by that way. The boys was thinking about moseying on over, see if'n perhaps you needed a hand getting it sound."

"I appreciate your concern," Callie said, quickly thinking up a lie, "but I have a hired hand. He's quite capable of doing whatever needs seeing to."

"Like unsticking your wagon here?"

She could tell by his voice that Denzell didn't believe her. "Like I said, whatever needs doing."

"Didn't know you'd took on a hand, Callie. What's his name?"

Callie's thoughts raced. But before she could respond a different voice broke the silence.

"Why don't you ask him in person?"

Rafe.

Callie didn't know if she should be relieved or furious that he'd shown up right this minute. Just in time to find her in a jam and catch her in a bold-faced lie, after all her insistence that she could manage fine on her own.

Denzell recovered first. "Don't believe we've had the pleasure. Denzell's the name. These are my boys, Junior and Red."

"Millar," Rafe said shortly, taking Denzell's outstretched hand. It seemed the boys didn't speak. At least not in the presence of their father, who was studying Rafe closely. Rafe returned the man's stare.

"You look more like an Injun scout than a ranch hand."

"I'm kind of versatile that way. Like Mrs. Lambert says, I take care of whatever needs doing."

"Been in these parts long?"

"Nope."

"Ever been here before?"

"Nope." Rafe turned to Callie. "You're finished sooner than I thought, Mrs. Lambert. I expected to have the wagon unstuck by the time you were ready to leave."

Denzell looked from Rafe to her and back to Rafe as if he didn't quite know what to make of things. "Fix that barn roof yet?" he asked finally.

"First up when we get back," Rafe said. "That's one reason we're here. To get the supplies for the job."

"Hmmph," Denzell said. "Well, be sure and holler if you need a hand. That's what neighbors are for. Look forward to seeing you again real soon, Callie." With that, he herded his sons in the direction of the saloon.

As soon as they were out of sight, Callie turned on Rafe furiously. "How dare you make a liar out of me?"

Rafe's eyes twinkled. "You were doing just fine on your own."

"I am doing fine on my own," Callie said through a clenched jaw. "I don't need any help from you."

"Not even to pull this wagon out of the mud?" he asked. "Think careful now. You'd be smart to ask me back to fix up your roof. Unless you'd rather Junior and Red show up with their pa to "help you out."

"Weren't you going to ask Denzell for a job at his mill?"

"I talked to the foreman already today. He said they won't be doing any hiring till the spring."

"Were you planning on sticking around till then?"

"I don't like to plan too far in advance. Kind of ruins life's surprises, wouldn't you say?"

"I don't believe I've ever had a nice surprise in my life."

Her words shocked even Callie with their candor. A revelation that didn't go unnoticed by Rafe, who glanced up at her from where he was bent over inspecting the underside of the buckboard.

Slowly he straightened and came toward her. Callie's heart started up again in that maddening way she was coming to expect whenever Rafe got within range of her senses. "Maybe," he said in a husky voice, "it's time we did something to change all that. Let you see what a nice surprise can be all about."

# CHAPTER 8

Rafe flicked the reins and the buckboard picked up speed. Alongside him Callie lurched slightly before regaining her balance. Rafe's horse was tied to the back of the wagon, which was loaded high with two bundles of shingles and several lengths of board. Once they crossed the bridge, the horses seemed to pick up the pace on their own, as if sensing they were close to food and shelter.

Rafe snuck a sideways glance at Callie, who sat stony-faced alongside him, clutching a near-empty basket on her lap. Mentally Rafe tipped his hat to lady luck, who one more time had intervened on his behalf, giving him not only a bona fide excuse to stay on Callie's spread but an introduction to the Denzell clan, as well. Things couldn't get much better.

At least not from where he sat. He had a sneaking feeling that, as far as Callie was concerned, there was real definite room for improvement. He studied her profile openly, as if daring her to turn and acknowledge his presence. Not by the slightest glance did she let on she even knew he was there, let alone staring at her.

He exhaled heavily as they rounded a bend and the cabin came into view. He decided it would be best to get this said now as later. "You're not planning to hold it against me for that one little kiss now, are you?"

"Of course not," Callie said quickly. Too quickly, Rafe thought. He would have been more convinced if she'd at least pondered his words a minute or two in her usual way. He noted the twin dots of color that stained her cheeks. The way she kept her eyes dead ahead, refusing to meet his gaze.

"Just wanted to get that out of the way between us," he said as he drew the wagon to a stop in front of the cabin. "I've found that's usually best."

She turned then and, for the first time since they left town, her eyes met his. "What are you stopped here for?"

"For you to get out," Rafe replied.

"Oh," Callie said. The red dots grew brighter. So did her eyes. "I suppose you're also planning to unhitch the wagon, feed and rub down the horses."

Rafe scratched his jaw. "Something wrong with that?"

"Everything!"

In that one word, Rafe judged, she let loose a whole gutload of frustration that had been choking her silent the entire trip.

He tipped his hat, leaned back slightly and took her measure. Sure had something stuck in her craw. "Meaning?"

"Meaning I'm soured on feeling like I have to depend on a man in order to get anything done. I've half a mind to fix that old barn roof myself."

"You know how?"

"Of course not," she snapped. "Bert never let me do anything he considered 'man's work.' Turned out woman's work meant everything he didn't feel up to bothering with himself."

"Strikes me there's one surefire way to take care of that."

"What?"

"I'll teach you."

"You'll teach me?"

"You're absolutely right. If you're going to survive on your own out here, you got to be able to do whatever needs doing."

He watched her agitation fade and hoped maybe her distrust was easing, as well. The one thing he wanted to avoid above all else was Callie's growing suspicions about him and his presence on her ranch. Bad enough, her finding those pages from the paper, especially the ones accusing Luke of Bert's murder. He wondered how much she knew about the happenings that day.

"I read a newspaper story just before I married Bert. Written by a woman. I don't remember the exact words, but it went something like, 'Any woman who likes her own company, sees the beauty of the sunset, loves to grow things, and doesn't mind putting in as much toil working the land as she does the washtubs, will succeed. She'll have independence, plenty to eat, and her own home.' It sounded like the answer to my prayers."

"You sure that's what you want?"

"Independence, my own home, and plenty to eat," Callie recited emphatically, "is everything I want."

"Looks to me like you already got that." Rafe waved one hand to encompass the entire ranch. "All that and more."

"Not yet I don't," Callie said as she climbed down out of the wagon. "Not so long as Denzell is hanging around like a vulture after my land, and I don't know how to fix a barn roof or build a henhouse."

"Those things are a cinch to learn." He let his gaze drift

lazily down her length. "You got any of Bert's trousers laying around?"

"Why?"

"Be a damn sight more practical than that skirt, if you're going to be climbing around on ladders and barn roofs."

"You're serious."

"Damn right I am. Matter of fact," he squinted at the sky. "Looks to me like there's more than a few good hours of daylight left. You and me ought to make the most of them."

Normally Rafe wasn't given to a whole lot of patience with teaching. Truth be told, he found it a damn sight easier to do something himself than to show anybody else how. But teaching Callie a few basic skills such as nailing on shingles struck him as being the least he could do. Besides, it helped salve the faint twinge from his conscience every time he thought about how his being here with her was simply a means to a far bigger end.

Callie couldn't for the life of her fathom what had made her open up to Rafe that way. She'd told him things she'd never shared with another living soul. Private things. Like the way reading that one woman's view of the West had influenced her decision to marry Bert and chase a similar dream, with no idea at the time that she was trading purgatory for hell.

Rafe had his own special way of making her say and do things she wouldn't have thought possible, she mused as she stepped into an old pair of Bert's trousers. Like wearing Bert's pants. They didn't stay up by themselves, so she cinched the waist tight with a hunk of rope. Bert's belt needed a new hole punched quite a distance in before she could wear it. Turning in front of the looking glass she thought it was downright scandalous the way the trousers hugged the shape of her rear and the length of her legs. But one thing was for certain. They were a darn sight easier to move in. Especially without those layers of bulky undergarments and her Balmoral petticoat.

Rafe's jaw dropped nearabouts clean down to his bootlaces when he saw her, and Callie almost giggled at his reaction. She caught herself just in time. Middle-aged widow ladies did not giggle, she told herself. That was a pastime suitable only in young girls. 'Course, back when she was a young girl she hadn't had anything much to giggle about.

"This what you had in mind?"

Rafe straightened, his eyes darkening with suppressed emotion. "Yes and no," he said. "How do you feel?"

"I'm not sure," Callie said. "Free."

"Free?"

"Light as air." She twirled experimentally. "I might even get to like it."

"Best not wear 'em into town," Rafe said. "Like as not to start a scandal."

"Might be kind of fun," Callie said.

Seeing Rafe raise his eyebrow, Callie clamped her mouth shut. What on earth had got into her? She was acting in a most unfitting way. And worst of all, it felt good.

"I'd think twice about it, if I was you," Rafe said gruffly. "Now how about we find us a ladder."

Rafe fetched the ladder and rested it against the side of the barn. Callie held it securely in place as Rafe started up, a bundle of shingles slung over his back. He was near the top rungs when she saw him slow down, hesitate, then stop. "What is it?" she called.

He didn't look down or up, but appeared to be staring straight ahead. Dear Lord. Surely he wasn't swaying from side to side. "Rafe?"

"I'm okay," he bit out impatiently. He glanced up, raised his foot to take another step, and froze.

"I'm coming up," Callie said, grabbing firm hold and planting her feet on the bottom rung.

"Don't."

Callie ignored him as she inched her way upward. She felt the ladder creak at the added weight. "Don't look down," she said softly, as her hand reached the rung where Rafe's feet rested. She craned her neck, her back arched, watching the rise and fall of his shoulders as he took a deep breath. Followed by a second. "I'm right here."

"Don't suppose your belly feels like it's down around your ankles?"

"Nope," Callie said cheerfully. "And if you go another rung up, you'll be able to see clear over to the other side of the valley. That ought to help some."

"I suppose." He shifted his weight from foot to foot but didn't move.

"You want me to get out of the way so you can come down?"

"No," he said, with what sounded like painful effort.

"I'll count you up, then," Callie said. "Three more steps is all. And I'm right behind you." As she spoke she edged farther upward, her feet on the rung below his, her arms cinching his hips as she held tight to the ladder. The bundle of shingles he carried grazed the top of her head. "Together now," she said. "One." Determinedly she nudged him along with her knee. To her relief, he edged up a step. She followed. "Two. That's very good. I'm right here now. Three."

On the count of three, Rafe flung himself, shingles and all, onto the barn's gently sloping roof. Nimbly Callie joined him.

"There now," she said brightly. "That wasn't so bad, was

it?" She watched the green tinge slowly fade and Rafe's face return to its normal tanned skin tones. "Why didn't you tell me you were afraid of heights?"

"Heights?" Rafe said scoffingly. "I'm not afraid of heights."

"Could have fooled me."

"Ladders now..." Rafe said, as he unhooked his hammer from his belt and took out a handful of nails. "Ladders I'm not over fussy about. Had one shot out from underneath me once."

"Who by?"

Rafe flashed her his trademark cocky grin. "Irate husband, as I recall. How do you feel about fetching those planks from down below?"

She made several trips up and down the ladder, fetching and carrying, while Rafe busied himself replacing the first row of shingles that had blown off in the storm.

"My turn," she said finally, impatient to actually swing a hammer, to feel like she'd made some real contribution. "Next I'll be thinking you got me out here just so you'd have someone to run up and down the ladder for you."

"Hold your horses," Rafe said, securing another shingle. "I want to get this finished before the rain starts."

"Rain." Glancing skyward, Callie saw what she'd been too busy to notice previously. Thick black clouds had rapidly filled the valley sky. "Looks more like hail."

"Could be." Rafe spoke around a mouthful of nails. "Hand me that board, would you? And pay attention." He nailed the board down with two swings, so she'd have some-thing solid to kneel on. "Always start from the bottom of the roof and work your way up to the peak. Seen folks do it backwards more times than I can count. Then they wonder why their roof leaks like a sieve every time it rains."

"Are those special shingles on the top edge?"

"Yes, very good. Those are called caps. Here, now. You try." He passed her the hammer.

Callie grasped the handle, unprepared for the weight of the tool's head. She bent and flexed her wrist experimentally. The hammer felt awkward and unwieldy, and she seemed to be one hand short when Rafe passed her a shingle and a nail.

"Place your shingle, so. Then position the nail. Next give it a light tap to engage. Followed by a solid blow to finish." Rafe claimed the hammer and demonstrated, then passed it back to her. "Now you try."

It didn't look very hard. Except—"Ow." The hammer completely missed the nail, painfully grazing her finger instead. On the next blow, she pulled her hand away too soon, and the nail went rolling off the edge of the roof. She exchanged looks with Rafe, who appeared to be struggling to keep a straight face.

"Hammer's too heavy," she said defensively.

"All it takes is some practice," Rafe said, inching his way around to kneel behind her.

"Just what do you think you're doing, Rafe Millar?" she asked in her most indignant tone, feeling his arms slide around her waist like a hug.

"Thought I'd start by showing you the right way to hold a hammer." His left hand guided her, readying the nail. "Grip a bit higher, like this." He curled his fingers around her other hand, supporting the hammer's weight. Callie could feel the heat of his breath against the back of her neck, shattering her concentration. With just the slightest movement she brushed against him, her spine contacting against the hard wall of his chest while her bottom cradled indecently against his powerful thighs and her shoulder nudged his. She felt his whiskers snagging slightly on the flyaway strands of her hair.

Even more disturbing than the physical contact was the way his scent filled her nostrils, a masculine smell of clean skin, leather, and the outdoors. Callie leaned back slightly and closed her eyes, conscious of the quickening beat of both their hearts. She thought her own heart might jump clean out of her ribs at the closeness.

She felt his arm tighten around hers, heard his sharply indrawn breath. She imagined his hand sneaking up and cupping her breast beneath the coarse fabric of the man's shirt. Her underpinnings were at a minimum, and to her mortification she felt her nipples tingle at the thought, seconded by a throbbing low in her belly.

He'd held her, kissed her even, but working together like this was different again. Disturbing. His breath against the back of her neck made it difficult to breathe or concentrate on what he was saying. She heard him clearing his throat.

"Now put your nail into position."

She snatched the nail from his callused palm.

"That's right." His hands guided hers as she raised the hammer, took aim, and connected with the nail. She snatched her other hand free. Together they drove the nail in.

"You got it. Hit it again."

"I can't hardly move. You're nearabouts on top of me," she muttered.

"I'm a hands-on kind of teacher," Rafe said. But he shimmied back a ways, and she got the nail halfway in before it bent clean over sideways.

"Just pull it out," Rafe instructed. "Can't," she said. "It's stuck."

This time his movements felt slow and deliberate as he

reached around her, took the hammer, banged the nail sideways to straighten it, then pulled it free and tossed it over his shoulder. "Don't give up now." He passed her another nail. "Practice makes perfect."

"That's what the nuns used to say when I was learning my letters."

"Nuns taught you to read and write? You're lucky. My brother and I taught ourselves."

"We had a shack in back of the convent. Pa worked around the place when he wasn't passed out drunk. They felt sorry for us, I guess."

"A long time ago I learned folks only feel sorry for you if you let them."

Callie didn't respond but continued with the next nail. By the time the rain started, she had mastered to some extent the art of hammering.

"You learn fast," Rafe said. "Now go on in before you catch your death."

"What about you?"

"I'll be along in a minute or two. I just want to cap off the peak."

"The ladder?"

"The ladder won't bother me going down. Go on in now."

"You sure?"

"Your hearing gone from all the banging? I said I'll be all right."

It probably wounded his male pride, her knowing he had a problem with ladders, Callie thought as she perched on the edge of the roof and watched Rafe nail on shingles at a speed she could only envy. His face was a study in concentration, and after observing him for a minute or two she conceded he was right. Sitting here getting soaked didn't make a whole lot of sense.

"If you're sure."

"I'm sure. Now get!"

By the time she'd toweled her hair dry, changed clothes, and made a pot of tea, the rain had turned to hail and back to rain. She peered outside where the dark clouds made it seem later than it was. Rafe should have come in long ago. Finally Callie couldn't stand the waiting any longer. She had just reached for her cloak when the door opened and in stumbled Rafe.

"Well," she said. "It's about time. I was set to send a search party out after you."

He looked at her through vaguely unfocused eyes. She was alarmed to see that his skin was the color of the leaden sky and shivers of cold wracked his limbs.

"Best come settle in by the fire and warm up." She led him to a chair and bustled about fetching towels, stoking up the fire, and fixing a cup of hot tea dosed with honey.

He took a sip and sat back, stifling a groan.

"You men are all the same." Callie knelt before him and briskly wrenched off his sodden boots.

"How's that?" His voice was huskier than usual.

"Rome wasn't built in a day, remember?" She watched the stiff way he rolled his shoulders. "You want I should fetch some liniment?"

"Quit fussing. I'm fine."

"You won't be good for anything if you don't get out of those wet things." As she rose Rafe stopped her, his hands encircling her wrist. Callie was shocked by the icy feel of his skin.

"I was enjoying the fetching picture you made in those man's pants."

"Speaking of pants," she gently disengaged herself, "I'll bring you a dry pair. And one of Bert's shirts."

After passing him the dry clothes, she busied herself in her bedroom long enough so he'd be able to change in privacy. When she ventured back, he was sitting right where she'd left him, eyes glazed, shivers coursing through him, still in his wet things.

# CHAPTER 9

C allie gave his shoulder an urgent shake. "Rafe, you must get out of those wet things. Do you hear me? Now!"

Her only answer was a wracking cough.

"What next?" Callie muttered as she grabbed a towel and started rubbing his hair. A deep-seated feeling of dread made her movements unnecessarily harsh. What if he was really sick? Typhoid or malaria or some exotic illness she'd never heard of? What if he up and died on her? Two deaths on the homestead in a few short months and folks would claim the place was hexed.

Rafe wasn't about to die, she told herself as she touched the side of his neck. His skin was much too cold. Feelings of inadequacy swamped her and she fought them down, forcing herself to function. She couldn't think about the folks she'd nursed in the past. Or the way nothing she did had helped ease their suffering. Not her ma. Or the woman who'd given birth on the journey west. The fever had taken them both.

Rafe didn't have a fever. He had the chills. Worlds apart.

She just had to get him warm, and immediately. No time to be running into town for the doctor.

He was still conscious, but not really with her. His eyes were unfocused, and he continued to shiver as another coughing spasm overtook him.

She grabbed three bricks from out by the woodpile and placed them in the fire to get warm. Next she fetched all her extra blankets and spread a thick layer of bedding on the floor in front of the fire. Finally she picked up her sharpest hunting knife. Nothing for it but to cut the wet clothes from his body. It seemed a shame to ruin such buttery soft buckskin, but his next cough decided her. Her hand was hovering over him, with the knife poised, when Rafe gripped her wrist.

"I must do this alone." Then he released her, uttering another deep, raspy cough.

She had no idea what he meant, but she was distinctly on her own as she took hold of the front of his shirt and split the buckskin from top to bottom. She peeled the clingy wet stuff from his arms and shoulders and discarded it in a sodden heap on the floor.

"Luke?" Rafe stared up at her through glazed eyes, obediently moving forward and back in his seat as she struggled to separate him from his shirt.

"Callie," she answered automatically. To her untutored eye, his skin appeared slightly blue-tinged. She bundled a blanket around his shoulders and rubbed till her arms ached.

Hadn't she claimed, just the other day, how a man on her property was an omen of bad things to come? She'd known Rafe spelled trouble right from the start. She should have listened to her instincts and hired someone else to come fix the roof. If she hadn't allowed herself to be cowed by

Denzell, she wouldn't be here like this, feeling helpless and beholden and resentful all at once.

While her hands were busy, her mind raced to the next step: removing his trousers. "You've got to do it," she said aloud. "There's no one but you." With unsteady hands, she reached for Rafe's belt, fumbling with the heavy buckle for what felt like forever.

Hard to say which was shaking more, her hands or Rafe's shivering body, as she unlaced the sides of his buckskins. Lucky for her he had no idea who she was or what she was doing. As she unlaced, she wondered about Luke. Funny. She would have expected to hear his wife's name. Or at least another female.

With Rafe's partial cooperation, she managed to hoist him out of the chair and onto the blankets on the floor. When she tucked a pillow beneath his head, he closed his eyes, which made him look younger and more gentle. Callie hoped he kept his eyes shut a spell.

After drawing a long breath, she peeled the buckskin trousers back, inch by sodden inch, to reveal woolen drawers beneath. *And what if he'd been buck naked?* she asked herself, rocking back on her heels and wiping a trickle of perspiration from her forehead. *Seen a naked man before, haven't you?* Of course, not one like Rafe. With his ropy, well-defined muscles and gold-tone skin and lean hips, not even the occasional scar—one near his shoulder and another down close to his hipbone—marred the smooth expanse of his skin or detracted from his rugged manly appeal. If anything, they added to his masculinity.

"Callie, girl," she admonished aloud, "the man's freezing to death and you're sitting here gawking." With sure, quick movements of her long-handled tongs, she retrieved the bricks from the fire, wrapped them in rags, and placed them next to Rafe for heat. Then she retrieved her knife and set to work separating him from his underclothes. She made the cuts as neat as she could in case she'd be the one sewing them back together.

That done, she bundled him in half a dozen blankets and laid her hand against his cheek. Cold as a corpse. But his chest rose and fell in a quiet, steady rhythm, which she took to be a positive sign.

It would be best to roll him onto his side—a trick she'd learned living with a pa and brother who were habitually drunk. If Rafe threw up, he wouldn't choke on his vomit or swallow his tongue or any of the other wonderful things people did when they weren't well.

Outside, the rain continued in major torrents. Thanks to Rafe she no longer needed to worry about the barn roof leaking, ruining her winter supply of hay. Small consolation if he up and died on her. She added more wood to the fire and checked the patient. He was still deathly cold, something Callie couldn't cotton to when it felt like a hundred degrees in the cabin. She was perspiring freely, yet beneath yards of coverings Rafe remained chilled and unmoving.

The fact that she had body heat enough for both of them struck Callie as totally unfair. On the heels of that thought tumbled a second one, so outrageous she tried to ignore it.

"Bad idea," she said aloud. But she'd seen it work with animals, especially if a foal or calf was born too soon. The mother took the offspring and warmed it with her own body.

It's scandalous.

Scandalous or not, she had to do what she could for Rafe.

*He doesn't have to know,* she assured herself. Soon as he warmed up some she'd scoot into the other room.

*What if he wakes up and finds me with him? What if he never wakes up?*

*He will,* Callie vowed, as she stripped down to her chemise and drawers. With a determined sigh, she pulled back the blankets and stretched out alongside him.

She felt the frigid dampness of his skin seep through to hers and began to wonder whether she did have enough body heat for both of them. The clock on the mantel ticked the minutes by with maddening slowness. How long could a body survive the kind of chills Rafe had? Eventually his shivering lessened, till it stopped altogether. She splayed her hand across his chest, which felt, if not exactly warm, at least no longer ice-like to the touch.

Outside the rain lashed the cabin's walls and windows, while nearby the fire hissed and popped in cheerful accompaniment. Callie's eyelids grew heavy. She felt cozy, warm, lulled by the rhythmic sound of Rafe breathing.

Her eyes flew open. How could she possibly relax? Nested here alongside Rafe as if they were two spoons in the sideboard drawer, their breathing keeping time. She'd learned the hard way never to trust any man. Rafe might be ill and sleeping and needing her care, but it didn't mean she could relax around him.

Even as Callie acknowledged the potential danger, she reached out and brushed a lock of hair from Rafe's forehead, only to watch it spring back to its original position. He was a tough one to figure. Something told her he was more used to being on the move than sitting still, yet he'd come back and fixed her roof, even taking the time to show her how. He'd risked his own health and safety staying out till the job was finished.

Occasionally she'd caught rare glimpses of what a body might call a tender side, something she'd never seen in a man. Yet he was tough. Tough of mind, body, and spirit. If he went after something, he wouldn't stop till it was his. Lucky for her he wasn't after anything of hers. Soon as he got well, he'd be on his way.

Or would he? He seemed genuinely worried about Denzell. Leastways, Denzell's intentions toward her. Funny. One wouldn't expect a drifter to care much about folks whose paths he crossed. Callie snuggled in closer, her legs tucked alongside his, her arm finding the indentation of his waist, her hands splayed wide across the breadth of his chest. His breathing sounded deep and even. Her own kept pace.

Eventually she must have dozed. She woke abruptly, sensing something desperately wrong. She pushed herself up on her elbows. What was she doing on the floor? The fire had gone out, yet she was hot.

So was Rafe!

Whereas before he'd been icy cold, he was now burning up with fever. Her underthings were stuck to her skin, damp with perspiration.

She bundled into her wrapper. Behind the curtains she saw that dawn was still hours away. She fetched a bowl of water from the bucket and grabbed a rag, which she wet with cold water, wrung out, and laid across Rafe's febrile forehead.

Snatching back the covers, she dabbed cool water down his neck and across his chest. He thrashed from side to side, muttering.

"Nishu."

Callie wondered if that was a name or a word from a different language. And how could a body go from being so cold to fiery hot? What she'd taken to be a simple chill was obviously something far more serious. Who knew what Rafe might have picked up in his travels, or what type of treatment he might require?

She sat back on her heels and studied him. Dare she leave him alone and ride to town for the doctor? His limbs thrashed as he clawed at unseen enemies. The sheet slipped and she pulled it up near his navel for modesty's sake. Her modesty's sake. She doubted Rafe had a modest bone in his body.

Abruptly he sat up and opened his eyes. "Luke," he said, just as clear as anything. "They won't get away with this. I promise."

"That's good," Callie murmured in soothing tones as she coaxed him to lie back down and continued with her gentle sponging motions. "Just don't worry about that now. Let's get you well first."

If she could. Ma had taken on just such a fever. Callie had been young at the time, yet old enough to experience a bone-chilling fear and helplessness as fever flushed the pale, delicate skin of her ailing mother. Unlike Rafe, Ma hadn't thrashed and moaned but simply given a peaceful sigh and slipped away, leaving behind her life of hardship and brutality.

Callie freshened her rag in the cool water. Her efforts didn't seem to be making any difference, but she had to try. When her mother went, she'd been allowed no time for tears and mourning. There was work to be done, even for an eight-year-old child. Her pa had taken to drinking worse than before, and her brother kept him company. Callie'd been forced to grow up faster than any girl should have to. Cooking and cleaning and keeping house. Earning the sharp side of pa's tongue if she slacked off, not to mention the occasional swipe with his belt.

Only at night, after the menfolk had passed out, their snores shaking the tiny one-room shack, did she pull out her school books from the nuns and continue with her spotty education. The one thing Callie recalled her mother insisting on was that Callie learn to read. Reading opened Callie's eyes to a whole different world, a world she was convinced lay out west, just waiting for her. And it hadn't taken much persuading from Bert that better things lay ahead in her role as his wife. After all, she was cooking and cleaning and working her fingers raw for her pa and her brother. Surely one man to care for was less work than two?

One day. That's all it took for Bert to completely shatter her youthful dreams. Callie wrung out the rag and laid it across Rafe's flushed skin. Her wedding night was one nightmare she'd never forget. And the lesson she had then learned remained uppermost in her mind: Any time a man came near her made for hardship and misery faster than she could shake a stick.

And if Rafe should die? She couldn't think like that.

Still, at the back of her mind was a deep-seated fear that such an occurrence would bring the sheriff back, skewering her with those mean little eyes of his, asking the same questions as before. The same things he'd asked about Bert's killing.

Callie fought down her panic. She was just lightheaded from lack of sleep. Rafe would get better and move on through her life, and she would finally be able to settle down and relax.

The sun was high in the sky and Callie was moving automatically, long past the stage of having any sort of feeling in her arms, when Rafe's eyes flew open.

"What are you trying to do, drown me?"

Callie started and glanced down to where the rag fluttered as she squeezed a trickle of cold water over his neck and shoulders. She'd been so consumed by her thoughts she'd failed to notice that his fever had broken. Some nurse she made. She rubbed a weary hand across her eyes.

"I thought you were going to die."

"Sorry to disappoint you." He tried to raise his head, then fell back to the pillow with a groan. "What the hell happened?"

"You caught a chill," she said, pushing a hank of hair back from her forehead. "Turned into a fever in the middle of the night. Never saw anything like it."

"Had you worried, did I?"

Callie gathered up her water bowl and rags. "Only when I wondered how I might bury your body so's no one would find it."

Rafe made a choking sound, suspiciously like a muffled laugh. "What other schemes were you hatching on my demise?"

"You mean like selling your horse and saddle? Denying I'd ever seen you pass this way?" Her eyes sharpened. "How long till someone came looking for you?"

"Nobody would have come looking for me," he said. "Nobody knows or cares where I am."

"Not even Luke?" Callie started to pull herself to her feet. Rate's hand snaked out and pulled her back down to him.

"How do you know about Luke?"

"You were muttering some with the fever. Most of it didn't make any sense."

His eyes narrowed. "What else did I say?"

"Who knows?" she said testily. "I was too busy trying to save your flea-bitten hide to pay attention."

"That so?"

"I said so, didn't I?"

He didn't answer but changed the subject with startling abruptness. "Did we get the barn roof finished?"

She paused. Didn't he remember being out there in rain and hail? "Far as I know."

"That's good," he said as his eyelids fluttered closed.

Abruptly they flew open. "Woman, what the hell are you wearing?"

Callie grasped the edges of her wrapper near her throat and drew it closed. She hadn't left Rafe's side long enough to get dressed. "I'm still in my night things."

"What am I wearing?"

"Birthday suit," she said shortly.

"You do that, Callie? Strip a man naked when he's too sick to see for himself?"

"Don't you remember?"

"Nope."

"You came inside. Said something about being cold. Took off your wet things. Lay down to rest a sec. Next thing I know, you're sawing logs." She shrugged. "Wasn't much I could do. So I went to bed."

"That a fact?"

"It is."

"Must have been some dream I had."

"Dream?"

"Yup. Dreamt about soft cool hands and soft cool words. A warm and willing body spooned alongside of me."

"You must have been delirious from the fever," Callie said. "Myself, I never heard tell of such imaginings."

# CHAPTER 10

From his position on the floor, Rafe watched Callie's graceful movements as she rinsed and dried the bowl, wrung out the rag and hung it on the line above the stove. Her hair was a riot of locks tumbling over her face and shoulders, and he had very vivid memories of that cloud of hair spread across his own shoulders, tantalizing him with her elusive fragrance.

It was mean of him to tease her when she looked plumb wore out. Despite what she said, he knew she'd been up most of the night tending him. Just as he knew the satin-smooth female limbs that had cradled his were more than a dream or fanciful imaginings.

Still, if he'd known a recurrence of malaria was waiting on him... Probably served him right, really, for pulling a fast one on Callie. Insinuating himself back into her life this way when they'd already said everything there was to be said between them.

He couldn't help it! He just couldn't cotton to men like Denzell preying on the fairer sex. The man was a viper, and Callie needed protection.

It had been so long since he'd worn his good-guy hat he wasn't quite sure he remembered how. But it seemed to him that fixing Callie's roof and making himself indispensable around here was a good start.

Indispensable. Right. And she winds up nursing him the whole night through. He wondered what he might have said during the fever's delirium. How much he might have revealed about Luke and Denzell. Probably too much, given that Callie had spent the night more or less in his arms. Damn shame he had no conscious memory of the experience. Just a hazy sensation of half-formed images, touches, and smells.

When his body reacted in typical male fashion, he stifled a groan and rolled over, turning his back on Callie and the room. Every muscle in his weary body ached. He'd been here before. Come tomorrow, he should be right as rain.

"Rafe, are you all right?"

Damn, she was right behind him, gentle fingers probing, giving him a shake. Reluctantly he rolled over and opened one eye.

"Can't a body get any sleep around here?"

"Of course. I'm sorry." Concern clouded her beautiful eyes. She was no longer holding the wrapper closed and he could see the fragile fabric of her chemise, the shadowed cleft between her breasts and the darker rosy hue of her nipples pressed against the thin, nearly transparent scrap of undergarment.

"Nothing to be sorry for. I'm the bear. I've been through this before, but it must have been scary for you." He couldn't stop himself from reaching up and threading his fingers through a down-soft strand of her hair.

"It was. Your fever was so high. I didn't know if I should leave you to fetch the doctor."

"Nothing the doc could do. It has to run its course."

"Are you in pain? I thought I heard you groan."

He dropped the hank of hair, feeling its silken bonds graze his fingertips in the softest caress. "Some kind of crime when a man groans? Just because every bone in his body feels like it was run over by a wagon train."

Well, maybe not every bone. Although a certain part of his anatomy ached, as well. He saw Callie flush as she noticed his aroused state beneath the thin covering. Her breath caught, doing fascinating things to the front of her bodice. He imagined the buttons popping from the pressure. Imagined himself sliding his hand inside, grazing her nipple with the pad of his thumb, rolling its velvety texture between thumb and forefinger and eliciting an answering groan of passion.

Watching the way she moistened her lips, he found the temptation too great, and gave in to his baser instinct. With one hand on her back, he urged her down until her mouth met his. She tasted warm and welcoming.

The blood thundered through his veins as he kissed her and ran his hands through her hair, gathering it up by the handful. From there it was a natural move to slide the wrapper from her shoulders and pull her down atop him so all that separated them was a thin cotton sheet and the transparent fabric of her underthings,

He clawed at the sheet covering his chest, pushing it out of the way. A button popped off her chemise and he felt the pressure of her breasts against his bare skin. Burning a feeling of rightness clean through to his soul. Incinerating him.

Her curves cushioned him in all the right places. He slid

his hands down her back and over her bottom, kneading her flesh through lace-trimmed fabric that was more of an enticement than a barrier.

She wriggled and the sheet slid lower. Waves of feeling slowly rippled through him. He caught his breath as she wriggled some more. In his dangerously weakened state, one more move like that and they were both about to be embarrassed.

With one desperate lunge he reversed positions so Callie lay beneath him. She stared up at him, eyes wide and glazed with passion. He parted her chemise, baring her breasts to his view, filling his senses with the sight of her.

Gently he brushed the tips of her breasts with his fingertips. She gasped at the sensation as her nipples tightened. Gently he pushed her breasts together before he lowered his head and grazed them ever so lightly with his lips. Hearing her gasp, he teased them mercilessly with his tongue before he parted his lips and tugged them deep inside his mouth, one at a time, then both together.

Callie's eyes were pressed tightly closed, yet Rafe could feel the little tingles of shock and wanting coiling through her limbs. The slight shifting of her legs against his, the faint arching of her back, the lifting of her hips.

He straddled her, his straining member seeking her feminine secrets through the thin fabric barrier. Gently, coaxingly, he rocked his hips. She rocked back, a rotating movement that was almost his undoing.

Fighting for control he closed his eyes against the waves of sensation that assaulted him. He leaned forward and touched his lips to hers, unprepared for the hunger with which she kissed him back. He felt the sharp pressure of her nails against his shoulder, reinforcing his earlier suspicion that beneath him lay a woman who had never been kissed properly. Never been loved properly.

He knew a fleeting moment of regret that he wasn't the man to love her the way she deserved, any more than the man who'd come before him had been. And while he might be several shades of a scoundrel, he couldn't possibly make love to her. No matter how willing she seemed at this moment. A woman of Callie's ilk wouldn't take kindly to his loving and leaving ways.

Once before he had committed himself wholly to a woman, taking her as wife, planting the seed of his son in her womb, with disastrous results. He wasn't cut out for settling down any more than Callie was cut out for a no-strings-attached romp. Regret and sadness cooled his lust. Yet as he prepared to end the kiss he felt her body beneath his shuddering in a way that told him she, at least, had found some measure of release from the tension that had been plaguing them both. And he was glad for her. She deserved more, but it was all he had to give.

Beneath him her eyes grew wide. Gently he eased down alongside her and held her as the tremors gradually abated. He felt her pull away and gather the torn edges of her chemise, holding them closed in her fist.

"What did you do?"

Her voice was edged in suspicion.

"What do you mean?"

"What just happened?"

There was genuine shock in her voice and he pushed himself to one elbow. "You really don't know?"

She shook her head. Rafe had a feeling that, once the shock subsided, she'd deny any of this had happened, let alone speak about it. He cleared his throat, wondering how to allay her fears yet at the same time not offend her.

"It's...you know. The usual thing that happens when a man and a woman get together."

Color flooded her cheeks. "But we didn't. That is... You didn't..."

"No, ma'am. I didn't."

"Then I don't under-..." Slowly she raised herself to a sitting position. While she might appear dazed now, Rafe had a feeling she'd wind up angry. He watched her struggle to her feet and collect her wrapper. Trouble was, he didn't know what to do or say to help. It struck him how he could easily make things worse instead of better. Without a word or backward glance she retreated to her room and shut the door.

Rafe stretched his arms beneath his head and stared thoughtfully at the ceiling. This was something he'd never forget if he lived to be a hundred and five. A woman like Callie, widowed and all, having no idea about her own body and the pleasures a man could give her.

*The right man,* he reminded himself grimly, as he rolled over and punched his pillow. A far cry from the kind of man Rafe Millar was.

Callie splashed cold water on her face and stared wide-eyed in the looking glass, amazed by the sameness of her reflection. A little dishevelled, maybe, lips a trifle swollen, skin puckered and red from rubbing against Rafe's beard, but basically she looked the same as yesterday and the day before. She raised trembling fingers to her still-throbbing lips, knowing she'd never be the same. Leastways inside.

She reached for the nearest clothes at hand, which happened to be Bert's old trousers. Being a newly changed woman, she might as well start acting the part, she reasoned, as she cinched the trousers around her waist and pulled on a blouse and a shawl. She didn't bother putting her hair up, just yanked it back and tied it with a piece of lace.

Then, keeping her eyes focused straight ahead, she charged through the cabin and made a beeline for the door and the relative safety outside.

Safe from Rafe. His eyes. His voice. His knowing looks.

Obviously he was no stranger to the responses he'd culled from her body. The intimacies. Her skin burned at the memory. There had to be something wrong with her, acting like that.

The rain had stopped. The clouds were breaking up, revealing a few faint rays of sunshine behind them, promises of better things to come. Turning left, Callie headed toward the creek. She reached the bank only to find the rain had swollen the waters unnaturally high and covered the steppingstones. She splashed across anyway, mindless of her boots and trouser bottoms getting wet. In one or two spots, the water came up past her knees, but she had to get away, and just ahead lay blessed sanctuary. She could hide amongst the trees. Lose herself in the sweet-smelling shadows of the woods.

After a spell she grew tired of wandering aimlessly and plopped down on a thicket of dried boughs, sliding her back along the rough bark of a tree trunk. Changing scenery hadn't made a difference. Her mind refused to settle. And she still had no answers for that thing that had happened.

Somehow, without engaging in the actual mating act itself, Rafe Millar's body had pleasured hers in ways she'd never dreamed existed.

Obviously he'd had plenty of experience, for he'd known instinctively where and how to touch her. To make her feel things she was powerless to prevent. She blushed at the memory of how she'd acted. Kissing with her mouth open, touching his tongue with hers, that was bad enough. But rutting against him like a bitch in heat? How would she ever be able to look him in the eye again?

Maybe he'd be gone when she got back. Surely he'd realize that would be best. Callie took heart from the thought as she followed the creek downstream.

Still sifting through her thoughts, she didn't at first pay much attention to the sounds of splashing water. Once her eyes tracked the sound, fear paralyzed her throat. A mother bear stood in the water, teaching her young ones to fish. The two cubs were not paying their mama much mind, frolicking on the bank a short distance from Callie.

Never get between a mother bear and her cubs.

Too late! All of a sudden the mother bear turned. She must have caught Callie's scent for, with a bellow of outrage, she rose up on her hind legs, then splashed down on all fours.

Callie didn't stop to think. She raced back to the woods, thankful to be unhampered by long skirts and petticoats. The first spruce tree she reached had spindly branches low enough to the ground that she could grab onto, but too high for the bear to reach. She hoped. Up she climbed, the long-forgotten skill learned as a child seeing her in good stead as the bear lumbered toward the spruce, sniffing the air.

When she reached the tree sheltering Callie, Mama Bear stood on her hind legs. Her front paws clawed the base of the trunk, slashing the tender bark as she roared. The sound of her challenge echoed clear through the valley and sent shock waves of fresh terror down Callie's spine. Callie clung to the tree's trunk, wondering how long till her pursuer got tired of the chase or remembered that she had young ones needing her attention.

The tree's trunk shook, and Callie closed her eyes and

prayed long-neglected prayers. Back when her mother had died she'd lost her faith in anyone listening to one frightened young girl, let alone answering her pleas. Maybe now she was a woman grown the Almighty might decide she'd had enough for one day and send the bears exploring someplace else.

She'd worked her way through the Lord's Prayer and two Hail Marys when she spotted Rafe on the far side of the creek. He must have heard the bear and known Callie was in trouble. Without wasting a second he grasped the situation, Callie clinging to her treetop perch, the bear circling down below. Raising his rifle to the sky, he fired a warning shot. The crack of gunfire echoed through the valley, sounding like an entire army rushing to her defense. It seemed to capture the mother bear's attention. With barely a backward glance, she herded the two young bears to cover in the woods.

Callie waited until she was sure they were gone, then shinnied down the tree. Her knees were shaking so badly she could barely stand, but she forced herself to run toward Rafe, who was splashing through the creek toward her. Callie didn't argue or pull away when he looped his arm around her waist and guided her back through the thigh-high creek waters. Once they reached the other side, she tried to pull away from him.

"Keep moving," Rafe said, urging her forward, his grip tight. "She might come back. And I'd hate to think what would happen to the young ones if I had to shoot their mama."

Callie stared at the heavens, waiting for a sign, wishing the ground would open up and swallow her. But nothing so dramatic happened. Eventually concern for Rafe's wellbeing overcame her embarrassment.

"Look at you. Soaked to the skin. You're not going to take sick on me again, are you?" she asked.

"I hope not."

She and Rafe continued on their trek, wet boots squelching with every step. Halfway back to the cabin their roles reversed, with Rafe breathing heavily and leaning on her for support.

His steps were slow and it would have been easy to dart off ahead, but she didn't, keenly aware that her actions would tell him more than anything she could put into words. She had to pretend nothing had happened. That would be best.

She turned her focus to the cabin. Her home. It should be a safe haven, the one place she felt secure. But it wasn't, not as long as Rafe was around.

When they reached the front steps, Rafe sat down heavily, his breathing labored. "Damn fever took more out of me than I thought."

"You shouldn't ought to be up," she chided. "You're weak as a newborn kitten."

"You're welcome." He flashed her a derisive, half-mocking grin.

Callie tried for bluster. "I would have been all right. Eventually she would have got bored and left on her own."

"You hope. I like those trousers, by the way. Bet they came in handy for climbing that tree."

"Just don't go getting it in your head that I can't manage without you. The wagon yesterday, and now this."

"That's right," Rafe said. "Stuck pretty good both times, weren't you?"

Callie turned her back and bit her lip. The horizon shimmered in the distance. She felt Rafe reach for her hand and snatched it away.

"No crime in needing a helping hand once in a while," he said in a low voice. "Doesn't make you less of a person. If anything, it makes you more human."

"Humans get hurt. I've had enough of getting hurt."

"I'm afraid that's all a part of living."

"I hate it. This land. These people. Most of all, I hate you, Rafe Millar." Pushing past him she ran inside the cabin, slamming the door behind her.

Rafe stared after her, well aware that hate is often a steppingstone to love. That was something he'd found out the one and only other time he'd opened himself up to the needs of another human being.

# CHAPTER 11

I t didn't take Callie long to realize two things: one, Rafe Millar had no intention of moving on, at least not for the time being, and two, it sure was nice having an extra pair of hands around the place. Through his efforts a multitude of unfinished projects got done. Lengths of fence were checked and readied for the winter. The woodpile grew to gargantuan proportions. The last of the carrots and potatoes were harvested and stored in the root cellar.

As she worked alongside him, Callie became aware of something else. He, too, had no intention of mentioning a word about what had happened between the two of them that day. And when he sometimes disappeared for hours at a time she told herself it was none of her business, as long as he pulled his weight around the place.

Fridays she left a pile of coins at his place at the table, a week's wages, her way of letting him know he was a free agent. He could leave anytime he took it into his head. And every Saturday morning he was up and about before her.

In her heart of hearts she'd known things were too good to last. So when he told her last night he was going into town, Callie felt her innards sink. She was all too familiar with Saturday nights. The menfolk going off drinking, coming home dead broke and foul-tempered, meaner than a bear with a sore paw, and stinking worse than the privy.

Rafe was no different from all the rest, she reminded herself as she pegged her freshly washed laundry to the line Rafe had strung out back of the cabin, even if she did forget it for a spell, now and again. He might be a hard worker. Didn't mean he didn't need his fill of liquor and whores like any other man. Nearabouts as she could tell, Rafe was no better than some and no worse than others. He just had better hold of his impulses was all.

*Better than Bert, you mean.*

Callie's movements slowed as she thought back to her husband. Bert hadn't been one for holding his temper in check or keeping his fists to himself. Eventually she'd get over her guilt about feeling glad he was dead.

She used to think he whacked her just to prove he could, or because beating on her gave him a sense of power. Other times he didn't seem to have any use for her at all, and acted as if she wasn't even there. Rafe didn't act that way, but if he ever did, she would be ready. Give him his walking papers, she would.

At the sound of an approaching rider she moved inside to where her rifle stood near the door. Now what? It was too soon to be Rafe coming back, and she was good and soured on folks dropping in unannounced. Denzell had been making a habit of it at least twice a week. Reverend Bligh had stopped by for a second visit, as well. And this time he hadn't been near so subtle in his hints that she should pack up and sell to Denzell. Rafe had just slanted her his smart-aleck, told-you-so look. Got her so wrathy, these men, pretending like they knew what was best for her. All she wanted was for them to leave her be.

Today's visitor was a stranger, a rough and dirty-looking fellow. She stood in the shadow from the overhang of the porch, rifle at hand.

"Good day to you, ma'am."

He dismounted, but prudently kept his distance. His smile revealed gaps left from several missing teeth. Without being able to say why, Callie knew she didn't trust him. Maybe it was the abused look of his mount. A man who would mistreat his horse was not a man to be trusted.

She aimed her rifle. "That's close enough, mister. State your business."

He stopped and unfolded a piece of paper, waving it toward her. "Looking for someone, ma'am. Wondered if you might have a look-see. Tell me if you've seen a chap looks like him around these here parts."

Callie kept her rifle trained on him.

A bounty hunter.

She had little affection for any breed of men who made their living hunting down others.

"What's he wanted for?"

"A list long as your arm. Including robbery and murder. Luke Rafael's his name. Least one of them. Has a dozen or more aliases."

"Put the poster on the steps." The man did as he was told.

"Now back off and stand on the other side of your horse."

He stood where she directed, both hands in the air, and spat a stream of tobacco juice in the dirt near his feet.

"Don't blame you none for being cautious, ma'am. Area's full of scalawags like this one."

Callie approached the poster and viewed the likeness pictured there. She kept her features impassive, despite the sudden lurch of her vitals. Even though it was a poor quality picture and the criminal clean-shaven and younger, it bore a striking resemblance to Rafe Millar. Same eyes, for sure. Hard to tell about the jawline. Or could that be the reason Rafe started to grow a beard?

"Ugly brute," Callie remarked casually. "A person would be hard-pressed to forget a face like that." She eyed the bounty hunter. "Is he dangerous?"

"'Fraid so, ma'am. Besides which, he's known for having a way with the ladies."

"Indeed. What makes you think he's headed this way?"

"I got a tip." He looked around with unconcealed interest. "Anyone else about I could maybe ask while I'm here?"

"My husband and the hired hand have gone into town. My bet is you'll probably pass them on your way out. Could ask them then."

"Much obliged to you, ma'am. Think I'll stop in at your neighbors to the south, first." The man remounted and turned his horse in the direction of Denzell's.

Once he was gone, Callie didn't waste a minute.

Abandoning the laundry, she jammed a hat onto her head, grabbed her gloves and a warm shawl, saddled her horse, and headed for town at breakneck speed.

She didn't bother asking herself why she was doing this. All she knew was that her instincts guided her. She didn't care for bounty hunters. For now, that dislike was reason enough.

Callie slowed her horse as she reached the town's outskirts, passing the church and the schoolhouse. Children ran through the schoolyard, engaged in noisy play. She really ought to hurry, Callie told herself. If Denzell happened to see the likeness between Rafe and the man on the poster, that bounty hunter would be on her heels like mud on a hog. Still she hung back, recalling her last foray into town. The hostile looks and whispers of the townsfolk. All because why? Because her husband had been murdered? Or because they thought she did it?

She rode down Main Street, wondering if she was imagining the looks coming her way from the bench of old men sitting just outside the barber shop, chewing tobacco and jawing away the day. Outside the first saloon she stopped, took a breath, and dismounted. Hateful memories came flooding back. Having to fetch her pa and her brother that they might say a final good-bye to Ma. She could still recall the tinny jangle of the player piano, the smell of ale and unwashed bodies, along with the cheap perfume of women who made their living entertaining men.

She glanced from left to right, hoping to spot Rafe's unmistakable gait somewhere up ahead. Straight in front of her fluttered the saloon's swinging doors, hinges squeaking ever so lightly. Callie swallowed her trepidation as she approached the doors and stood on tiptoe, hoping to catch a glimpse of Rafe inside.

"Oof!" The door rammed into her chest as a patron left the establishment. Callie reeled backward trying to catch her balance.

"I do apologize, ma'am." The well-dressed stranger caught her elbow, drew her close, and smiled...intimately. There was no other word for it. "I didn't see you there. Are you all right?" Without releasing her, he stood back a pace and gave her a thorough onceover, in a way that made Callie feel he could see right through her skirts to her drawers. She blushed.

The stranger's smile widened. "You look all of a piece,

and very fetching, if I may say so. Allow me to introduce myself." He removed his hat and bowed from the waist, still without letting go of her arm. "Frank Abbott's the name. Were you looking for someone in particular?"

"Yes." The word was the barest squeak. Callie cleared her throat and tried again. "Yes, my—"

"Don't tell me your husband," he interjected, "or my poor heart will be just shattered."

Callie had little doubt the man before her was a gentleman. His manner of dress declared him one, from his starched white shirt and cutaway frock coat to the brocaded vest and striped linen trousers. The gold chain of his pocket watch blinked encouragingly at her.

"Actually, I'm looking for my hired hand. Name of Rafe Millar. I don't suppose you know him?"

"I can't say as I do. However, I would be honored if you would permit me to act as your escort. If you'll forgive my bold speech, a lady such as yourself must be careful where she goes."

"I..." Callie fondled the brooch pinned to the throat of her blouse. Normally she'd resent what Mr. Abbott was implying. That a woman couldn't manage without a man. But his chivalrous manner inspired her confidence as she acknowledged the sense of what he was saying. "I don't want to be any bother."

"On the contrary," replied Mr. Abbott. "I welcome the distraction." Tucking her elbow securely to his side, he led the way toward the center of town.

"Any idea of the gentleman's favorite haunts?" Mr. Abbott inquired.

Callie shook her head.

"Well, let's see now. There's Belle's, up on the hill. A lot of the hired hands stop up there on a Friday or Saturday night. There's Dodger's place over yonder, if a game of chance is what stirs the lad's blood. And if his tastes run a little more...shall we say exotic, then there's—"

"I really don't know." Callie spoke hastily, not interested in learning whether or not Rafe's tastes ran to what Mr. Abbott termed "the exotic."

"Not to worry." Thoughtfully Abbott stroked his mustache with his middle finger. "If he's here, we'll find him sooner or later." He beamed down at her. "I take it you're a landowner?"

Callie nodded. She'd just opened her mouth to impart further details, when someone grabbed Abbott from behind and spun him around. Callie whirled, aghast to see Rafe holding a fistful of Mr. Abbott's impeccably pressed jacket.

"Rafe! Stop that!" she cried.

Rafe gave the man a threatening shake and released him. "On your way, Abbott. Find yourself another mark."

"Well, I never," the other man sputtered, brushing ineffectually at the wrinkles in his lapel. Callie rushed to his side and tried to minimize the damage Rafe had wrought.

"Don't trouble yourself on my account, dear lady. I take it this," he indicated Rafe, "is the gentleman you seek?"

Callie privately thought "gentleman" was a bit of a stretch, but she nodded.

"In that case I shall bid you a regretful adieu. Until we meet again."

Without a backward glance, he turned on his heel and strode away.

Callie folded her arms across her chest. "Would you mind explaining just what it is you think you're doing?"

"Saving you from being robbed or swindled," Rafe said. "The man's a con artist."

"He was a perfect gentleman," Callie retorted.

"That's the way he operates. Finds himself a single lady, preferably widowed, makes himself indispensable, then leaves her high and dry and quite a lot poorer for having made his acquaintance."

"Folks hereabouts could be saying much the same about you."

"I doubt that."

"Why?"

"Because I don't dress like a dandy, that's why."

"Are you saying the main difference between you and Mr. Abbott is your tailor?"

"One difference. And I'd be counting my money, if I was you." He started to leave.

"Wait!"

He half turned, leaving Callie with the impression he was poised on the edge of flight. "It's you I came looking for." Glancing over her shoulder, she instinctively edged closer. "A man came by the ranch this morning."

Callie swore Rafe didn't move a muscle, yet tension radiated from every limb as he waited for her to go on. "A bounty hunter. Carrying a wanted poster." She lowered her voice. "Claimed he was looking for a man by the name of Luke Rafael. You ever heard of him?"

"And if I have?"

"I couldn't help but notice the man bears you an uncommon likeness."

"You tell him that?"

"No."

At that moment a large group of people jostled past where they stood, steps from the entrance to an alley. Rafe nudged her to one side till they stood just inside the alleyway, out of the way of passersby and with no danger of being overheard.

"Why's that?"

"I don't cotton much to bounty hunters." Callie knew there was more behind her action than that one stated fact. She chose not to look too closely at the whys and wherefores.

"Just con men," Rafe said.

"I came all this way to warn you. Least you could do is act the slightest bit appreciative."

"Thanks," Rafe drawled. "I suppose you're expecting me to light out of here before he catches up with me. That way you'll be quit of me for good."

"I...I never thought of it that way. You leaving maybe. I just didn't want him taking you by surprise is all."

"Hang me first and ask questions later?"

"Something like that."

Disbelief edged his words. "You really came all this way just to warn me? No other reason."

Callie inspected the toe of her boot, silent for once.

"Why?" Rafe placed one finger under her chin and tilted her face up till her eyes met his. "Why'd you do that, Callie? What do you care?"

She shrugged and looked away, staring intently at the mortar edging a brick just behind his right shoulder. "Figured you ought to know, is all."

"Was he heading this way?"

"Denzell's. What are you going to do?"

"Nothing."

"Nothing?" Callie squeaked. "But that man—"

Rafe stepped right up to her and silenced her with a hand across her mouth. She could feel the heavy beat of his heart in his chest.

"It isn't me on that poster, Callie. I swear to you. And

you're the only one who's been around me enough to notice any resemblance."

He released her slowly, and Callie moistened her lips.

They tingled with the pressure from Rafe's hand, the taste of his skin. "Does that mean you're coming back to the ranch?"

"Why wouldn't I?"

"I don't know. Except this is the first time you've stayed away all night."

The skin around his eyes crinkled as he smiled. "Funny. I didn't think that would bother you none."

"Did I say it did?"

"I took it that I was a free agent. That we had an understanding."

"We do and you are."

Rafe gazed down at her in a way that made Callie suspect a joke was being played out without her knowledge or consent. She didn't like it. He must have sensed that and decided to change the subject.

"Saw your friend Reverend Bligh, last night. For a man of the cloth, he's got mighty expensive taste in whores."

Callie's jaw dropped. Hastily she closed it and brushed at an imaginary speck of dust on her sleeve. She knew those kinds of things went on. She just didn't happen to feel like standing here discussing them with a hired hand. Besides, more than likely Rafe's comment was his way of letting her know he'd found a woman more than happy to suffer his attentions.

Callie drew herself erect. Rafe Millar could bed an entire houseful of whores for all she cared. It had nothing to do with her. Nothing at all.

"I don't need an escort," she informed him as he followed her back to her horse.

"Frank Abbott seemed to think you did."

"Unlike yourself, I have no knowledge of the location of every saloon and whorehouse in the state. His services would have been invaluable."

"And lightened your purse considerably." Rafe said as he boosted her into the saddle. It seemed to Callie that his hands lingered at her waist longer than necessary, and the wash of feelings only confused her further. She told herself she didn't care if he came back to the ranch tomorrow or not.

"My purse is hardly your concern," Callie said loftily." Anymore than it's my concern where you choose to squander your earnings."

Rafe took a step back and tilted his hat off his forehead. "Ride careful," he said. "I'll see you tomorrow night. And Callie..." He paused. "Thanks. I'll be on my guard."

Callie jerked the reins and sent the horse prancing in a tight circle. A man on her territory. The last thing in the world she needed right now. So why didn't she just send him away? Specially when all he was doing was complicating her life.

# CHAPTER 12

As Rafe watched the swaying back end of Callie's mount, his gaze strayed from horse to rider, admiring the way she sat in the saddle. Fancy her coming all this way just to warn him about a bounty hunter flashing Luke's picture around the countryside. Whether Callie realized it or not, her actions told him she had feelings for him. She might not have faced up to it herself yet, but he'd seen the signs before. And he'd have to do something about it as soon as he got back to the ranch.

What he really ought to do is pull up stakes and leave before Callie came to depend on him. She deserved better than finding out the hard way Rafe Millar wasn't the kind of man a body could depend on.

Trust Callie to pick up on the likeness between him and his twin. They weren't identical, but they did have similarities, easiest to see when the brothers were standing side by side. He sighed. No chance of that happening ever again.

Over a year had passed since his brother first walked these streets, and Rafe was having the devil's own time tracing his steps, or even figuring out how Luke had got himself tied up with Lambert and Denzell in the first place.

One of the girls up at Rosie's had got to know Luke some, at least in the biblical sense, and Rafe had spent most of last night liquoring her up, trying to learn what secrets, if any, his brother had spilled between the sheets. It was a safe bet Denzell had informants all over town. Rafe had to have a care who he talked to and what kinds of questions he asked if he didn't want to disappear off the face of the earth the way Luke had.

So far, all he'd done was buy up a few of Denzell's gambling debts from disgruntled moneylenders. Which left him a long way from seeing any sort of justice brought to his brother's murderers.

Taking a deep breath, Rafe shouldered his way into Dodger's. Just as he'd heard, Denzell was in the middle of a poker game. And winning big, by the looks of it. Cheating big was more like it, Rafe decided, as he sidled closer just in time to see one of the players throw down his cards in disgust.

"I'm cleaned out." Grabbing a whiskey bottle from the table, the man lurched to his feet, spat in the direction of the spittoon, and ambled away.

Rafe watched Denzell rake in his winnings and shuffle the cards. "Millar," he said without looking up. "We seem to have an empty seat. Care to join us?"

"I don't know." Rafe hung back, determined not to look too eager. "Seems like you're on some hard winning streak."

"Maybe you're the man who can change all that."

"Suppose I could at least try," Rafe said, straddling the vacated chair. He removed a handful of money from his pocket and laid it on the table.

Denzell raised a brow. "Mrs. Lambert must be a generous employer."

"Being a ranch hand's not exactly my life ambition," Rafe said, reaching for the whiskey bottle and pouring a measure into the empty glass someone sent his way.

"What is?" Denzell slid the deck of cards toward him to be cut.

Rafe cut them and leaned back in his chair, observing Denzell's dealing practices. Wouldn't do to go appearing too eager. Best to take his time. Feed Denzell crumb by crumb rather than an entire handful. "I'm known for being a man of many and varied talents. Prospecting for gold's more along the line of what I had in mind, for one."

The other players guffawed loudly. Denzell flipped down a card. "You're in the wrong state for that, boy. Even California's plumb cleaned out."

"I dunno," Rafe said as he thumbed the cards Denzell dealt him. "I got a gut feeling about the valley, here. It's got that special smell."

"So's a two-dollar whore," Denzell retorted, to the amusement of the others. "We here to jaw or play cards?"

Rafe hid his smile of satisfaction as he settled down to the game. Denzell might have no problem cheating these half-drunk small town players, but no matter what tricks he pulled, Rafe could go one better.

"I'm challenging you to a rematch real soon," Denzell blustered some hours later as Rafe nonchalantly collected his winnings. He'd been winning slowly and steadily since he joined in the game, aware that Denzell knew he was cheating but couldn't figure out how. Anything Denzell might say would only expose his own less than honest tactics.

"'Nother time," Rafe said easily, as he pushed back his chair. "Got me a lady waiting on my attentions."

"Wouldn't be yonder widow, I don't suppose?" Denzell asked cagily. "I seen her come into town earlier."

What else had the man seen? Had Denzell been behind Abbott setting out to sideswipe Callie?

"I make it a habit never to mix business with pleasure. Mrs. Lambert, now. That lady's all business."

"'Magine she is, at that," Denzell said, as he rose and tucked in his shirt. "You heading over to Rosie's? 'Cause if you are, I'll keep you company. Got to roust those two boys of mine. The pair of them'd spend their whole lives whoring if I gave them leave to." He laughed uproariously at his own wit and slapped Rafe on the back.

Rafe felt the hair on the back of his neck prickle in warning before they set one foot outside the saloon. He should have known Denzell wouldn't watch him walk away with a fistful of his money. And he'd seen the old man's barely perceptible signal to a couple of his ranch hands at the bar who'd left the saloon just minutes ahead of them. Unless he missed his guess the two were holed up in some alley ahead, just waiting for Denzell and him to pass by before they jumped him.

Slowly Rafe's eyes adjusted to the darkened streets.

The moon was hidden behind the clouds. The night air felt damp and dangerous. Rafe turned up his collar. Half a block later he stopped abruptly. He put out a hand to detain the older man. "What was that?"

Denzell frowned and glanced over his shoulder. "What was what?"

"Thought I heard somebody call for help from that alley across the way."

"I never heard nothing."

Rafe cocked a hand to his ear. "Real faint. Best I check it out." Stepping off the boardwalk, he cut directly across the street to the other side. "Don't wait for me," he called as he disappeared. Shouts and raised voices followed him as he hopped the fence at the end of the alley and kept going. If Denzell mentioned the incident later, Rafe could pretend he'd become disoriented in the dark.

CALLIE FELT grateful her horse could automatically find its own way home. Right now her mind was so distracted she could likely get lost in her own backyard. What in tarnation had come over her, anyway? Chasing off into town after Rafe like some...like some...she didn't know what. All she knew was it was one of the dumbest things she'd done in her life. Now Rafe would think she gave a damn what happened to him.

Nothing could be further from the truth. A dozen bounty hunters could string him up, for all she cared. Why should she believe it wasn't him on the poster? When had any man, Rafe included, given her one single reason they could be trusted to speak the truth?

Didn't make a hog's hair of difference to her, one way or the other, whether Rafe was an outlaw. Rafe Millar's business, past or present, was nothing to her.

So why did the thought of him leaving give her a funny, empty feeling in the pit of her stomach?

She flicked the reins.

Hunger. That's all it was. She was hungry.

Rafe waited in the shadows a few doors down from Rosie's until he saw Denzell leave, his two sons in tow, stumbling and cursing and falling all over themselves. A sharp word from their pa and the two shut right up like trained monkeys.

Once Rafe felt certain the Denzells were long gone, he tipped his hat low over his eyes and made his way inside. The madam greeted him effusively, managing to rub against his arm with one watermelon-sized breast.

Minutes later, Rafe climbed the stairs two at a time and paused before a door at the end of the hall. He knocked lightly.

"Go 'way."

"Maisie, open up. It's Rafe." He rattled the knob. To his surprise, it wasn't locked but turned easily beneath his hand. Inside, the room was lit by a single gas lamp casting a dim circle of light on a pouty young girl with dyed black hair.

"I tole herself I couldn't work no more tonight."

"Not to worry. I bought you off the floor."

Her bravado slipped. For a brief moment she looked like a little girl, playacting at being a grownup.

"Why'd you do that? Herself said just 'cause I took the Denzells on two at a time didn't mean I could shirk the rest of my customers. What's shirk mean?" One sleeve of her tattered silk wrapper slid down her pale arm.

"Shirking is something most men are darn good at, hon. Avoiding responsibility." He produced a bottle and placed it on the table next to the bed.

Maisie flopped back down onto the bed and poured herself a drink. She took a long swallow and peered at Rafe over the rim of her glass. "Their pa was asking about you tonight."

Rafe tensed inwardly, Outwardly he was careful not to show any sign of concern. "Whose pa?"

"Junior and Red. I guess herself must have told him you were here last night."

"What did you say?"

"I told him one john's the same as the next. I'm not too good with names."

"I know a gold prospector came to see you about this time last year. Name of Luke. New in the area. About my size and coloring."

"What's this fella to you?"

"Old friend," Rafe said easily. "We lost touch, is all."

"Him and me got in touch. Deep in touch."

"Tell me."

"At first he used to come around regular-like. Him and the Denzell boys' pa. Till one day old Bert showed up dead and Sheriff said it was Luke that done it. Never saw Luke again after that."

"What else do you remember?"

Maisie stared at the ceiling. "Used to talk about his girl-friend. Lotta the guys talk about their wives and sweet-hearts. So's we know they're not going to get serious about us and marry us out of here."

"Girlfriend?"

"Yeah. Not one of us, you know. A real girlfriend."

"You remember her name?"

"He never said."

The noonday sun had come and gone by the time Rafe reached the ranch the following day. His eyes felt gritty from lack of sleep, and his mouth tasted stale. It had taken some doing, pretending to match Maisie drink for drink until she passed out.

Unfortunately he hadn't found out anything more about

Luke's dealings with Denzell, or his supposed girlfriend. Still, it shouldn't take too much to hunt her down in a town the size of Springfield.

He still wasn't sure what to do about Callie. He could wait and take his lead from her, or he could deliberately increase the distance between them. Inwardly he blamed himself for the fact that they'd gotten even a little bit close.

He should have known better. Seen from the very first that she was the settling-down type, while he was anything but. He thought of the vulnerable look in those big soft eyes of hers, and the way she insisted on doings things her way even when it was the wrong way. Then he gave his head a shake to clear it. Callie and her problems were nothing to do with him.

He spotted her around back, pegging clothes on the drying line he'd strung between two trees. Down near the creek, he could just make out the retreating backsides of a horse and rider. Only one person likely to be heading in that particular direction.

And gone were all Rafe's good intentions of keeping Callie at arm's length.

He rode right up to her before he dismounted.

"Who was that?" He directed his question at the stiff lines of her back, since she didn't turn to face him.

"Neighbor." She still didn't turn around.

Rafe scratched his jaw thoughtfully. His gaze moved from Callie to the departing visitor and back to Callie. Looked to him like the little lady was rightly puckered at him. Yet he couldn't for the life of him think why.

"Denzell?"

"That's right. Chummy, the two of you are now, aren't you? He mentioned what a right delightful time you'd had playing poker before the two of you lit out over to the whorehouse together."

Rafe frowned. This wasn't the type of behavior he'd expect from Denzell, "He stopped by to fill you in on my activities in town?"

Callie turned. "Don't flatter yourself. He came to invite me to a party."

"A party?" Rafe echoed. Now he knew something was up.

"Wipe that look off your face," Callie said crossly. "It's nothing unusual for folks to get together in the fall. Celebrate bringing in the crops and all. Everyone around these parts is invited. Even you."

Rafe kept his face void of expression. "Even a no-account drifter like me? That can't be usual."

Callie picked up her laundry basket and pushed past him on her way into the cabin. "Said something about you and him having a date with a deck of cards."

Rafe stopped her with his hand on her arm. "I don't like it, Callie."

"Don't like what? Being invited to the neighbors'?"

"He's up to something. I can feel it."

"Funny," Callie retorted. "He said the exact same thing about you."

## CHAPTER 13

I t was Rafe's first look at Denzell's sprawling ranch house from the front, and an impressive sight at that, complete with Mexican influences where wrought-iron gates led to a brick-walled courtyard. From around back came the sound of fiddles and banjos, and he could hardly wait to take advantage of this opportunity to scope the Denzells out on their own turf.

"Quite the get-together," Rafe said as he halted the buckboard near the courtyard entrance and surrendered the care of the horses to a black-eyed youth who couldn't have been more than ten or eleven. At Callie's insistence they had taken the long way, via the road, rather than follow one of the trails through the woods between the two properties, and he'd chafed at the extra travel time.

He resented every extra minute he spent alone with Callie, for it was impossible to be anywhere near her without recalling the way he'd made her burn and then melt, the way her body had responded to his. So open. So giving. Holding nothing back. He hated himself for taking advantage of her response.

That's why it was for her own good, him holding her at arm's length ever since his bout with malaria. For not only had Callie nursed him with gentle concern, her every word and act showed she was capable of great depth and caring. Along with acting too impulsive.

Take the way she'd hightailed it into town to warn him about the bounty hunter. He knew right then and there that he needed to maintain some mighty careful distance between them. He'd taken to eating in the barn and generally doing his best to keep clear of Callie's way. If she was hurt or puzzled by the sudden changes in his habits she never spoke about it. He had a sense that maybe she was relieved.

The smell of roasting meat hung heavy in the air, along with the unmistakable scent of ale. Dozens of wagons ringed the space in front of the house. "I suppose everybody's here who's anybody?"

Callie gave him one of her looks. "As well as a few who aren't."

"Looks like half the state made the guest list."

"And why not? Denzell can afford to entertain in style."

Rafe frowned at her words. Not only was Denzell in debt up to his bloodshot eyeballs, since when had Callie started speaking the man's name with the type of reverence one reserved for the pope? When he'd first arrived on the ranch she'd mentioned her neighbor with distrust and dislike. Yet ever since Rafe had spent those days and nights in town, something had been different between him and Callie. More than one something.

He stood back and surveyed the front of the house, wondering once again just how Luke had got tied up with the likes of the Denzells. Tied in so tight Denzell had ordered him killed. Had to be something big. Something involving Callie's ranch to the point that first Bert was in the way, and now Callie.

So who was he here for? he asked himself crossly.

Luke or Callie? The answer wasn't half so obvious as it ought to be.

Not when he knew in his heart that he couldn't just up and leave Callie on her own. At least, not until Denzell no longer posed a threat.

Thoughtfully he joined Callie near the open front door.

Damn, he was tired of seeing her in black. She was no more in mourning than he was. Still and all, she looked exceptionally pretty today, and he was tempted to tell her so but stopped himself in time. *Luke,* he reminded himself. *You're here for Luke.*

"How many of these little dos does his lordship throw?"

"I'm not sure."

"How many you been to?"

Her regal air slipped just a notch, and he caught an unexpected glimpse of the true Callie. Insecure behind her bristly air of confidence. "This is the first one."

Rafe whistled softly. That must rankle. Past times she'd been overlooked. Finally she made the guest list, along with her hired hand.

"Callie!"

It was obvious Denzell had been watching for them, and that alone was enough to arouse Rafe's suspicions. With only the briefest acknowledgment to Rafe, he appropriated Callie and swept her away. Rafe would have to be deaf and dumb to miss the proprietary way the older man kept Callie pinned to his side as he escorted her from guest to guest, performing introductions. So that was the way things lay, was it? Had a bad smell, through and through.

No one bothered introducing Rafe around, and he was

glad. Passing on the small town chitchat, Rafe fetched himself a glass of the free-flowing ale and decided to take a closer look around the home of the man who'd arranged to have his brother killed.

The first room he came across was a study, filled with shelf after shelf of books. Cynically Rafe wondered whether anyone had ever opened any of them or if the gold-stamped leather volumes were just for looks. A scarred wooden desk occupied a place of prominence near the window, and Rafe had barely sidled closer to take a gander at the papers strewn across its unwaxed surface when he heard a noise behind him. Junior and Red glared suspiciously from the doorway, practically joined at the hip like Siamese twins.

"Howdy, boys," Rafe said casually. "Nice room."

"Party's thata way." Red jerked his thumb back the way they'd come. Junior nodded.

"How about that. I must have taken a wrong turn."

Rafe smiled jovially as he squeezed past them into the hallway. He could feel their glares digging into his back just below his shoulder blades. It wasn't a good feeling.

CALLIE GLANCED over her shoulder and wondered where Rafe had got to, hating the fact that she even cared. Denzell was insufferable. Not only had he attached himself to her side the second she'd arrived, he'd taken it upon himself to squire her around.

He insisted on introducing her as "poor Bert's widow from next door" and she'd got a funny look from a few of the ladies, although they'd said "how d'you do" nice enough. Did they think she was out socializing too soon after Bert's death? Perhaps four months was considered an indecently short period of mourning. Trouble was, she had no one to ask about these things. Surely Denzell wouldn't have invited her if it was a social faux pas. Of course, he was a man. What did they know about such niceties?

Alongside the female guests in their smartly fashioned, brightly colored gowns she felt shabby and dowdy in her one black dress. She found her thoughts straying back to that bolt of taffeta she'd seen in town. Closing her eyes, she pretended she was wearing a gown made from it. She could almost hear the crisp rustle of new fabric with each step she took. Smell that new-fabric smell.

"Mr. Denzell says you're staying on alone next door to him here."

Callie's eyes flew open to rest on a small woman she recalled being introduced to, although she couldn't remember her name.

"I declare I'd be too nervous, out here in the middle of nowhere like that. Lucky for you to have such caring neighbors close by."

"It's not so bad," Callie said. "Mostly I'm too busy with the ranch to have time to be lonely." The woman's face registered the fact that Callie had said the wrong thing. She ought to be still mourning the loss of her husband. But it wasn't in her to be so insincere. Foundering, she tried to undo the damage. "I mean, Bert would have wanted me to stay on and keep busy." Actually she suspected that if Bert had had his way it would be her six feet under, instead of him. But the fates had decreed otherwise.

"Indeed?"

"Truly. It was one of the last things he said to me."

"Were you there when he was killed? Weren't you scared?"

Callie swallowed hard. "It happened so fast. It's all rather a blur."

The woman appeared to thaw slightly, patting Callie on the arm as if to comfort her. "Well, I think you're very brave. Tell me. Who is that dark-haired man watching us from across the room? I don't believe I've made his acquaintance." She managed a coquettish smile. "He does look quite the rake."

"His name's Millar." Callie kept her voice even, despite the way her insides quivered at the sight of Rafe, dark and dangerous and eminently capable. She should have been repelled, but instead a warm liquid excitement percolated through her veins. "Showed up at the ranch a few weeks back, looking for work. I've managed to keep him busy lately, but with winter coming..." She let her words trail away, implying, she hoped, that Rafe Millar was just another of those drifters. No one terribly important.

"A ranch hand, you say?" The woman subjected Callie to a searching look. "Maybe there's something to be said for widowhood after all."

Callie managed her sweetest smile. "I confess, I do feel quite safe having Mr. Millar in the barn."

"To be sure." With one last look the woman drifted away, something in the way she looked at Callie leaving her with a sudden urge to go and wash her hands.

The need to wash was compounded by the appearance of Reverend Bligh sidling up to her. He was almost beaming, quite the change from his usual dour expression.

"I'm happy to see you and Mr. Denzell have patched up your differences, my dear. And I wish you all the best."

Callie opened her mouth to ask him what he meant, then closed it again. Let the reverend think what he wanted.

Bligh frowned as his gaze settled on Rafe. "Something

about the hand of yours. Looks real familiar to me. Like I've met him before, only..." He scratched his head.

"Drifters," Callie said noncommittally. "They all have the same look about them."

"Perhaps that's it," Bligh said. But he didn't sound overly convinced.

She glanced across the room to where Rafe had stood just seconds earlier. The spot was vacant.

RAFE WANDERED OUT BACK, pulling on his ale. Musicians strummed their instruments. Several haunches of meat roasted slowly over a huge fire pit, attended by a short Mexican man. Impulsively Rafe addressed the fellow in Spanish. The man's face brightened like the sky after a rainstorm as he responded in rapid-fire Spanish. And while he was out of practice some, Rafe managed to catch most of what the fellow said. When the little guy ran out of breath, he finished up with a hopeful smile. Rafe smiled back before he responded in the other man's mother tongue. Never could tell when it might be helpful to have an ally in the enemy camp.

And Rodriguez proved to be a veritable gold mine of information. Seemed he understood more English than his employer suspected, so Den and the boys spoke freely in front of him. None of what he heard made much sense to Rod, of course. What, for example, was a betrothal dinner? Rod didn't see anyone in the household heading in the matrimony way.

Rafe echoed his sentiments. Together, they had a good laugh over the gringos' weird behavior. Then Rod confided how a different señor used to come around, one who also spoke in Spanish to Rod when they were alone. The señor and Rod had more in common than Spanish, actually. They both had a nose for the gold. Rod's face darkened, and Rafe interpreted more in that look than anything Rod said. One day the señor didn't come any more. And there was no more talk of finding gold.

Rafe masked his reaction to what he had just learned.

Rod had to be talking about Luke, and he was wondering how he might pry out further information without seeming overly eager when a couple of the guests strolled past, their voices clearly audible.

"What's old Den up to, keeping company with Bert's widow?"

"Haven't you heard the rumors?"

"Rumors? What rumors? Do tell." The rest of their exchange was lost in the background noises of the party, and Rafe was left with warning signals flashing through his brain. When he turned back to talk to Rod some more, the Mexican had vanished.

"There you are, Mr. Millar." The Denzell boys were upon him again, leaving Rafe to wonder if they'd been instructed to keep an eye on him. "Pa says to tell you there's a game starting up in the barn."

"The barn?" Rafe echoed. "Funny place for a game."

He wondered if he was being set up the way Luke must have been. Hustled out of sight.

"Few of the fellows don't want their wives to find them. Seems the ladies disapprove."

Rafe nodded. "Thanks. I'll look in a little later."

The boys exchanged looks, which clearly told Rafe that he'd been expected to trot after them, obedient as a trained hound. If Denzell was spreading rumors about himself and

Callie, it made good sense that he'd want Rafe out of the way.

It didn't take much maneuvering to give the boys the slip. Then Rafe circled the outskirts of the attending guests, keeping his ear open to the murmurs. The poor, unfortunate widow. Nice of Denzell to take her under his wing. And word was that wasn't all he was taking her under. Woman shouldn't have to be out here all alone. Lucky to have someone like old Den who cared what happened to her.

Eventually he spotted Callie out near the musicians, a hungry longing on her face as she watched several couples who had begun to dance. He halted just in front of her and extended one hand in invitation.

"What?" Confusion pinkened her skin.

"Would you care to dance?"

"I... No. I never—"

Come on, Callie," he said with his most persuasive tone. "It's been quite some time for me, too, but it seems a shame to waste the music."

Slowly, coaxingly, he drew her into his arms, cursing inwardly as he did so. He shouldn't be doing this, holding her like this. Feeling the rightness in the way her body snugged his at every juncture. He knew he was holding her closer than propriety dictated, and he didn't give a tinker's damn.

The smell of her hair and her skin wafted up to him and he felt drunk with the scent of her. Intoxicated. He shifted, his body doing its bit to acknowledge her feminine allure. He drew a shaky breath, rested his cheek atop her head, and guided them among the other dancers.

Abruptly he felt her stiffen in his arms. He became aware of the couple behind him, making no effort to keep their voices low.

"...that gown. Really. Looks like it was dragged through the war..."

"...can't imagine why he invited her."

It took Rafe a minute to read through Callie's fence-post rigidity that she was the one under discussion. He squeezed her hand tight in silent support, but she didn't seem to notice.

"Come on," he said gruffly, guiding her off the floor. "Maybe dancing wasn't such a good idea after all."

Callie's face was flushed with humiliation. "Please excuse me." Then she turned and fled.

Damn! Rafe stared after her, knowing he would give anything for Callie not to have heard that malicious old biddy. Trouble was, what else had she overheard? Surely it took more than one snide comment about a frock to send a gal into a tailspin. Women. He'd never understood them and never would.

He hung around waiting to see if Callie returned, and when she didn't he headed over to the barn. The air above the poker table was blue with cigar smoke, echoing the muted sounds of men's voices. Denzell was sitting with a big pile of cash in front of him. He gave an exclamation of satisfaction when he saw Rafe.

"'Bout time you gave me a chance to win back some of my money, boy. Junior, give Mr. Millar your spot."

"Pa!"

"Just do it."

Rafe straddled the chair still warm from Junior's butt, and eyed Denzell as the older man shuffled the cards.

"Be fun to up the stakes a little, don't you think, Millar?"

Rafe took a toothpick out of his vest pocket and stuck it in his mouth. "Depends what you got in mind." He reached across the table as Denzell started to deal. "I'll cut the cards, if you don't mind."

"You don't trust me, Millar?"

"Stayed alive this long by listening to my instincts," Rafe said. "Don't see much reason to stop now."

"And your instincts tell you I'm a cheat?" Denzell rose and hitched his belt, slung low underneath his belly. If he was a cow, he'd be set to calf, Rafe mused, glancing up at the older man with a studied lack of concern.

"I never said you were cheating, Mr. Denzell. I just don't trust a whole lot of folks, is all."

Slowly Denzell resumed his seat. "Ain't seen you giving folks a whole lot of call to be trusting you. In fact, more than a few of us are concerned how long you've been hanging around over at Callie's."

"Is that a fact?"

"It is."

Nods and grunts from the other players. *Puppets,* Rafe thought. *And Denzell pulling the strings.*

Luke had never been anyone's puppet in his life. Which could well be one of the reasons Denzell had him killed. It seemed a safe bet that Luke must have witnessed Denzell killing Bert, which Denzell pinned on Luke before he sent the boys to hunt him down and kill him. Life at the Double D goes on. Except Denzell still hankered after Callie's spread.

Denzell's next words gave credence to that fact. "You best be making plans to be moving along."

"Oh. Why's that?"

"'Cause pretty soon you won't be welcome around here. And Callie'll have a real man to look out for her. She'll be living under my roof. As my wife."

"That's funny," Rafe said. Just the thought of Denzell

after Callie made him see red, fired enough to kill the man with his bare hands.

"What's funny about it?"

"'Cause her and me agreed to get hitched just as soon as the banns have been read."

Denzell let out a bellow like a wounded cow, while Rafe asked himself what on earth made him say such an outrageous thing.

"I ain't playing cards with no cheating liar."

"I won't bother to qualify that." Rafe ambled to his feet and left the barn, a heated buzz of conversation following him. What would happen once Callie got wind of the whopper he'd just told? He'd better find her first, so he could explain. If he could explain. Even as he pondered, the idea started to grow on him. Not the marrying part, mind, but the other part. Denzell coming through him to get at Callie. Could be just the edge he'd been looking for.

He found her out back, sitting by herself looking puckered and miserable by turns. Was he too late? Had the gossip spread this far this fast? He squatted at her side, searching for the words to explain. True, he'd always felt for the underdog, but he'd always been good at not getting himself involved. Until now.

Callie glanced at him, her eyes a deep, sea-washed green, full of troubled thoughts. "I overheard some folks saying I fixed it to have Bert killed."

Rafe shot to his feet like an arrow. Damn Denzell! Roughly he pulled Callie to her feet. "We're getting out of here. Right now."

Callie shook her head. "I can't spend my life running. I've done too much of it already. It's best to put paid to the gossip."

How could he tell her the gossip was only getting started? "There's something I need to tell you. In private."

"I think I know what you're going to say."

"I doubt that, somehow."

"It was you the bounty hunter was looking for, wasn't it?"

"I told you it wasn't." He inhaled raggedly and took hold of her wrist. "I also told a whole roomful of good folks here today that you and me are getting hitched."

# CHAPTER 14

"*A*re you insane?" Callie stared at Rafe in disbelief. First Denzell and now him. Had the entire world gone mad? Rafe's grip loosened, and for a second she was tempted to pop him one, but she thought better of it. She'd been on the receiving end of too much violence in her life.

He scratched his jaw. "Beats the hell out of me. It just popped out."

"Well you can just unpop it." Then, with more control than she felt, Callie smoothed the front of her skirt. "I think this is something best discussed in private."

Not until they were almost home did she speak to Rafe again.

"I hope you're proud of yourself. You've made me a laughingstock."

"That wasn't my intention."

"I can only begin to imagine what folks are saying."

"Doesn't bother me what folks say behind my back or to my face. Never has."

"Obviously I'm different from you in that regard."

"Callie, they're nothing but a bunch of stuffed shirts and

two-faced biddies. You said so yourself, to Reverend Bligh. I heard you. And when we were dancing, what those two said? Folks always talk. Today it's you they're talking about. Tomorrow it's some other joe."

She gave him a sidelong glance. Rafe was a man who walked his own path. It wasn't important to him what others said or thought. And she'd almost convinced herself that it didn't matter to her. Until today.

Today she realized that growing up the daughter of the town drunk left her wanting more than independence. She wanted respect—as a person, a human being with feelings, not some poor pathetic widow in need of protection. Or worse yet, the town laughingstock. But that was something Rafe would never understand.

He sat alongside her, looking solid and uncompromising. She envied him that stance, along with his need to be unfettered. All of which made his outrageous statement that much more incongruous. He couldn't be serious in his talk of getting hitched. Must be he'd heard the rumors started by Denzell. Quite a reaction those rumors had, on a man who didn't get involved.

"It's interesting. Denzell offered me something no man has offered me before." She watched a muscle jump in Rafe's tightly clenched jaw.

"What's that?"

"Respectability."

"Respectable? Him?" Rafe snorted. "I've seen rattlers more respectable. At least a rattler knows he's a snake. No pretending otherwise." Callie picked up something in the undercurrents of his tone. Could it be jealousy? Hardly. Still, she decided to string him along just a bit and see what happened.

"Actually, he seemed very sincere," Callie mused, as if

more to herself. "No flowery protestations of love. I would have turned him down for sure if he'd tried to pull any of that."

"What do you mean, you would have turned him down for sure? You didn't agree, did you? Not after everything you said."

"Maybe I figured there's more to life than independence. Maybe it's more important to have folks look on me as a person deserving of respect."

"It's possible to have both those things."

"For a man, yes. For a woman, I'm not convinced it isn't a matter of choosing one over the other. Denzell suggested his name would bring me the respectability of his standing in the community."

"Might as well make a deal with the devil himself," Rafe said sullenly.

"Well, I thanked him very nicely, of course. Told him I was flattered beyond all measure, but that it was too soon after Bert's passing for me to make any sort of decision along those lines." Was that a sigh of relief she heard from Rafe, or did she just imagine it?

"He won't leave you alone, you know."

Callie pulled on her lower lip thoughtfully. "What's so appealing about my land that Denzell would marry me in order to acquire it?"

"That's one of the things I aim to find out." They both knew he didn't need to marry her in order to do that.

As always, the countryside soothed Callie's restless spirit. The undulating hills and valleys stretched as far as the eye could see, interrupted only by the winding ribbon of the river. She should be content here. And she would be, if only...

In that second an arrow sliced the air between them and

landed with a hollow thud on the front of the wagon, scant inches from Rafe's boot. "We're under attack!" she cried.

Callie dove toward him. The horse reared and Rafe sawed on the reins. As the buckboard ground to a halt, Callie felt Rafe's arms close around her, and the rest of the world ceased to matter. Every time she tried to tell herself she had imagined these feelings, something like this would happen, catapulting her into Rafe's arms and making her aware just how good it felt to be held.

His hands were gentle, reassuring, as he stroked her back, and in spite of herself she felt her fear recede. Rafe fostered a feeling of safety and serenity like no one in her life.

"We're not under attack," he said, pulling the arrow free. A hunk of paper was stuck to the point, and Rafe ripped it off, skimmed it, then stuck it in his pocket.

"What, then?" Callie asked, twisting this way and that in her seat, on the lookout for wild savages. Not a breath of movement stirred the landscape. But they could be anyplace. In a tree. Behind a rock.

"Just a message from a friend." Leaving his arm resting comfortably around her, Rafe flicked the reins and the wagon set off.

"Something wrong with the telegraph?" Callie asked as she pulled away and straightened her shawl.

"Never know who's reading those telegraph messages."

As he spoke, Rafe removed his arm, and she hated to admit how much she missed the warmth and security of the contact.

"I haven't seen many Indians hereabouts."

"I doubt Wounded Bear will show up at the ranch. But don't be shocked, just in case."

"The ranch?" Callie gasped. "My ranch?"

"Yours till Denzell manages to get his dirty hands on it."

"That won't happen."

"Your experience with men of his caliber is sorely lacking. They set their sights on something, they get it. Over your dead body if need be." His lips thinned. "Or anyone else who gets in his way."

"You're just trying to scare me, Rafe Millar."

"Scare you, Callie? Now, why would I want to do a thing like that?"

"I don't know." Just the way his gaze rested on her stirred up all sorts of emotions, including fear.

Fear that he would leave any day now. Fear that he wouldn't.

What if she grew tired of fighting these feelings that arose any old time she thought about him? Would she eventually give in to him?

Better him than Denzell!

But why did it have to be either of them? Why did she have to give in at all? She didn't need a man. Men were the root of all her past miseries. A fact she'd do well to remember.

Before she knew it they reached the cabin. "One thing I do know is that I'm tired of being bossed and bullied and pushed around." Almost before Rafe brought the wagon to a halt she jumped down. She landed awkwardly on the ankle she'd injured when Rafe first arrived, and the joint gave a twinge, as if trying to remind her not to be so impulsive. She glanced back at Rafe. Her impulses had gone cockeyed the minute she'd first laid eyes on him. And she still hadn't the slightest idea who Rafe Millar was or what he was all about.

She'd barely straightened before Rafe rounded the wagon and reached her side. "You okay?"

On top of everything, he made it sound as if he really

cared. "Fine," Callie said tightly. "At least I would be if everyone just left me alone."

Rather than pick up the hint, Rafe followed her inside and tossed his hat onto the table in an infuriatingly familiar manner. You'd think the man owned the place or something, the way he acted. Owned both her and the ranch.

She watched as he washed his hands at the kitchen sink and dried them on her good dish towel. She wished she knew the right thing to do. Sending Rafe packing didn't help her any in dealing with Denzell, but she still had to deal with Rafe. She hated feeling this way. She'd sworn "never again" the day Bert died, yet here she was, vulnerable as ever. In an entirely different way.

She was aware of Rafe watching her, almost as if he could reach inside her mind and read her thoughts. "Guess you're feeling pretty confused right now, huh?"

"Nope," she said shortly. "I'm just puckered that folks assume I need a man in my life. I don't."

"Well, just don't go setting your mind till you hear what I've got to say."

"That's all I need," Callie said. "Listen to another man."

Rafe ran a hand through his hair as if he was having trouble wrapping his tongue around his words. It was a new pose for him. She'd thought the man had been born knowing what to say and how to say it.

"The way I see it, is this." Rafe paused for a breath. "Denzell wants your ranch, for whatever reasons. And he wants it pretty bad if he's willing to marry you to get it."

He made it sound as if marriage to her was a bad bargain for Denzell. Or maybe Rafe just considered marriage a bad bargain no matter who it involved.

"You need to find out why he wants the land, and get

him off your back. Plus, up your standing in the community if, as you say, folks' respect is important to you."

"I don't see what your particular interest is," she said. "Here one day, gone the next."

"That's true," Rafe said. "But I got a real thing against folks who flex their muscles against someone weaker. Kinda gets my dander up, if you know what I mean."

She eyed him speculatively. Was he willing to go so far as to marry her just to one-up Denzell? "So you'd aim to see Denzell thwarted, if only for the sake of it?"

He squared his shoulders, hauled in a breath, and faced her. "Made sense what I told folks today. That you and me get married."

"Not on your ever-loving life," Callie said flatly.

"Wait." Rafe raised a hand. "At least hear me out."

"Why should I?"

"I don't want your land. I'm sure any judge could draw up a legal paper saying the land stays yours after we're hitched. You being respectably married ought to please the old biddies in town and get Denzell off your back at the same time. 'Cause then Denzell has to deal with me."

"That's what this is all about, isn't it? You and Denzell. You've got some kind of quarrel I don't even know about."

"Not like that."

"I won't marry. Not ever again."

"I know how you feel," Rafe said, "on account of I feel like that myself. Once was enough. And I wouldn't even be talking about it now, except I don't see any other way after I leave."

"You mean, you'd still plan on leaving?"

"Once I knew you'd be all right on your own, I'd hit the trail for good. You tell folks I'm off prospecting or something. After a time, they'll stop asking. Or, if you'd rather, tell them I died. How's that sound?"

"It sounds pretty damn fishy to me. You want something, and I don't know what."

"I swear to you, I don't. Oh, I admit, I've done some things in my life that I'm not exactly proud of. But offering you my name and my protection for as long as you need it is one way I can make up for it. I like the idea of doing something I can be proud of."

"Find something else to be proud of," Callie replied. "Or some other widow you fancy needs protecting. I'll fight my own battles."

"You're outnumbered, Callie, right from the start. Denzell's got his two sons, the reverend, the sheriff, and Lord only knows who else in his pocket. Maybe even the governor."

Callie studied Rafe, trying to gauge the level of his sincerity. "How come you know so much about a man who you claim is nothing to you?"

"I know enough to know he's dangerous, Callie. What if Denzell was behind Bert's getting killed?"

Callie's mouth dropped open. She closed it again with a snap. "Of all the outlandish notions I ever heard, that one takes the cake."

"There's something on this land that Denzell wants powerful bad. Say Bert refused to sell. Denzell gets rid of him with the idea that you'll sell out and skedaddle back home. 'Cept you don't. You plant yourself tighter. And he has to find another way to get his hands on the ranch."

"You really think Denzell arranged to have Bert killed."

"Don't you?"

Callie drew a shaky breath. She didn't. But she couldn't say why. "What about the man they claim did it?"

"Far as I can gather, Denzell's the one said that. The sheriff sent out a posse. But they never found him, did they?"

"What are you saying?"

"It's not important. What is important is for you to think things over. I'm going out scouting for a few days with Wounded Bear. See if maybe we can figure out what's so attractive about this here chunk of the valley."

"Wounded Bear? Is that the Indian who almost hit us with his arrow?"

"If he wanted to hit us he would have. My brother-in-law's one hell of a shot. Might as well make the most of him being nearby."

"You have a brother-in-law who's an Indian?"

"Shoshoni. I lived with their tribe a spell."

As Callie digested this latest scrap of information, her next words popped out before she could stop them. "What happened to your wife?"

Rafe was silent so long Callie feared she had offended him. She was just digging about for some way to withdraw the question when he spoke. There was a darkness in his eyes she'd never seen before.

"Nishu died in childbirth."

"You must have loved her a lot." The thought of Rafe in love made her insides drag some place down near her bootstraps.

"More than I ever dreamed it was possible to love another human being."

"You're lucky," Callie said. "I never loved anyone that way."

Rafe shook his head. "You're the lucky one. It's hell on earth, caring more for another than you do your own skin. 'Specially when something bad happens."

Callie took advantage of his disclosure to make her own point. "So how can you even think about getting married again?"

The bleakness in his eyes surprised even her. It was a bleakness she shared, a sense that something important was missing from her life.

"Simple. Our marriage would mean nothing more than a piece of paper."

# CHAPTER 15

C allie wasn't so sure she agreed with what Rafe had said, her being lucky 'cause she'd never cared about anyone with the bottom-of-your-soul love he'd obviously felt for his wife. Sometimes she had a sense that never having loved that way left an empty, dead space inside of her.

To love someone so much you'd willingly die for them, and at the same time you put their needs well and truly before your own. She'd heard songs proclaiming such emotion, such feelings existed, but she hadn't believed it. Not until she'd looked into Rafe's eyes and seen the bleak ruin of his soul, having lost the one woman he'd loved. He'd never be whole again, while she'd never been whole to start with.

She knew for a certainty she couldn't marry Rafe. No more than she would seriously consider marrying Denzell. She was a woman on her own, bound and determined to stay that way.

At least that's what she told herself as she watched Rafe saddle up and ride away. Truth was, she missed him more than she cared to admit, had gotten used to having him around, and found herself storing up little things to tell him when he got back.

"Man's already been gone three days," she told herself out loud as she tossed the last of the table scraps to the chickens. "Who's to say he's even coming back?"

He said, replied a soft inner voice. And she believed him.

As she put Rafe firmly out of her mind for what had to be the twelfth time that day, Callie decided, since the weather was fine, she'd treat herself to a bath in the creek.

Carrying a towel and a sliver of lavender soap, she wandered upstream to the deepest part of the creek, where the bottom dipped close to twenty feet and made a splendid bathing spot. With scarcely a thought past how good it would feel to be squeaky clean from head to toe, Callie stripped to her skin. The creek water was biting cold. It stung her skin and brought tears to her eyes as it lapped around her knees, her hips, and finally her waist.

"Don't be a sissy," she scolded herself. "A little discomfort is good for a body."

Glancing down she noticed how her breasts were covered in goose bumps and her nipples puckered from the cold. The sight brought to mind one of those memories she was hoping to banish forever. The hot moist hollow of Rafe's mouth, his lips gentle as he suckled her the same as any babe. She felt the wanton warmth flood her limbs in response to the image branded into her brain. Rafe's dark head against the milk-white skin of her breasts.

Resolutely she splashed herself with cold water and waded deeper, not stopping till the water was nearly chest high. She dampened the soap and lathered it between her palms, shocked at the raw sensuality of' the sensation radiating outward from her fingertips. Slowly she lathered her arms, then her neck, with her head back, throat arched as if she'd never felt her own limbs before.

She took a deep breath and ducked her entire head below the surface to wet her hair. She wouldn't think about Rafe, she promised herself, or his outrageous offer of marriage. She'd prove to herself and to the township in general that it was possible for a woman to manage alone.

To work hard and produce something she was proud of. To carve a life and a home from this barren wilderness with or without a man at her side.

Her scalp tingled as she raked her fingernails over it, distributing the lavender-scented lather through to the ends of her hair. A heavy swath of wet hair brushed her shoulders, and she rolled her head from side to side, enjoying the sensual freedom. One strand of hair dragged across her breast, and the nipple tightened with a pleasurable intensity that was almost unbearable. She imagined Rafe in the stand of bushes across the creek, observing her actions, wanting her, and the scalding rush of heat that coursed through her limbs was downright embarrassing. What on earth had come over her?

She felt the tiny hairs stir and lift at the base of her skull. What if someone was watching? *Ridiculous*, she told herself as she tipped over to float on her back, rinsing the soap from her hair. Overhead the sky was a soft and gentle blue, dotted with the occasional fluffy wisps of cloud. Soon, she knew, the sky would be perpetually dark with winter clouds, bringing more rain and maybe even snow. She wouldn't mind. In past years she'd dreaded the approaching winter, if only because Bert couldn't make the journey to town as often as he liked. Being cramped up inside made him edgy and tense. That's when he did the most drinking, often all day and into the night. She tried to keep busy and stay out of his way, praying he'd pass out before he took it into his head that somehow• the weather was her fault.

Sometimes her prayers were answered. Sometimes not.

But this winter would be different. She'd be tucked up inside her cozy cabin, blessedly alone, snugged in for the winter with plenty of firewood and food and good hot tea. Trade that peaceful picture for the misery of marriage? Marriage to any man? She thought not.

When she stood and tossed back her wet hair, she thought she heard a noise in the bushes.

"Jumpy today, girl," she muttered. She had taken one step toward shore when she heard a shout, followed by the Denzell brothers riding into the open with a whoop of laughter. Callie swallowed the instant rise of panic and backed away till the water reached her chin. Too late to try and hide. They'd already caught sight of her. Side by side they rode to the edge of the creek and stopped to water their horses.

"Well, well, what have we here?"

"A bathing beauty?"

"Nah, it's just old Bert's widow."

"Hey, Junior. Looks like women's clothing on that bush over yonder. What do you suppose the widow's wearing?"

"I dunno, Red. Don't suppose she's naked, do you?"

"I dunno. Why don't we just set a spell and see."

"Water must be cold. Wouldn'cha think?"

"I'll find out." Red dismounted and strutted to the edge of the creek where he made a big show of bending over and dipping his baby finger into the water. "Damn cold," he turned and reported to his brother.

Next he grabbed up Callie's towel and flicked it through the air. "Come on out, Miz Lambert. Don't be bashful."

"Yeah. We'll even close our eyes." Both brothers laughed uproariously.

Callie crossed her arms over her chest and shifted her feet against the gravelly creek bottom. How long before they grew tired of tormenting her? Could she wait them out?

Her feet were beginning to go numb and a chill chased through her legs, rendering them heavy and sluggish. She knew she needed to get out of the water and warmed up fast.

"What you waiting for, Miz Lambert? Don't worry. We both seen a naked woman before, ain't we?"

"You boys are trespassing," Callie said with more assurance than she felt. "I'll thank you to get off my land. Now."

The brothers eyed each other and hooted with laughter. "Trespassing, are we? Does that mean she's gonna sic the sheriff on us?"

"It might."

"But first she has to come out of there."

"Thought I heard the lady ask you two boys to leave." Callie glanced over her shoulder to the far side of the creek. Denzell!

"Go on. Get back to the ranch. Both of you. I'll deal with you later."

"Hell, Pa. We were only funning her."

"Yeah. We didn't mean no harm."

Red remounted, and both boys sullenly turned their mounts in the direction of the Double D ranch. Callie eyed the white scrap that was her towel, which Red had dropped near the edge of the creek.

Denzell blew out an impatient breath, crossed the creek at the shallow point, and dismounted near her clothing. He made a big show of turning his back toward her.

"Come out of there, Callie. Before you catch your death."

Callie didn't need a second invitation to scramble from the creek and dive for her towel. Her hands were shaking so much she fumbled and dropped it twice before she managed to wrap it around herself in some semblance of modesty.

Without bothering to dry herself off, she pulled on her underthings and was lacing her chemise with numb, clumsy fingers, when a sudden choked sound from Denzell made her look up. He'd turned and was staring at her. Callie felt herself grow even colder. With stunning clarity she was reminded of Bert and the times her husband had looked at her that exact same way.

When Denzell started toward her, Callie turned tail and darted through the brush. The ground underfoot was rough against the soles of her feet, and she hadn't gone far when she heard the harsh rasp of his breathing. Seconds later he tackled her, slamming them both to the ground. Callie lay there, the wind knocked out of her, unable to move.

Denzell's squinty black eyes gleamed with lust and meanness a second before he backhanded her across the face.

"Don't run away from me. Ever. You hear?"

She lay there, conscious of his weight pressing her into the hard earth. She couldn't drag enough air into her labored lungs to move, let alone fight back.

"Now then," Denzell said. "I asked you once, nicely, to marry me. This time I'm telling you. And just in case you might be thinking otherwise, we'll be anticipating our wedding vows, starting here and now." Spittle formed on the corners of his mouth as his eyes raked her body. "Might even manage to plant a bastard in that barren womb of yours. Something old Bert was never man enough to do."

Callie closed her eyes and wished she could die.

Desperately she sought refuge in that one hidden corner of her mind where, in the past, she'd found a safe haven from a man's brutality. But another part of her screamed to fight back. She didn't have to take this any more. Not from Denzell. Not from anyone.

Her chest rose and fell with each labored breath as she closed her fist around a sizable rock. As Denzell lowered his mouth to her throat, she raised the rock and slammed it into the back of his head with all the force she could muster.

He let out a ferocious roar that echoed through the countryside, then grabbed her arm and twisted it above her head until she thought the bone would snap. The rock fell from her fingers, and Callie had just steeled herself for the retaliation that she knew was coming when Denzell let out a shocked gasp and released her.

He straightened up, his eyes glazed in shock. "What the hell?"

Callie gasped and covered her mouth at the sight of an arrow sticking from his shoulder and blood beginning to soak his shirt.

Indians!

Desperately she wriggled from beneath him and scrambled to her feet. Turning blindly, she ran straight into Rafe. He reached out and dragged her against him. Callie screamed and lashed out, clenched fists and bare feet making contact with buckskin-sheathed limbs.

"Callie. It's me. Rafe. It's okay. Everything's all right." She felt the pressure of his grip gentle as he cradled her protectively, both arms wrapping her close. He smoothed the damp tendrils of hair back from her face as Callie sagged against him with a muffled sob.

"It's over."

She swung about in time to see Denzell pull the arrow

from his shoulder and lumber to his feet. The circle of blood from the wound was widening. A black-haired Indian stood, bow and arrow at the ready a short distance away. Denzell spoke to Rafe. "Call off your Injun, Millar. I'm going."

"Stay clear of Lambert land, Denzell. Or Wounded Bear will demonstrate exactly how his people got known as bloodthirsty savages."

Stiffly Denzell mounted his horse and splashed back across the creek. Not until he was out of sight did Callie become aware that she was trembling from top to toe, clad only in her underthings.

Rafe retrieved the rest of her clothing, which he bundled up and passed to her. His Indian companion melted soundlessly into the woods. Hastily Callie pulled her dress over her head. She didn't bother with her shoes.

"Ready?"

Callie nodded. Rafe whistled and Marshall trotted into view. Rafe lifted Callie onto the horse and swung himself up behind her. His arms circled her with comforting warmth as he reached around her to pick up the reins.

Callie was too drained to do more than lean limply back against him. Silence lay heavily between them. As the horse climbed the uphill slope, Callie felt herself sliding backward into Rafe. His nearness combined with the gentle swaying motions of the saddle beneath her were having a most disturbing effect as a warm, heavy lethargy spread through her. Rafe's breath warmed the back of her neck, and when his arms tightened around her as they went over a rough patch of ground, her entire body reacted. The saddlehorn chafed the juncture of her thighs in ways that made her blush, keenly aware of her semi-clothed state.

Through the distraction of Rafe's nearness she wrestled with what she could possibly say. "Thank you" sounded much too inadequate. Besides, it was her own fault. She hadn't listened when Rafe warned her that Denzell wasn't about to be deterred.

They were nearly at the cabin before either spoke. "I'm sorry I didn't get back sooner," Rafe said. She felt his arms tighten with suppressed emotion. "I would have done anything to spare you that."

"I owe you and your friend a huge debt of thanks." It required tremendous effort not to turn and curl herself against him. To somehow attempt to hold the world at bay.

"Wounded Bear gets most of the credit. He heard the ruckus long before we reached the creek."

"You tried to warn me," Callie said miserably. "Only I was too pigheaded to listen. You know the kind of man Denzell is. The things he's capable of."

"It doesn't matter. Listen, I think Wounded Bear and I discovered why Denzell wants the land so bad."

"I don't care any more," Callie said. "I'm going to do what I should have done when Bert died."

"What's that?"

"Sell the ranch to the highest bidder. Move someplace different, where I can start over fresh."

"You might change your mind when you see what we found." Rafe took out a buckskin pouch and tipped the contents into her palm.

Callie frowned. "It looks like—"

"Gold dust," Rafe agreed. "We found it in the creek bed a few miles north of here. On Lambert land."

Callie was silent for a long time.

"Don't you see? Bert must have told Denzell about it. So Denzell had him killed."

Callie emptied the gold dust back into the pouch and returned it to Rafe. "This does tend to complicate things."

"It could also make you a very wealthy woman."

"How do you feel about it?"

"I'm thrilled for you. Money means power. And Denzell won't ever be able to touch you again."

Callie nodded, a feeling of resignation leaching through her about what she had to do next. "Folks'll say you married me for my money. That bother you any?"

"I beg your pardon?"

"You said, before, you'd marry me. This hasn't changed your mind, has it? We can keep to the original agreement where I keep the land, except you deal with the gold. Whatever gold you find we split fifty-fifty. You move on when you're ready. I stay behind and keep my ranch. Sounds like a good deal all around, wouldn't you say?"

Rafe frowned. "You sure that's what you want?"

"You said it yourself. It's for the best," Callie said. "Otherwise, soon as word of the gold leaks out, I'll have a whole passel of Frank Abbott types falling all over themselves to woo me. I couldn't stand that. You and me are different. Cards on the table going in. No false promises or declarations. A business deal is what we'll have." She tapped the gold pouch. "And a profitable one at that."

Rafe was silent so long when she finished speaking that she wondered if he'd changed his mind about marrying her. That's when she realized that marriage to Rafe Millar might not be so bad after all. Not that she was in love with him or anything, but she had got used to having him around.

"I'll have Bligh read the banns starting this Sunday."

"Good. Oh, just one more thing."

"What's that?"

"My pa had a beard. So did Bert. I'd be obliged if you'd shave yours off the day we exchange our vows."

# CHAPTER 16

"Mrs. Lambert. Callie." Reverend Bligh stepped between her and Rafe and lowered his voice. "You sure you know what you're doing, gal? Marrying this man? Nobody around these parts even knows him."

His concerns echoed the many nagging doubts that had plagued her since she'd agreed to this. She didn't want to think about it any longer. She just wanted it done. "I know precisely what I'm doing, Reverend. Now can we please get on with it?"

The reverend blew out a sternly disapproving breath.

"Very well. But it goes against my better judgment." He stepped back and cleared his throat, then opened his prayer book and started to speak. As Callie looked past Rafe and out through the church's one stained-glass window, her mind drifted, memories fueled by the distant drone of Reverend Bligh's voice.

Her first marriage had started out under similar circumstances. Her pa and brother had gone off on a drunk the day before and missed the ceremony. She hadn't known squat about the man she was marrying, still naive enough to think that marriage meant living happy ever after. It hadn't taken but one night as Mrs. Bert Lambert to alter her perceptions forever. And she'd never be that naive again. About anything.

She heard her name and turned her attention to the two men, automatically reciting the responses fed to her by the preacher. She'd been raised to respect the nuns and their teachings of the Almighty. Listening to Rafe repeat his vows to love, honor, and cherish, she wondered if he was recalling the first time he'd made that pledge, and she couldn't stop the sudden surge of shame that crept clear through her to the tips of her toes.

This was all wrong! Marriage wasn't meant to be a sham. It was a sacred promise between two people who swore to love each other till the day they died. She'd never known that kind of love, or any other kind, had no need to love and be loved. Give her independence and freedom, a roof over her head, and enough to eat. What more did she need?

Rafe thought she needed his protection. His name. But he was wrong!

As if waking from a dream, she felt Rafe reach for her left hand. Felt the cold edges of metal. Glancing down as if from a great distance she watched him slide a thin gold band onto her finger. A ring? He was giving her a ring? He must have won it in a poker game and didn't know what else to do with it.

Reverend Bligh pronounced them man and wife, reluctantly adding that Rafe could kiss the bride. Rafe replied that he'd save that honor for when they were alone. Callie flushed. They both knew this would be a marriage in name only.

She turned and all but ran down the center aisle to burst through the church doors. As she skidded to a stop at the top of the steps, she took a deep lungful of outside air, as if she were about to suffocate. Behind her she heard Rafe, and the suffocating feeling grew, even as she dragged more air into her lungs. She was Mrs. Rafe Millar. And despite the agreement they'd had the solicitor draw up, she was nonetheless wife and possession of a man she barely knew.

Her fingers clenched and unclenched, conscious of the strangeness of the new ring on her finger. She had to restrain herself not to rip it off.

Rafe joined her, shoved his hands in his pockets, and glanced up and down the street before meeting her eyes. She still wasn't used to him clean shaven. He'd honored her request that he shave before the ceremony, and as a result he looked younger, more approachable. More like the face in that damned wanted poster she hadn't been able to get rid of.

"Where to now? Over to the hotel for a bite of lunch?"

Lord, he was acting as if this was a proper wedding, instead of a mere formality. "I'd just as soon get back to the ranch, if you don't mind." She felt as if every person who passed their way was staring, knowing exactly what kind of deal she and Rafe had struck.

He eyed her closely, as if weighing her words. She forced herself to meet his gaze and felt a brief victory when he looked away first and said, "Whatever you say."

When they reached the wagon he pulled out a package wrapped in brown paper, which he extended toward her.

"What's that?"

"Marriage gift."

"From you?"

"Something wrong with that?"

Callie accepted the parcel reluctantly. "I didn't get you anything."

"No mind." He crossed his feet at the ankles and leaned against the side of the wagon, watching her. "Aren't you going to open it?"

"Right here? Now?"

"Why not?"

"I guess." Under the first layer she found two separately wrapped packages. The first was heavy, a funny, lumpy shape, and her hand shook as she tore the paper aside to reveal a hammer. She glanced from the hammer to Rafe, not knowing what to say.

"I saw it over at the hardware store," Rafe said. "It's not so heavy as most and has a smaller handle. Give it a try." His warm strong fingers positioned hers on the wooden handle.

"It feels real good." She expected him to let go, but he didn't, choosing instead to lightly stroke the soft skin of her bare hand. Why hadn't she left her gloves on? "The hammer I mean," she added hastily.

"I know what you mean. Open the other one."

Callie bit her lip hard. No one had ever given her any sort of a gift, at least not since her mother had died. She set the hammer on the seat of the wagon and turned her attention to the second package. The contents felt soft and floppy and she pulled the paper away to reveal a length of blue-green taffeta. The exact fabric she'd admired in the dry goods window.

She glanced up at Rafe, who was watching her with a knowing grin on his face. "How did you know...? "

"Man's got his ways," he said. "Besides. I'm tired of seeing you creeping around in all your blacks and browns. Thought you might have time to do a little sewing this winter. Make yourself a new gown or two." He took the fabric from her and held it up near her face, nodding to himself. "Yup, Matches your eyes real nice."

Callie felt herself flush again, felt it creep up her neck to her overheated cheeks. She cast her gaze down, hardly trusting herself to speak. Emotion clogged her throat. "Thank you."

"You're welcome. Sure you want to go back to the ranch?"

Lord, yes, she needed the security of her home and familiar things around her to offset what was becoming a very emotional day.

DRIVING HOME in silence was getting to be a real regular thing for them, Rafe thought as they reached the ranch. Then he caught himself. Callie's spread wasn't home. No place was home. Best he remember that, and not get too caught up in the trappings of society. Marrying Callie was no more than a means to an end, same as his staying on here in the first place.

Callie climbed down from the wagon and turned to face him. "The fact that we're married doesn't change things between us any. You'll continue to sleep in the barn and be paid for your labors. Any gold prospecting you do, you do on your own time. I won't have the ranch neglected while you're off chasing fool's gold."

Rafe felt his temper flare out of control. He jumped down, three long strides bringing him flush with Callie. He wasn't blind to the way she cowered from him, but he was beyond caring. Whatever had happened to her in the past was ancient history. And he wasn't about to have any skirt bossing him around.

"You listen up and listen good. I aim to sleep wherever I damn well please. I'll work when it suits and take off whenever the urge strikes. This place was a damn sight worse off before I got here than it is now."

"In your opinion, perhaps. Myself, I liked things just fine the way they were. Before I was invaded by you and your alter ego, Luke Rafael."

Rafe caught Callie's upper arm, conscious of the fragility of her limbs. He could break the bone in a heartbeat, but he didn't ever want to break her fiery spirit. He released her slowly. "Let it go, Callie."

"Let it go?" As she spoke she fumbled in her reticule, pulled out the wanted poster, the poster with Rafe's face on it, and waved it in the air between them. "Quite a resemblance. wouldn't you say? However, I'm sure you have a ready explanation."

Rafe snatched the poster from her and with only the barest glance, crushed it in his fist. To his chagrin he felt a sudden stinging sensation behind his eyes. With one sharp breath he dispelled the sadness that swept over him whenever he thought of his brother's untimely end. Instead he allowed the rise of good, clean anger, anger directed with renewed ferocity toward the Denzells, to take its place.

"Luke was my brother," he said shortly. "He's dead." With that he turned and stomped into the barn.

Callie stared open-mouthed after Rafe. His brother?

She supposed it was possible. But it didn't explain why the name had been niggling in the back of her mind ever since the day of the bounty hunter's visit. She had a sense that the name ought to mean something to her, yet she couldn't for the life of her fathom what.

She'd just started inside when she caught sight of the brown paper packages on the front seat of the wagon. Rafe's gifts to her proved him a thoughtful and caring man. And the look in his eyes as he crushed the poster... Yes, it was believable that Luke Rafael had been Rafe's brother. Which meant Rafe's being here in Oregon was more than a coincidence.

In a rare move, Callie delved into her carefully rationed flour and sugar and baked a cake for the evening meal. Now the cake was cooked and cooled, dinner ready long ago, and still no sign of Rafe. As darkness fell Callie went out looking for him, telling herself she had to make sure he hadn't fallen, maybe lying some place with a broken leg, helpless and in pain.

She found him neither helpless nor in pain but sitting on an old keg in the barn, repairing a leather bridle. A lantern hung on a nearby beam, spilling a circle of light across him, while behind him the barn was shadowed and still, save for the occasional whinny from one of the horses. The hay muffled her footsteps and she didn't think he was aware of her presence, but he spoke without turning.

"What do you want?"

"I—" Callie knotted her hands in her apron. "I wondered if you were coming in for supper. I made a cake."

"Wedding cake?" Rafe asked cynically. "Ought to have saved yourself the bother."

When it appeared he had no intention of turning to face her, Callie made her way to stand in front of him. "I thought it was the least I could do. You getting me a gift and all." She twisted the still unfamiliar wedding ring around and around on her finger as she spoke.

"Don't go setting a whole lot of store by it, Callie. It didn't mean anything."

"Bert never gave me a ring," she continued softly. "I was real surprised when you did."

"Doesn't sound like Bert ever gave you much of anything except grief."

"That's the truth of it."

"Don't be looking to me for anything different." Rafe squinted up at her. "I already loved and lost the only woman for me. When the time comes for me to go, I aim to do it without a backward glance."

In a purely impulsive gesture, Callie flopped down into the hay and hugged her knees to her chest. This way they were almost on an eye level. "You're lucky," she said. "At least you know what love feels like, if only for a short while. What was she like? Your wife."

Rafe pressed his lips together tightly, and for a moment Callie thought he was going to ignore her. To demand she leave.

"She was a princess in every sense of the word. Beautiful. Exotic. Demanding. Spoiled. I adored her. Everyone did."

Callie pulled on her lower lip and picked up a piece of straw, bending it into short lengths. "And she died in childbirth. Your first child?"

Rafe nodded.

"Your brother, Luke. How did he die?"

Rafe's eyes met hers. "You sure you want to hear this? I'm warning you. You won't like it."

"I asked."

Rafe threw down the bridle he'd been working on.

"The Denzell boys hunted him down in the mountains and killed him."

Callie smothered a gasp. "You know that for a fact?"

"Wounded Bear was keeping an eye out for him till I got here. He was too late." His voice dropped so low she could barely make out the words. "At least I know where he's buried."

"Why was the sheriff not informed? I mean if there was a witness and all?"

"You think the sheriff would take the word of an Indian over Denzell's sons?"

"I guess not. Do you know why they killed him?"

"I've got a few different theories." The look in his eyes chilled her with its intensity. "Denzell accused Luke of killing your husband, Bert."

The straw between her fingers snapped in two. With startling clarity, Callie saw the remaining pieces of the puzzle, the niggling details that had eluded her, fall into place with a click.

"You don't believe Luke killed Bert, though, do you?"

"I know my brother. Killing's not his style."

Callie clasped her hands together tight to stop them from shaking. "You know for sure what happened that day?"

"Not for sure. Not yet. But Luke always had a nose for gold. My guess is that he fell in with Bert and Denzell, probably saw Denzell kill Bert. Denzell and his boys figured he was going to blab, so they said he did the killing, then they hunted him down and made sure he'd never talk. Ever. All the sheriff knows is that his suspect got away, never to be seen again."

"You sound awfully certain about all this."

"I've been asking around. One fact I got no doubts on is who killed Luke."

"What good is knowing, when you've got no way of proving it?"

"I got no call for proving anything."

"You're not going to just sit back and let the Denzells get away with this, are you?"

"Nope."

"Then what—?"

"I got my own ideas about justice."

"I see why you didn't want me marrying Denzell."

Rafe shot her a look more than tinged with impatience. "He would have made your life hell. Marriage to Bert would have looked like a Sunday school picnic by comparison."

"It was no picnic," Callie mumbled.

Rafe nodded and stood. Stretching down a hand he helped Callie to her feet. "Myself, I got no truck with men who beat up on their women."

Callie's eyes widened. Instinctively she tried to pull her hand free. "Who said Bert beat me?" She felt his hand tighten on hers, then release her to slide, slowly, insinuatingly, up to her elbow. Callie trembled at the gentleness of his touch. The understanding look in his eyes.

"Nobody had to tell me anything. It's there in your eyes. Every minute of every day, if a body takes the time to look." Softly he touched her face near the corners of her eyes.

Callie locked her gaze onto his, conscious of the reassuring warmth of his touch. "What's in your eyes, Rafe Millar? If a body takes the time to look?"

"Nothing." Rafe released her abruptly. "I play poker too good."

Callie continued to study the expression in her new husband's eyes. "I don't think you're half so tough as you pretend, Rafe Millar." In a bold move that shocked even her, she ran her fingertips across his cheekbones to the clean shaven angle of his jaw. Her fingers lingered there, reluctant to let go. "I see things. Things you'd best prefer to leave hidden. Things that tell me you care about people. That you're a man of honor. Someone I can trust. I wouldn't have married you otherwise."

"Don't go trusting me, Callie. Or getting too used to

having me around. Once I'm done with Denzell, I'm down the road for good."

"What have you got planned for Denzell?"

"It's best you don't know."

"I don't believe you could kill the man in cold blood."

Rafe gave a harsh laugh that chilled her to the marrow of her bones. "Who said anything about killing him? Killing's way too good for a man like that."

# CHAPTER 17

The echo of Rafe's laughter continued to chill Callie's blood as she huddled in her cold bed later that night. If Rafe considered killing too good for the likes of Denzell, what on earth could he have in mind? She rolled onto her stomach, balled the pillow beneath her chin, and stared at the headboard. What had she been thinking, to up and marry a man she didn't know?

Especially after all her brave talk about independence.

Managing on her own. "You're a coward, Callie Lambert. Millar," she corrected herself. The first sign of anything unpleasant and she ran for protection to the nearest man! Yet men had always been the cause of everything wrong in her life.

She'd wished Bert dead more times than she could count, and when it finally happened she'd known it was too good to be true. No way she'd be left alone, allowed to live out her days in peace. The sense of freedom she'd felt seeing her husband lying dead in the dust had been as short-lived as the happiness she'd experienced as a married woman.

Her gaze moved to the highboy, where moonlight

spilling through a crack in the curtains accentuated the bolt of taffeta pooled on top. Her wedding night. The one bright spot was that she was spending it alone. She rolled to her back, propped her hands under her head, and stared at the ceiling. In spite of herself she gave a deep, heartfelt sigh. Life had a funny way of refusing to turn out the way a body thought it ought to.

On the whole, life as Mrs. Rafe Millar proved a fairly minor adjustment. Rafe continued to confer with her as to what-all needed doing, before winter set upon them, rather than take over the way she'd half expected. She had the sense that when the time came for him to up and leave, he aimed to see her better fixed than before he came.

Today he'd set off at first light to check the fencing through the north pasture. Callie was poring over seed catalogues, trying to decide what to plant come spring, when she heard the approaching sounds of a horse and wagon.

Upon hastening to the front door, Callie spied a lone woman driving a wagon hitched to a tired-looking gray. Her heart gave a hopeful leap. No one had ever paid her a social call before. Could it be the townsfolk had decided to accept her as one of them, now that she was married and respectable-like?

"Good day," she called brightly, and made her way down the steps. The wagon lurched to a stop inches from running her down.

"To some, perhaps." The gray-haired woman threw down the reins and picked up a basket resting near her feet, which she thrust into Callie's arms. "I've brought yer husband's bastard."

Callie's arms instinctively tightened around the basket as it started to slip. Speechless, she gazed down at the wrinkled red face of a newborn infant.

"Homely critter," her visitor announced. "Mandra only drew enough breath to give him a name." Her eyes suspiciously red-rimmed and moist, the woman drew a shuddery breath. "Myself, I've got eight other mouths to feed. Can't be taking care of another brat."

"This...this can't be. You're making a terrible mistake."

"No mistake," the woman said. "Mandra spotted Luke and you coming out of the church the other day as man and wife. Whole town's talking about it, even if he does call himself by a different name."

"No, really. You see—"

"Kind of a runt, anyway. He might not make it," the woman said as she picked up the reins and started off. "Mandra named him Luke," she called over her shoulder. "After his pa."

Callie's legs refused to carry her past the front stairs, where she collapsed onto the bottom step and sat as if frozen into place. Baby Luke almost opened one eye, then seemed to change his mind. Either he'd gone back to sleep or he'd already died on her, Callie wasn't sure which. Dark hair peeped from the crown of his badly knitted blue cap. The same dark fuzz continued down past his ears almost to his tiny jaw. He was wrapped in a clean, if threadbare, blanket. Just then he wrinkled his wizened face, letting her know he was alive. His lips were red, ringed with a thin milk-like film.

Milk! Oh no! How would she feed him? She knew nothing about the care of infants, except for one thing: Luke Junior was bound to be hungry when he woke up.

Ever so gently, so as not to disturb the sleeping infant, Callie placed the basket near her feet. Her mind was totally blank save for the rise of palpable, blind panic. A sudden urge to turn tail and run. Her gaze slid back to the basket and its contents. It wasn't fair. This baby wasn't her responsibility. Let Rafe deal with it. Take it to the orphanage or wherever one took orphaned newborns. She was having no part of it.

She picked up the basket and made her way to the barn, where she lost no time in saddling her horse. Mounting a horse while balancing a baby basket was no mean feat, but at last she managed it. With the reins in one hand and the basket settled across her knee on the other side, Callie shifted in the saddle, trying to get more comfortable, before she turned her mount in a northerly direction.

Miraculously, the baby didn't wake. Maybe he liked the jostling gait of their trip. At any rate, Callie felt an overwhelming sense of relief when she spied Rafe in the distance, down off his horse, mending the fence. He glanced her way and straightened, pushing the brim of his hat back off his forehead as he started toward her.

"Whoa!" Callie stopped inches away from him. Now that she was here, she hadn't a clue what to say.

He reached up and took hold of the bridle, rubbing her horse's sweaty neck. "Don't tell me you rode all this way just to have a picnic with me?"

"Hardly." Callie passed him the basket and slid from the saddle, anxious to stretch her cramped muscles.

Rafe glanced casually into the basket and did a double-take. "Whoa. This here's a baby."

"Brilliant observation," Callie said. "What I want to know is just what you're planning to do with it."

Rafe glanced from Callie to the basket and back again.

"Callie. Where in tarnation did this baby come from? Can't be much more than a day or two old."

"His gran brought him out and dumped him on the doorstep like so much dirty laundry."

Rafe's forehead wrinkled in a frown. "Why'd she do that?"

"Claims she doesn't want him."

"Where's his folks?"

"Both dead. If you believe Luke was his pa."

"Luke?"

"So the woman claimed. Has a notion in her head that you're Luke."

She couldn't believe the change that transformed Rafe's features.

His face softened into a half-smile as he gazed down at the sleeping baby. "Well, I'll be. What do you know about that? Little Luke Junior."

As if on cue, the baby opened both his eyes. They were the dark, deep-set blue of a sky about to storm. Screwing up his wee mouth, he uttered a frail cry. Which he repeated a second time with more gusto.

Rafe laughed with delight.

Callie was less enthused. "You've got to take him back to town, Rafe. There must be an orphanage or some place that'll look after him. Maybe the church."

Rafe meanwhile had the basket hooked comfortably under his arm. He slid a finger into the rosebud mouth and laughed again. "He's hungry, that's all. Feel him suck. Strong little cuss."

"Exactly," Callie said. "I don't see any wet nurse hereabouts, do you? Poor little tyke'll starve to death if you don't take him back right away."

"Don't tell me you're scared of a helpless little newborn baby."

"Not scared," Callie said. "Terrified. Look how small he is. Even his gran called him a runt. She said he might not make it. Sounded fair hopeful of the fact."

Rafe just shook his head and pulled the blanket back in order to inspect the newborn from top to toe. "He's no runt. He's just right. Look at this." He pulled off a knitted bootie and lifted one perfect miniature foot for Callie to examine. "You ever see toes this small?"

"No. And I got no need to."

"I'll bet the little tyke needs a change." Rafe set the basket down, knelt beside it, and fished out a dry diaper. "Don't you worry none, little Luke. We'll get you fed and changed in just a jiffy."

Callie stared open-mouthed. "You're going to change him? Right here?"

"You got a better idea?"

She clamped her mouth closed.

Rafe flashed her a knowing grin. "You want to do it?" Callie shook her head.

"Fine. You take my cup over to yonder field. Bring back some goat's milk for his highness. It'll be a sight easier for him to digest than cow's milk."

In spite of herself, Callie felt her mouth drop open again. Rafe was turning out to be a man of many surprises. First he changed the baby as natural as if he'd done it a hundred times over. Then he picked the infant up with one hand beneath the miniature head, raised him to his shoulder, and started rubbing the baby's back in soothing circles. Callie couldn't tear her gaze from the sight of that huge, sun-browned hand stroking the tiny back.

"What are you waiting for? Go fetch the milk. He's hungry."

Callie did his bidding, mostly because she thought it might be amusing to watch Rafe's consternation when he realized the baby couldn't drink from a cup the way he did.

"Thanks. Hold the cup for me, will you?"

He took a clean handkerchief and twisted the end into a bulb-like knot. Luke fussed and squirmed, red-faced with disapproval as Rafe settled him in the crook of one arm. With his free hand he dipped the handkerchief into the cup of still-warm milk and transferred it to the baby's mouth. Luke sucked noisily, then let out a fretful wail.

"Easy, greedy guts," Rafe crooned, as he resoaked the hankie and put it back in the baby's mouth. "You remind me of your pa." With painstaking patience he repeated the procedure until the cup was near empty and it seemed Luke had eaten his fill. Settling him back over his shoulder, Rafe patted his back. The baby responded with a satisfied burp. Followed by a second. "Good boy." He looked up at Callie and inquired innocently, "You want to take over now?"

Callie scrambled to her feet. "No sirree. You're doing just fine. I have to get back."

"What's your hurry?"

"No hurry." As she spoke she leapt for the stirrup and completely missed her footing. She forced herself to slow down before she tried again. Not until she was firmly in her saddle did she look at Rafe. "Where'd you learn all that baby stuff, anyway?"

Rafe shrugged. "Plain old-fashioned common sense. A few things I picked up when I lived with my wife's people. Mostly you need to remember that all a baby really needs is love."

Callie kneed her horse harder than she intended, sending the mare into a skittish dance. Damn Rafe and his easy talk of love, when he'd already made it abundantly clear there was no room in his life to love again. Yet she saw the way he took to that little tyke. He loved that little baby the instant he laid eyes on him. How dare he shower a stranger's child with a love he denied her? She gave him one last look, her heart overflowing with sadness. She'd never know the opportunity to experience such a love. Not as a wife or a mother.

"Callie!" he called after her.

Frantically she urged the horse into a full-blown gallop, knowing she couldn't face Rafe. Not right now!

Callie pretended to be engrossed in kneading the bread dough as she heard Rafe's step on the porch, followed by the sound of the door swinging open.

"Callie?"

Unconsciously she hunched her shoulders up near her ears, her back toward him. "You finish mending the fence?"

"No, I damn well did not finish mending the fence. Now, would you turn and look at me?"

Before she could decide whether to turn around or ignore him, Rafe decided for her, taking hold of her shoulders and forcing her none too gently around to face him. Resolutely she avoided his gaze and stared over his shoulder at the chair where the baby basket rested.

"You're a really nice piece of work, you know that? You show up out of the blue, drop off a baby for me to tend, then ask me why the fence isn't mended."

"I don't know anything about babies," she said, continuing to stare past him, across the room and out the window.

"Look at me, Callie."

When she didn't comply he took hold of her chin and forcibly tilted her face around to his. Eyeball to eyeball, Callie took little care to hold back the defiance she was feeling. "So I'm looking at you. So what?"

"I expect that having the baby thrust on you like that was kind of a shock."

It wasn't the baby that had her so spooked. It was the mixed-up way Rafe Millar, a man she didn't even know, made her feel. A man who married her with scarcely a second thought and no intention of sticking around a minute longer than he had to. Callie tried to lower her gaze, but Rafe wouldn't let her, ducking his head just slightly, his compelling blue eyes holding hers with an intensity Callie could feel, an invisible force with the power of a lightning bolt. She felt drawn to him, yet compelled to pull away before it was too late. Before she said or did something they both regretted.

He still held her shoulders, only his touch had softened, shifted to a caressing motion, as gentle as she'd seen him rub the baby's back.

Callie sucked on her bottom lip. Felt her limbs quivering right down to the toes of her boots in response to his touch.

"I lost my brother, Callie. My best friend in the whole world. The one person I always knew I could count on. I can't just abandon his son."

"I never had a best friend," she blurted out, then stopped, mortified by what she'd just said.

Rafe's fingers tightened ever so slightly, his voice low, his gaze compelling. "Let me, Callie. Let me be your friend. The one person in the world you know you can count on."

Even as she felt a part of her longing to say yes, Callie reminded herself she'd never been able to count on any man. Rafe Millar was no different from the rest. Her stomach might be doing somersaults and her heart might be beating double time. None of that mattered. She couldn't let herself get drawn in by false promises. They'd made a pact.

"You told me yourself you never settle in one place. Some help you'd be if I was ever to need you."

She watched the shutters fall across Rafe's face. He dropped his hands and stepped back a pace. "Tell me. Have I let you down yet?"

"It'll happen. Sure as the sun rises and sets. It's only a matter of time."

Rafe left her side. "One thing I have learned," he said, "is that in order to have a friend you have to know how to be a friend. I suspect that's part of your problem. You never learned how to be a friend to anyone. You say you want the townsfolk to like and accept you, and then you put on those standoffish airs of yours. Wait for them to come, hat in hand, to you. That's not the way life works."

As he spoke he picked up the baby basket and tucked it under his arm.

"Where are you going?" She spoke before she could stop herself. Anything to avoid thinking on what he'd just said.

"Luke and me'll get ourselves settled in the barn."

"You can't take a baby out in the barn. It gets cold at night."

"You were ready to leave him in an orphanage, where no one cares who he is or what happens to him." Callie was shocked by the dark anguish revealed in Rafe's face.

"Luke and me spent some time in one of those places. And I can tell you, soon as we were able to fend for ourselves, we opted to sleep in a barn any day."

Callie felt a lump form in her throat, making it hard to breathe and nearabouts impossible to swallow. "Then you and Luke better plan to sleep inside."

His gaze skimmed her face. "You think a spell on what you're saying. Make sure of how you feel."

Making sure of how she felt was the last thing she wanted to do right now. Instead, she slipped on her shawl.

"Where are you going?"

"Out to get more goat's milk. Your nephew's got some growing to do if he doesn't want to be called a runt."

That night Callie woke to unfamiliar shuffling sounds in

the cabin. A crack of light wedged under her door and pried her eyelids open. She shrugged into her wrapper and stepped from her room only to stop, frozen, at the sight before her. Rafe and Luke occupied the rocking chair before the fire. She watched Rafe lower his face toward the small one. When he spoke it looked for all the world as if the baby was drinking in every word, his dark eyes intent on Rafe's face.

Callie heard the soothing rise and fall of Rafe's voice rather than individual words as she watched him snuggle the infant against him, then lean his head back and close his eyes. Callie's insides were a muddled ball of mush. A log fell in the fire, sending a shower of sparks dancing up the chimney. The only other sound in the room was the steady breathing of man and child, underscored by the rhythmic creak of the rocking chair in motion.

Silently Callie returned to her bed, where she had the devil's own time falling asleep.

# CHAPTER 18

"Can I get you anything while I'm in town today?" Rafe asked, as he sipped his morning coffee.

"I didn't know you were going into town." Was that wariness he saw? It seemed she'd been on edge lately, that is, when she wasn't jumpy and watchful by turns, as if she half expected him to up and leave for good. Then she'd go someplace else entirely and he'd end up repeating everything two or three times. He'd never been able to figure out women, and Callie was no different in that regard.

"Got some things need doing."

"Oh. What kind of things?"

He set his cup down on the table harder than necessary and swore inwardly at seeing her flinch. It seemed like the two of them had been tiptoeing around each other of late, and the strain was jangling his nerves. He sighed and leaned toward her.

"Damn, this is hard." He ran a hand through his hair. "I'm used to coming and going as I please. I'm no good at being married."

"Neither am I." She forced a laugh that sounded strained

to his ears. "You want to maybe see about getting an annulment?"

Rafe shook his head. "Just 'cause Denzell seems to have let up for the time being doesn't mean we should start feeling too cocksure. Not as far as he's concerned. We know he's got his sights set on the gold."

"Is it Denzell stuff you're seeing after in town?"

"Some." Rafe glanced to where the baby slumbered in his basket near the stove. "Luke stuff, too."

"What kind of Luke stuff?"

"I thought I'd stop by the solicitor. Find out about adopting the boy. Ought to see about getting him christened, as well."

"Christened?"

He'd really surprised her on that score, Rafe judged.

"You're the churchgoer here. Isn't that the way things are done?"

"I guess. Suppose I just never saw you for following any kind of organization, religious or otherwise. What about Luke while you're in town?"

"I thought I'd take him with me."

"Best you leave him be here," Callie said. "Can't have the poor little tyke jounced around like a sack of spuds on the back of your horse."

"I admit, it's kind of hard to keep a low profile with a baby hanging from one hip like a six-shooter."

"Low profile? Why do you need to keep a low profile?"

He stood before she had a chance to try to grill him further. "I'll be back soon as I can. You sure it's okay about Luke?"

Callie nodded. "You mean to find out what happened to your brother, don't you?"

"I know what happened to my brother. What I need is a way to prove it."

"You said it yourself. The Denzells are a law unto themselves in these parts."

"Well, they've met their match this time. No mistake about it."

Seeing the solicitor had been more of an excuse than his primary mission, although he figured to look into that, too, while he was about it. Damn, he was even starting to act married, dreaming up a plausible story for the little woman so she wouldn't worry while he was gone. He didn't care one whit for the way it felt.

Rafe was greeted by name by the two old boys on the bench outside the barber shop, chewing their tobacco and passing the day away, and he didn't like the feel of that, either. Once a town started feeling familiar, it was a sure sign it was time to move on. Past time. Trouble was, he couldn't just pick up and go right now. Not without finishing what he came here to do.

On impulse, he stopped at the telegraph office and found out where baby Luke's grandma lived. It wouldn't do to go getting too attached to the little tyke if the woman was inclined to change her mind and want him back.

But when he reached the house where he'd been directed, there seemed little chance of that happening. The woman who came to the door appeared anything but pleased to see him.

"I wondered how long before you showed your sorry face."

"I beg your pardon, ma'am?"

"You can drop that act with me, boy. I know why you're here. Wait."

Rafe stood on the sagging porch, conscious of several

pairs of eyes in the front window peering from behind a yellowed lace curtain, watching him. He glanced over his shoulder, wondering how many other houses up and down the street had their curtains wagging, as well.

"Mandra said you'd show up. Made me promise on her deathbed that I'd see this got into your hands and no one else's." She held out a thin, leather-bound journal. When Rafe reached to take it, she snatched it back. "I want your word you'll do the right thing."

"Have you read it?"

"'Course I have." Her eyes narrowed. "You really aren't Luke, are you?"

"No, ma'am. But I cared for Luke as much as your daughter did. And I know for a fact who killed him."

Her steely eyes bored into his. "We both do." She slapped the journal into his outstretched palm and, without another word, closed the door in his face.

Tucking the book safely inside his shirt, Rafe made a slow, sweeping glance up and down the street, assuring himself no one else had witnessed the exchange.

A BABY in the house proved a dreadful distraction. Every two minutes Callie tiptoed to the basket and peered inside, reassuring herself he was still breathing. She found herself gazing hopefully at the clock on the far wall. Surely Rafe would return soon—before she had to change or feed her young charge. Upon hearing a faint stirring from the direction of the basket, she rushed to the baby's side. He was shuffling around, eyes closed, tiny red face contorted.

Callie took hold of the basket and jiggled it slightly, making hushing noises which seemed to quiet him down some. She plopped into the chair next to him and continued to rock the basket. Without conscious thought she started to hum a long-forgotten lullaby, one she must have heard as a child. To her surprise, the words popped into her head like beads on a string, and she sang them softly, humming the parts she couldn't remember as she gently rocked the basket in accompaniment.

In her mind she heard Ma's voice singing to her, as if trying to make up for everything wrong in their lives. Her mother had loved her, she realized. Callie had known how it felt to love and be loved. Closing her eyes, she recalled her mother's arms, their warm, safe shelter.

As she sang and rocked she felt the warm miracle of love surround her, spilling out of her. The baby's face relaxed. His tiny fists uncurled. Callie reached to stroke one downy-soft palm, startled when the baby's miniature fingers closed around hers. She recalled Rafe's words. "The thing a baby needs most is love."

"Well, I'll be," Callie said softly to herself as she watched the little one sleep. "I'll be."

RAFE RETURNED to the ranch pondering what Mr. Barnaby, the solicitor, had told him. First and foremost was the adoption—which wouldn't proceed unless Callie agreed to become Luke's adoptive mother.

"The boy's kin to me, not Callie," Rafe had protested.

"Doesn't make no mind. Folks don't cotton much to the idea of a man caring for a child. 'Specially a newborn. What's the problem, anyhow? You and Callie are husband and wife."

"Yeah."

"And she's got the ranch where the boy'll be living. I drew up the papers on that one, myself. Still don't understand it, mind you."

"That's beside the point."

"Anyway, I don't see a problem. Bring Callie and the tot in here, and I'll see the papers drawn up. You sure the gran'll go along with it?"

"Positive."

Barnaby had clapped him on the back and shown him the door. "Then it's as good as done."

Except it wasn't, Rafe mused. Callie had no interest in taking on another woman's child. 'Specially if anything should happen to Rafe himself somewhere down the road, leaving her Luke's guardian.

And while he felt strongly about not consigning his brother's son to life in an orphanage, would life with him be any better? Moving around all the time. Always on the road from here to there. Be much better for the boy to have a stable environment. Some place he could call home. The ranch would be perfect, and Rafe liked the idea of giving the boy all the advantages denied him and Luke when they were young. But it wouldn't be fair to Callie, expecting her to raise his nephew.

Damn, but life had a way of working itself into snarls.

He'd come hightailing to Springfield with the single-minded intention of seeing justice served for Luke's death. Nothing was ever as easy as it should be.

He patted the journal that still rested next to his heart.

At least he had proof, after a fashion, anyway. Luke had confided Denzell's entire scam to Mandra, who had painstakingly documented the facts. While the journal alone wasn't enough to take to the magistrate, it was at least something to make Denzell squirm.

He was imagining this, aware he should be feeling more elated, when he felt a puff of moving air as his hat was lifted clean off his head. He reined in his horse. With a triumphant laugh Wounded Bear rode past him and leaned down to retrieve the hat, which he tossed to Rafe after pulling the arrow free.

"What the hell did you do that for?" Rafe grumbled, fingering the arrow hole in his favorite hat.

"To show you, you must be on guard," Wounded Bear responded. "An enemy would be feasting on your heart at this minute. Or at least be trophying your scalp."

"I got things on my mind." Their horses fell into step like old friends.

"So I hear. A wife and son in less time than it takes to skin a buffalo."

"A damn sight more trouble, too."

"With my people you learned to make life simple. It is the white man's way to complicate his thinking."

"Amen to that," Rafe said.

"Myanta sends this." Wounded Bear tossed him a carrying cradle that Rafe recognized as being used by the Shoshoni.

"Myanta made this?"

"I'm to remind you: A warrior's son learns from his father the ways of the world."

"We both know I'm not cut out to be anybody's father."

"You're wrong, my brother. You are wise brother and wise father to many."

"I did wrong by your sister. I'm still puzzled you haven't lifted my scalp in retaliation."

Wounded Bear stared off into the distance. His face could have been carved from stone. "I miss Nishu. As I know you do. But I hold you no blame. Nishu's spirit speaks. She saw the way. Now destiny joins you to the white woman and brings you a son."

"Destiny also sends me the way of Denzell."

"Denzell." Wounded Bear's face darkened. "He is *t'ishek*. Evil. The world shall be soon rid of him and his seed."

"You see that message in some smoke signal?" Rafe drawled. "Or is that your own particular interpretation?"

Wounded Bear grinned. "Your woman waits with little patience."

Rafe turned to him. "When are you going to get a family of your own and quit worrying about me?"

"I do not understand. First you sleep in the barn. Now you sleep inside but do not share the woman's bed. She grows weary of the wait."

"Quit spying on me."

Wounded Bear managed to look hurt. "I watch. Ensure the *t'ishek* that took your brother does not end your bloodline, as well."

"I appreciate your concern. But Callie won't cotton much to you hanging around."

"I take my truth from the Great Spirit. And go where he says."

Up ahead, smoke curled from the chimney of the cabin.

Rafe grew impatient. There'd be a fire waiting. A meal. A woman and child. The domestic scene flashed through his mind and his gut burned with it, like a knife twisting. Every day that he stayed was going to make it that much harder to leave.

"Your sister's spirit. Does it speak of me?"

"She sees your happiness at long last. The white woman is your way now. Beware the evil one. He spreads his mischief far."

"Yeah, well, he's about to get his in spades. My great spirit tells me that."

"Remember the lessons learned from my people. You must listen with your heart instead of your ears. That is how you find the true way among those who would lead you false."

Abruptly Rafe guided his horse from the road toward a small stand of trees. He turned to Wounded Bear. "It's better you don't come with me, my friend. I've got something that needs a safe hiding place. Away from all evil."

"I understand." Wounded Bear turned in the direction from which he'd come. "I await your signal."

"What signal?"

"You'll know."

Rafe wasn't so sure on that score. Continuing through the woods, he eventually came to the site of a hollow tree stump. Pulling a piece of oilskin from his saddlebag, he carefully wrapped up Mandra's journal and tucked it deep inside the crevice between tree and root. Then he covered any sign of his passing with a handful of loose moss and, using a tree branch, erased his tracks.

Back on the road, he smelled the wood smoke from the fire underscored by the crisp fall air. Beneath him, his horse picked up the pace without being told. Damn it, he had to have it out with Denzell and get the hell away from here before he got too damn comfortable to leave.

## CHAPTER 19

Rafe stomped into the cabin without giving Callie or the baby a second look and tossed what he was carrying on the table, where it landed with a thud.

Callie looked up from her needlework. "Ssshh," she said. "You'll wake the baby."

"Any baby who can't sleep through a little noise deserves to be woke up," Rafe said shortly.

"What is that?" As she spoke Callie put down her needlework and approached the table warily.

"Handy little gadget," Rafe said. "You strap the baby in it and wear it on your back so your hands are free to ride or shoot or hoe the fields."

"Where did you get it? It looks Indian." Callie reached out and fingered the butter-soft leather straps woven sturdily onto a stiff wooden backing.

"Damn it all and thunderation," Rafe snapped. "Can't a man walk into the house without getting a hundred questions thrown at him?"

"My, my. We're in a bit of a temper, aren't we? What happened in town today?"

"Nothing happened."

Callie appeared to digest his words, then tried a different track. "What did Mr. Barnaby say about the adoption?"

Rafe took a minute to compose his features. "Nothing to it. He's drawing up the papers."

"Did you talk to the girl's mother?"

Rafe sent her an impatient look. "Questions and more questions. Next time maybe you ought to be the one who goes. I'll stay behind and babysit."

"I'm not the one who has a score to settle with the Denzells."

Her words reminded Rafe of the carefully hidden journal. The words Mandra had painstakingly penned as she and Luke shared everything. His brother had fallen in love at long last, and fallen hard. As he recalled what that felt like, Rafe's insides knotted with remembered pain. Luke's son might have lived to see the light of day, but the father hadn't. The pain intensified, white hot. The women they'd loved, him and his brother, neither had survived birthing their young. And now it was just him. Him and baby Luke. His hands balled into fists. "Denzell'll get his."

Callie crossed the room and took his hands in hers as if seeking to ease some of his torment. He felt tension race through him like an overwound clock. Her touch was winding him tighter.

"And Luke's gran? She won't be changing her mind about the baby? 'Cause I'd hate to get attached to him and then lose him."

"What the hell do you think's going to happen when I leave?"

Callie loosed her grip. "I didn't... That is..."

"You didn't think I'd leave him here with you, did you? You, who were all set to send him to the orphanage."

"I can give him a better home than you can, always on the prowl the way you are."

"He's my blood. He goes where I go."

"Fine," Callie said, giving Rafe what he sensed was a far too easy victory. "And the christening?"

"Shoot. I forgot all about that."

Callie gave him a satisfied look, as if she had proven her point. *Not much of a parent after all, are you?*

"Perhaps on Sunday after the service we can talk to the reverend together."

"I guess."

She made it sound a foregone conclusion they'd attend Sunday services together. Just like a real family. Could it be she was bound and determined to make him and Luke into the family she'd never had? Now he knew he'd made a mistake staying this long.

Callie returned to her seat and resumed her sewing.

"I'm making this christening gown for him to wear." She held up a scrap of white fabric. "It's been nearabouts impossible to get cotton since the war, but I had this piece tucked away, saving it for a special occasion. It's a bit yellowed, but it should wash up real nice."

"That's good." Rafe jammed his hat onto his head and crossed the room to the door.

"Dinner's just about ready. Where are you going?"

"Out," Rafe said shortly. "Don't bother waiting dinner on me."

For the life of her, Callie couldn't figure out what was bothering Rafe these days. He was taciturn, surly, and restless by turns. Seemed to Callie as if something was stuck in his craw but good. He spent most of his time out in the barn, away from her and the baby. The way he'd been spending his time became apparent the day he came in lugging a handmade wooden cradle.

Callie felt tears fill her eyes as he set the cradle in the middle of the room and gave it a nudge with his toe to set it rocking. She couldn't recollect the last time she'd shed a tear. Not even when her mother had died. She swiped at her cheeks with the back of her hand, hoping against hope Rafe hadn't seen.

"Tell me where you want it and I'll set it up for you."

Callie bit her lip in indecision. She'd dearly love to have little Luke in with her at night, but how would Rafe feel about her usurping his place caring for the infant?

"I wonder," she said, picking her words carefully. "If he should be out here near the fire, or in my room where it's quieter."

Rafe gave her a studied look. They both knew it wasn't noisy near the fire. Silent as a tomb, often as not. "You want him in with you, it's all right by me."

"You sure?"

"I'm more than happy not to be getting up in the night with him. That way I can go back to sleeping out in the barn."

"That's not necess-" Callie bit off her words. "I guess you miss your privacy, hmm?"

"Damn right." Rafe picked up the cradle and hauled it into Callie's room. "Where do you want this thing?"

Callie followed him. "I think in that corner there, away from the window. Wouldn't you say?"

"Up to you." But despite his nonchalant manner, Callie noticed the time he spent positioning the cradle just so.

Making sure it was far enough from the wall so the rockers didn't bang.

She reached out and ran a hand over the satiny wood curves. "Must have taken a long time getting this so smooth."

"Couldn't have my nephew getting splinters, now, could I?" Rafe straightened and turned abruptly, mere inches from Callie. In spite of herself she felt color flooding her cheeks at their unexpected proximity. The whole scene smacked of intimacy. The two of them. In here. Close to her bed. Next to the cradle.

She felt heat suffuse her entire body. Her breathing grew shallow. Little pinpricks of awareness raced across her skin. She couldn't have moved if she wanted to.

What she wanted was for Rafe to take her into his arms. To tumble her down on the bed. To peel back her clothing. To chafe his naked skin against hers. To...

"'Scuse me." Rafe attempted to pass. All he succeeded in doing was brushing against her. She felt the hard edges of his belt buckle press into her stomach. Her senses swam in response to his familiar masculine scent. She ran a tongue around the edge of her suddenly dry lips. Rafe's gaze followed the movement.

"Damn it, Callie." His chest rose and fell with the exertion of keeping himself in check. "You're not some innocent school-girl who doesn't know what happens when you're in a bedroom with a man, looking at him with those big, wanting eyes."

"'Specially when he's my husband," Callie said huskily.

Rafe drew in a long shuddery breath and released it slowly. "You don't mean this, Callie. You think you do. But I know you're no tease. Come tomorrow you'll be awful damn sorry."

"Maybe." Callie tilted her head to one side and took a tiny step closer. Close enough to seal them together from hipbone to thigh. To feel the heat from his loins, the stirring of his hard male length.

His hands sliced the air between them, seemed to hesitate, then draw close to her, close enough to settle on her shoulders and the soft warmth of her throat. He could feel the accelerated beat of her pulse.

"I'm only going to ask you this once." The husky timbre of his voice gave away the depth of his emotions. "You sure?"

Callie blinked. He wasn't making this easy on her.

She'd rather he tossed her down and set about the business of seducing her. But that wasn't his way. He wanted her to at least have a share in the control every step of the way. It was a totally new experience. A man who shared instead of just taking what he wanted.

She couldn't speak. She tried. But the words just seemed to catch in her throat. "Bert was..." She stopped and tried again. "I never enjoyed having him touch me."

"Are you saying you enjoy it when I touch you?"

Wordlessly, she nodded.

"Where?"

She looked away. It wasn't something she could talk about.

"Here?" His fingertip outlined the shape of one ear, sending a radiating flood of feelings through her bloodstream.

She nodded and stared at the way his Adam's apple bobbed.

"What about here?"

Gently he traced her jaw with the backs of his fingers.

His knuckles were softer than the callused pads of his fingertips. She swallowed deeply.

With his pinky he followed the outer curve of her lips.

She closed her eyes against the flood tide of emotions and felt herself swaying toward him. "What about here?"

His palm cupped the rounded shape of one breast straining against the fabric of her blouse. Surely he felt the eager pebbling of her nipple as he shaped and reshaped her softest curves.

From her breasts his hands slid down her ribs and spanned her waist before taking hold of her hips. Bert had always told her she was too skinny, but Rafe made low murmurs of masculine approval as he outlined her shape, and her heart warmed to the sound.

"You like it when I touch you, Callie?"

She opened her eyes and nodded, trembling. He needn't know she loved him. All he had to know was that she craved his touch. The closeness of his body pressed to hers.

"How about when I kiss you? You like that, hmmmm? You going to kiss me back this time?"

She felt his breath against her lips, as sweet as a summer breeze, followed by the slow, steady pressure of his lips molding hers. Deliberately she held herself back from returning the kiss, afraid that if she did her true feelings would be revealed.

Before she could fully enjoy the sensation of his lips atop hers, he ended the kiss and stood staring down at her.

"You'll have to do a damn sight better than that." As he spoke he put her from him. "I know you're hoping you can seduce me into staying. But I'm telling you now it won't work. I'm a man who's got leaving on his mind."

"True enough," Callie said, swallowing her disappointment as she stepped back and gave Rafe room to move past her.

"It's for the best," Rafe continued. "It's not like our being together would change anything. I'd still be on my way. Soon as I finish what I set out here to do."

From the doorway she watched as Rafe picked up the baby from his basket. It was a sight she wouldn't soon forget. Made all the more precious by the fact that she knew it wouldn't last.

"YOU SURE YOU want Bligh to be the one doing the christening?" Rafe whispered from the corner of his mouth. It seemed as if Bligh's deadly dull sermon would last forever. All around them on the uncomfortable wooden pews the members of the congregation stirred and fidgeted. Other babies cried. But not Luke. His boy slept like an angel in his mama's arms,

Callie's arms, Rafe amended quickly. Although she certainly looked the part of a mama today. She was handling little Luke as if she'd been born with the skill.

"We got no choice," Callie whispered back. "He's the only minister in town."

"Could go to a different town."

"Doesn't that strike you as extreme?"

"Maybe. Maybe not." Just then Bligh wound down his monologue on the evils of the flesh and signaled to the choir. The piano player started up, the choir joined in, and the churchgoers obediently shuffled to their feet, as if grateful for the excuse to move around.

"I'll talk to him after the service."

"Alone?" Callie asked. "Don't you think—"

"Alone," Rafe said firmly. "You take Luke and meet me at the wagon."

"But—"

"I wonder. Think it might be possible for you to do as I say without getting into a big question and answer spell?"

Callie listened to Bligh deliver the final blessing. The music changed to the recessional hymn. Bligh gave his incense burner a final flick, and the sweet-smelling smoke wafted through the air over the heads of those assembled before he made his way down the center aisle of the church. Beginning at the back of the church the congregation filed out in an orderly fashion. Bligh stood just outside the door at the top of the steps. Callie sidled past while Rafe hung back.

She felt horridly conspicuous as she descended the stairs with Luke bundled securely in her arms. Out in the street, the townspeople gathered in little bunches, the women to gossip and exchange recipes, the men to have a chew of tobacco or discuss the weather.

At least when she'd come here with Bert he'd had his cronies to jaw with. She'd almost felt a part of things. Today she'd been conscious of the many speculative stares that started from the time she and Rafe took their seats. Head down, arms protectively holding Luke cradled against her middle, she had started to make her way past the little groups of people when she found her way blocked by Miss Simon, the schoolmarm.

"Let's see what you got here, Callie." Her booming, no-nonsense tones carried through the entire throng. "Won't be long till this little man is clapping my erasers and learning his sums."

Callie gazed into Miss Simon's clear blue eyes and wondered if she was misinterpreting the friendly note in the other woman's voice. She bit back explanations of how Rafe would leave this winter and take the boy with him. Instead she offered a hesitant smile.

"I'm afraid I have little experience with young ones."

"You'll learn." Miss Simon pounded her heartily on the shoulder. "I think it's a real fine thing you've done, Callie, taking on another woman's babe and raising him as your own."

Her words were audible to those nearby, and to her amazement Callie heard murmurs of agreement from some of the other women, at which point the ice had clearly been broken. They huddled around her and Luke three deep, clucking at the baby. Nothing would do but that Callie peel away the blankets and display him like some sort of prize turkey.

"Got a few knickers my youngest has grown out of. I'll see that you get them for his nibs."

"If his teeth start to bother him, a half a spoon of quinine will do wonders."

"And if he has gas, don't hesitate to give him a little sugar in warm water."

"He's bonny fine, ma'am," said a young pigtailed girl before she darted off to join her playmates.

"Now, then," Miss Simon said, taking Callie's arm once the crowd had melted away. "I've been meaning to ask if you might spare an hour or two this winter to help me in the school library."

"Oh, I don't—"

"It's not good for you being holed up on the ranch day after day. We all understood how you wanted your healing time after Bert died, but you got yourself a new life now. New husband. New baby. Time you started getting out in the community. Mixing a little more. School library'll be a good place to get started. Get Mr. Millar to bring you in with him when he comes to town." Looking past Callie, her face brightened at Rafe's approach. "I was just telling this wife of yours how she needs to get out once in a while, I could use a helping hand in the school library. Say, every second Wednesday, for a few hours in the afternoon?"

Rafe laid his arm across Callie's shoulders in a possessive gesture she knew was solely for effect.

"I've been telling her that very thing, Miss Simon. Getting out will do her the world of good."

"That's settled then." Pulling her shawl snugly around her, Miss Simon turned and made her departure.

"Don't do that to me," Callie hissed as soon as they were alone.

"Don't do what?" She noticed how Rafe dropped his arm and took a step back from her.

"Pretend like you're going to be here forever. We both know different."

"Where's the harm?"

"I won't be party to any more deception."

"That a fact?" Rafe's eyes narrowed. "Did it ever occur to you that by wearing my ring you're the one doing the deceiving?"

"Is that so?" Shifting the baby to her other arm Callie went to tug the ring from her finger.

"I wouldn't," Rafe said. His breath tickled the inside of her ear and set off a ricochet of signals up and down her spine. "Everyone's watching. Give a smile so they know things are fine."

Callie glanced up. They were indeed subject to a variety of looks, ranging from curiosity to frank interest to narrowed speculation. She managed a tremulous smile. Glancing up at Rafe she spoke tight-lipped. "One of these days this house of cards you've built yourself is going to come tumbling down. Mark my words, Rafe Millar."

# CHAPTER 20

The inside of the barn echoed Callie's gray and gloomy mood. Not even the smell of warm animal flesh and sweet hay, usually a comfort to her, erased the heaviness in the pit of her stomach as she watched Rafe saddle his horse and pack his bedroll, along with a canteen of fresh water and enough food to last for several days. "I thought you said you'd be back by nightfall."

"I said I'd try to be back by nightfall. Plans have been known to change along the way."

Callie took a hesitant step closer. Close enough for her senses to take in the familiar, stirring scent of Rafe. Warm skin, underscored by leather, tobacco, and the futility of love. She'd been on her guard against revealing her feelings, especially now she knew firsthand the helplessness that results from caring more about another than oneself. It was hell on earth. Pure, torturous hell. She knew, too, what Rafe had meant when he told her she was lucky to have escaped. "I guess there's not much use my saying I wish you wouldn't go."

Rafe blew out an impatient breath and turned to face

her. There was no softness or caring in his look, but she couldn't stop herself from hoping. "We've been through this. One way or another I aim to settle this score with Denzell and his boys through to the finish."

"They haven't come around again since we got married."

"That's only one of the things that gives me a bad feeling. I don't trust them. And I don't cotton to setting around wondering where the enemy might strike next."

"If he strikes." Callie buried her hands within her skirt. Anything to prevent her from making a fool of herself—launching herself at Rafe, begging him not to go, vowing her undying love. Nothing would push him out of her life faster than if he suspected she'd fallen in love with him.

"Oh, he'll strike, all right. Unless I get to him first."

"And when you get to him, what then?" Worry sharpened her voice. If he got Denzell to admit Luke didn't kill Bert, would Rafe start looking around to find out who did, so he could clear his brother's name? Or would he remain convinced Denzell had pulled the trigger, despite what the older man might say?

"Damn it, Callie. I'd feel a whole lot better about this if I didn't have to put up with your nagging right now."

"I'm simply concerned for your safety."

"Don't waste your time. Remember our deal. You go about your business. I go about mine. End of story."

Easy for him to say. "Didn't I hear you say plans sometimes got a way of changing on a body?"

"I was talking about a completely different matter."

"Doesn't make much difference, far as I can see."

Rafe turned, not fast enough that she didn't hear the soft string of curses he uttered. When he turned back to her his face was impassive. "I know what you're trying to do, Callie. I've seen it coming for a spell now. And I'm telling you it won't work. You'd like to have you, me, and Luke turn into some kind of fairytale family that lives happy ever after. And I'm telling you, here and now, stuff only turns out that way in books."

"What about little Luke? What kind of pa you going to make him if you up and get yourself killed?"

Rafe swung into his saddle. "I'm only going out to check and see what those boys are up to. Like as not I'll be home for supper."

RAFE GUIDED his horse across the creek and into the woods on the other side. He hadn't traveled far before Wounded Bear joined him. As they rode side by side, Rafe appreciated the way men were able to share a companionable silence. No need to be discussing and examining every little detail of what they hoped would happen. It was pretty damn obvious that the sooner he finished this chapter with Denzell and got the hell out of here, the better for all parties concerned. Living with Callie was driving him crazy in a whole number of different ways.

He'd started sleeping in the barn again, if only to spare himself the sight of her in her thin night rail. He was sure she had no idea when she stood in front of the lamp that he could see clear through a fabric that was little more than a gauzy enticement, revealing the length of her legs, the curve of her waist, the rounded weight of her breasts. All told, his self-control had worn mighty thin.

"The white woman is not pleased." Wounded Bear spoke first.

Rafe shot his companion a speculative look. "That a guess or an observation?"

Wounded Bear glanced skyward where thick foliage provided a leafy canopy and obscured the sky from their sight. "Females. And you ask why I'm not married."

"Got yourself a point there, my friend. You sure Bligh's visiting the ranch house?"

"Positive."

They continued on their way, soon passing from Lambert land to the Double D spread. Leaving Wounded Bear back in the woods with the horses, Rafe belly-crawled up near the terrace in back of the house. Seemed Denzell was indeed entertaining. Rafe frowned as he concentrated on the faint snatches of conversation. It sounded like Denzell was interrogating the foreman of his lumber mill, with the poor bastard trying to explain why the huge profits from the earlier years had dried up and turned into debts. Denzell informed him things were about to change and admonished him to keep his mouth closed. What was the old goat up to now?

The next voice he heard was that of Reverend Bligh, and Rafe nodded to himself as he followed their conversation with ease. He'd suspected Denzell of blackmailing the good reverend, and his suspicion was confirmed when he heard Bligh complain about congregation donations being down, so he couldn't quite meet the dollar amount set by Denzell. Denzell only laughed humorlessly and told the reverend to ante up. Unless he wanted the entire town to find out about his penchant for young, dark-skinned boys.

The reverend took his leave, and Rafe did a double-take at the sight of Frank Abbott joining Denzell. Unfortunately, the wind shifted and he couldn't hear a single word they exchanged, but Abbott looked suspiciously comfortable at the Double D. After Abbott's departure, Denzell bellowed for his sons, and Rafe made his way back to Wounded Bear.

"You were right," Rafe said. "Abbott dropped by. And Reverend Bligh just made a generous donation to the Denzell gambling fund. Now what?"

Wounded Bear directed Rafe's attention to the boys riding across the field away from them. "Damn," Rafe muttered. "If we follow them, they're sure to see us."

Wounded Bear looked unconcerned. "I know where they're going. I'll take you there."

Rafe chafed with impatience, but it wasn't long before the boys returned to the ranch house. Taking a circuitous pathway to avoid being seen, Wounded Bear led Rafe through the woods, across an empty field, and halfway up a craggy mountain gorge to a natural rock crevice. At the bottom of the crevice was a plot of recently turned earth. Dismounting, Rafe bare-handed the soft dirt.

"We should have brought a shovel."

Wounded Bear remained astride his horse, watching Rafe's efforts with an inscrutable expression.

"Don't suppose you feel like lending a hand here?" Wounded Bear gave his glossy head a shake. Barely two feet below the surface Rafe's fingers reached something that didn't belong. Grasping hold, he pulled out a canvas draw-string bag. He glanced up at Wounded Bear. "I suppose you know what's in here."

"Denzell doesn't believe in banks."

The bag was heavy in his hand. Loosening the top, Rafe emptied out the contents. Gemstones gleamed up at him, watches, coins, gold nuggets. But it was the last item to tumble free, his brother's watch, that caused a huge lump to stick in his throat. His fingers closed over the familiar object, and Rafe raised his eyes to the heavens as he renewed his vow for revenge.

WITH BABY LUKE strapped securely onto her back, Callie fetched a pail and made her way to where she'd spotted a late crop of blackberries earlier this week. This carrying thing was a godsend. Luke gurgled happily while she filled her pail. He was such a good baby, really. Hardly a scrap of bother.

Rafe, on the other hand, was a terrible lot of bother. She was afraid he'd ferret out her deepest, darkest secrets, for he had that way of looking at her, peering straight into her soul. At least that's what it felt like.

"Ow!" She pulled back her hand as a thorn bit into the fleshy pad of her thumb. These old berry bushes were as thorny as Rafe. She hoped fresh blackberry-and-apple pie would help smooth things over between them. At least put them back on a more comfortable footing.

Later, just after she pulled the pies from the oven to cool, she heard the sound of a wagon approaching. From the doorway Callie watched, open-mouthed, as two wagons disgorged nearly a dozen ladies from town to swarm up her front steps, arms laden with packages. Leading the way was Miss Simon, who grasped Callie's hand in a bone-crunching handshake.

"I do apologize for showing up unannounced, my dear, but I just couldn't stop myself. Ever since Mr. Millar stopped by the schoolhouse and asked me to be little Luke's godmother, I've been just tickled pink. And when I told the others, why, they all agreed it was high time to pay a call. You remember Mrs. Hughes? That there's her daughter Lily. Mrs. Bell. And her daughter Bernice." By the time Miss Simon had completed the introductions, the cabin was full of the excited sounds of female chatter and Callie's head was reeling.

Miss Simon paid no speck of mind, simply breezed inside as if she'd done it every day of her life, and put the kettle on to boil.

"We'll just stay for a quick cuppa, although I must say, is that blackberry-apple pie I smell?"

"Yes, ma'am. Fresh made." Callie grabbed hold of her long-forgotten manners as she bade the women sit and rest while she brewed a large pot of tea and cut wedges of the still-warm pie.

Just then Luke started to fuss, and Callie fetched him from the bedroom. Miss Simon took him over as if he was already one of her charges, while the younger guests laid out the layette and baby things that the women had brought.

There were several knitted outfits. "Blue to match his eyes," said Miss Simon. A beautiful patchwork quilt, bibs and booties. even a tiny toy clown.

"He'll be grabbing onto that in no time. Just you wait." Callie was awash with emotion, her gaze moving from guest to guest. It seemed they all spoke at once vying for her attention until, as if by a prearranged signal, the ladies downed their tea and rose to take their leave.

"Don't want to be taking up too much of your time," Miss Simon said. The others nodded as they clambered back into the wagons. "You won't forget about helping in the school library now, will you?"

"Not at all. Thank you all so much for the gifts and for coming out here. I really don't know what to say."

Miss Simon sliced the air with her hand. "No need to say a thing. It's been too long since you've been a part of things. And much of the blame's ours." She patted Callie's hand.

"Just don't go getting overwhelmed as we try to make it up to you."

RAFE AND WOUNDED Bear were making their way single file toward the ranch when Wounded Bear stopped and signaled to Rafe. He nodded. "Over the next rise. They wait."

"Who waits?"

"The evil one's seed."

"The two boys. Alone?"

Wounded Bear nodded.

"Well then," Rafe said, "why don't I go see what they want?"

"We could return a different way." No emotion showed in Wounded Bear's black eyes.

"What? And ruin their fun? You take the other way. Watch my back." Rafe made sure his rifle was within easy reach as he rounded the rise to where the Denzell boys had positioned themselves so they blocked the way.

"You're trespassing, Millar."

"That a fact. Does your pa know you're out here talking to me?" He watched them exchange wary glances. They were puppets of the old man, scared stiff of their parent. While Rafe knew from Wounded Bear that they were the ones who killed Luke, they never would have done it without their pa's say so. "'Cause he doesn't take kindly to you boys going it on your own, does he?"

Junior straightened in his saddle. "He don't own us."

"I think you're wrong about that. He owns your horses. He owns your soul. He even owns your whore. Isn't that a fact?"

"Pa wants you to get," Red said in a whiny, nasal tone.

"I'm getting," Rafe said easily. "Soon as you boys move aside."

"Outa Oregon, he means," said Junior with a sneer. "You don't fit in here. What kind of man would marry old Bert's widow, anyway?"

"Your pa asked her, if I recall."

"He don't have to now. He figured who killed old Bert. And the widow'll do whatever he says to keep him quiet."

"We all know your pa killed Bert. Let's not kid each other."

"You're wrong, Millar. And you're going to find yourself dead wrong when the truth comes out. Best be leaving while you have the chance." That said, the Denzell brothers rode cockily past him, leaving him thinking on their words.

CALLIE WAS STILL STANDING on the porch, Luke propped on one hip, a dreamy smile on her face, when she heard the frantic hoofbeats of riders coming at the cabin hard and fast.

She saw Rafe and the Indian ride into the barn. She went across the yard to the barn, but hesitated on the threshold. The two men were talking low-voiced, their words too muffled for her to make out, but she sensed a fair amount of agitation and urgency in their speech. Reluctant to intrude, she'd just stepped back from the doorway when the opening was filled by the looming shadow of man and horse.

Seen this close up the Indian appeared huge astride his mount, and threatening. Cradling Luke protectively against her chest, Callie gasped as she took a step back.

He gave her the once-over from top to toe, then raised

one hand as if in greeting and wheeled his horse in the direction of the creek. Callie stood rooted to the spot, watching his retreat.

She sensed rather than heard Rafe come up behind her.

Then she swung about, agitation making her voice sharper than she intended. "Your friend nearly mowed me down."

"Somehow I doubt that. Wounded Bear is the best horseman I've ever come across."

"He could use some brushing up on his manners."

"He meant you no disrespect. Don't make the mistake of judging him by white men's standards. Here, let me." Rafe retrieved the baby from her and laid him over one shoulder. Callie felt the imprint of his fingers where they'd grazed her bosom and arm. White heat. As intense as if Rafe still touched her.

"Company today?"

She shot him a quick sideways glance. "You don't miss much, do you?"

"Fresh wagon tracks up to the front door."

"Your friend Miss Simon with a contingent of the local ladies. Pleased as punch about her assigned role as Luke's godmother. I wish you'd told me, I felt quite stupid not knowing what she was talking about."

"Sorry. It slipped my mind."

"To be sure."

Rafe's hand on her arm stopped her, swung her about to face him. "I got a sense that this isn't working out between us."

"What's that?" Nervously, Callie scuffed at the dirt with the toe of her boot.

The baby started to fuss and Rafe shifted him to his

other arm. "You and me living here. Pretending to be man and wife."

"Is it the living together part or the pretending part that's bothering you?"

"Seemed easier when I was just your hired hand."

"Things were far less complicated before you showed up."

"I expect they were."

Callie swallowed the sudden rush of emotion that threatened to choke her. Before Rafe arrived everything was less. Less color in the sky. Less scent in the air. Less feeling running through her. She'd been truly half dead, prepared to wither up out here and blow away.

He'd made her feel. Made her love. Made her care. Even pain was preferable to feeling nothing at all.

RAFE FOLLOWED Callie to the cabin, but the second he stepped inside he felt the roof hover about an inch above his head and the walls close in on him from all four sides. Panic was laced with the smell of fresh-baked blackberry-and-apple pie. The settee was stacked with baby clothes and toys. A pot of something hearty-smelling simmered on the back of the stove alongside the coffeepot. The perfect picture of domestic bliss.

Even as he fought for breath the feeling closed around him as insidious and venomous as any cobra's coils. Hearth and home. A trap with tentacles so subtle a body didn't realize until it was too late just how good and well he was stuck.

The baby had gone to sleep in his arms and Rafe laid him in his basket, near the stove where it was warm, smoothing the blanket atop his relaxed and curled-up body. Had he himself ever been so relaxed? Somehow Rafe doubted it.

He straightened and slipped his hand inside his pocket, feeling the cold hard edges of Luke's pocket watch. One day he'd hand it over to Luke's son, along with all the memories he'd stored up about his twin. It was important a boy know his pa. What kind of man he was.

Callie faced him with a falsely bright smile. Except when you had a pa the likes of hers, Rafe added to himself. A youngster was better off not knowing they'd been sired by the town drunk. It was well and truly amazing how she'd managed to rise above her beginnings. It certainly proved her mettle.

"Want to take a look at the things the ladies brought out for little Luke?"

"Not much."

Her smile wavered slightly. "You hungry?"

"Not much."

Arms clasped about her waist she gave herself a small, comforting hug.

He watched the way her gaze darted about the room, careful to light on just about anything, save him.

"I'm...ah, glad you made it back so quick. I wasn't sure. You know. How long you'd be. If you'd be hungry."

He couldn't stop himself. He closed the distance between them, grasped her shoulders and held her still.

She stared up at him, eyes glazed, full of doubt.

"Quit it," he said from between clenched teeth.

"Quit what?"

"Quit acting like a wife."

She seemed taken aback. "I don't know what you mean."

His fingers tightened. He had to be hurting her, but she didn't let on.

"Sure you do. Supper waiting on the stove. Fresh-baked pie. A bunch of church ladies over for tea. You're loving every minute of this, aren't you?"

"I don't understand. What have I done wrong?"

He gave a harsh laugh. "Why do you have to do anything? Why can't you just leave things be?"

Her head snapped up straight. "Might I remind you, getting married was your idea in the first place."

He released her abruptly. "You didn't have to up and go along with it." He watched her eyes cloud over, saw her face lose all animation.

Slowly she drew her entire body erect, as if a pole was wedged down her spine. "Who's keeping you here, if you're so out-and-out unhappy?"

"Good question." Pushing past her, Rafe went to the cupboard where she kept the whiskey, grabbed the bottle, ripped out the cork, and took a long drink. Lowering the bottle, he wiped his mouth with the back of his hand. His eyes met hers across the room. He read the way shock, horror, and a load of bad-time memories washed over her, rocking her clean down to her toes.

"Sooner or later the men in your life all choose whiskey over you. Isn't that a fact, though?"

Before she had a chance to answer, he took the bottle and headed for the barn, slamming the cabin door behind him.

# CHAPTER 21

Callie stared at the back of the cabin door, knowing full well she'd turned as chalk white as the half-made christening gown. Her hand flew to her throat, settling over the rapid beating of her own pulse. Were Rafe's cruel words true? She'd blamed bottled spirits for making the men in her life act that way. Her pa. Her brother. Bert. Could it be something in her that forced a man to seek the solace of drink? She paced the cabin, her thoughts awhirl.

What should she do?

What could she do? Short of going out to the barn and wrestling the bottle from Rafe. Or holing up inside here and waiting him out. What if Rafe proved as mean a drunk as Bert or her pa? Suppose the firewater in his veins made him decide to claim his husbandly rights?

Rafe wouldn't do that.

Or would he? Bert had never touched her unless he was falling down drunk.

Her thoughts startled her to action. First she slid the bolt into place across the door. Next she tipped a chair under the door handle for good measure, even though she knew full well that if Rafe took it into his head to gain entry, nothing she did would keep him out.

Hands on hips, she surveyed the homey interior. Was it a refuge or a prison? The shotgun was next to useless. Rafe had been right when he said she wouldn't be able to turn the gun against him. She'd sworn to never again use the weapon for the taking of a human life. And she wasn't confident enough in her aim to trust she could only slow him down. She dragged out her heavy black-bottom fry pan. It wouldn't hurt any to have it close at hand, just in case.

She was sitting motionless in the slat-backed rocking chair when she heard the dreaded sound of boot heels coming up the front steps and across the porch. She heard the rattle of the door knob. Followed by the sound of Rafe's voice.

She started to rock, aware she'd been unconsciously waiting for this moment. And finding herself no better prepared now that the time was here.

"Callie." More knob rattling. "Callie, let me in."

"Go away," she said. "Go sleep it off."

"Callie," His voice dropped so low she could scarcely hear him. "I haven't been drinking, I swear. The bottle's full."

She continued to rock, the seesaw pace speeding up.

"I can't talk with the door between us like this. I need to explain. I had no call to say those things I said earlier."

The chair bobbed at near dizzying speeds, echoing her agitation.

"I guess I don't blame you for not wanting to talk. I haven't given you much call to trust me, I know. I'm going. The bottle of whiskey is right here outside the door." She heard movement on the porch. "I'd like for us to talk.

Anytime you're ready. We got some things need saying. Both of us."

Callie held her breath as she heard his steps retreat.

Slowly the chair creaked to a stop, and Callie let out her pent-up breath. She forced her fists to uncurl against her lap, then rose and made her way to the window. The moon provided just enough light to reveal Rafe returning to the barn. The leather chaps he wore stirred little puffs of dust near his feet. He didn't walk like any drunk Callie'd ever seen.

She unhooked the chair from the door, slid back the bolt and opened the door. Just as he said, the whiskey bottle rested on the top step, full as when he'd plucked it from the cupboard and taken his first drink.

As Callie stood and took in huge gulps of raw evening air, her gaze strayed to the hulking dark silhouette of the barn. What was Rafe doing in there? Chasing his thoughts, same as her? She wavered in indecision, knowing she ought to march back inside the cabin. To let things settle between her and Rafe, sort themselves to rights over time.

Or until he left. She didn't much like to think about him leaving, even though she knew he would, soon as it took his fancy. He and Luke would leave. The church ladies would frown at her in disapproval. One husband dead. The second one run off. And blame her for both those failures.

She didn't want to be thought of as a failure. Just because Rafe Millar didn't care for her the way she cared about him didn't make him a bad person. And, despite what he thought to the contrary, she did trust him.

Resolutely, she went to the barn, where she found Rafe stretched out atop his bedroll, hands stacked under his head. He lay so still she thought he might be asleep, till she ventured close enough to see how his eyes were wide open, staring straight ahead, focused on nothing.

Not even the flicker of an eyelid acknowledged her presence, yet Callie knew he darn well saw her. Had to. He just wasn't of a mind to make this easy on her. Not one whit.

A candle stood anchored onto a nearby stump, upright in a puddle of melted wax, and spilled an uneven pool of light across Rafe's sprawled limbs. He'd unfastened his shirt and Callie could see the ridges of muscle from his chest to his stomach, dissected by an arrow of soft black hair. Her mind teased her with hazy memories of how that hair had felt beneath her fingers, soft yet crisp. At the same time she couldn't keep her fascinated gaze from straying to the shadowy hollow of his navel. The hair grew thicker there, before it disappeared into the top of his pants.

Strengthening her resolve to get things square between them once and for all, Callie settled herself upright in an unbundled mound of hay. Her perch was uncomfortable as the dickens, but she didn't let on. She took a deep breath. Nothing for it but to jump in with both feet. "We're quite the pair, you and I."

Rafe didn't move any part of him except his lips. "How so?"

"Both of us with our prickly little guards up. Things in the past we'd just as soon be forgetting."

He moved then. Rolled his head to one side so he faced her. "I had no truck saying what I did. A man's life as a drunk has nothing to do with any woman. It's a pact made between him and the devil."

"You ever drink more than your share? Regular-like?"

Rafe shook his head. "I saw what whiskey did to too many of my wife's people. The ones who were too weak to leave it alone, even after they knew it was bad for them."

Callie digested his words. She'd never thought of liquor in those terms, as a sign of weakness in a man. Unbidden, her gaze returned to Rafe. His strength was only one of the many things she'd come to admire about him. Not only his physical prowess but his inner strength as well. A force in no way tempered by the gentle way he had with a baby that wasn't even his.

He'd been gentle with her, too, braiding her hair, tending her hurts. She'd never known before that a man could be strong and gentle at the same time. Sensitive to someone else's needs the way Rafe was.

If she could make just one wish upon a falling star it would be to know the love of a gentle man. Maybe such a love could help ease all the hurts and disappointments she'd known.

"Quit looking at me that way." His voice was almost a growl.

"What way?"

In the blink of an eye he pounced. So fast his movements were little more than a blur. One minute he was lying there, still as you please. The next second he knelt directly in front of her, powerful arms on either side of her, trapping her in place, nothing gentle in either his look or his stance.

"Looking at me as if I'm somebody special."

He was more than special. Did she dare tell him? "In my eyes, I guess you are."

"I'm just an ordinary man, Callie. No better, no worse than the next. And not immune to the sins of temptation when they come my way."

"Temptation?"

"Some might call it that."

His eyes were dark as a midnight sky. Bottomless.

Fringed with spiky lashes. Underscored with a myriad of indecipherable emotions. Except one.

He wanted her, Callie realized with a growing sense of wonder as she caught her breath. Desired her, at least in a primitive physical way. And while he might come to regret that desire, he was through with fighting it. His look told her that, and a lot more besides. It stated that she was his woman, and he was laying claim to that fact.

She froze where she sat, even as the heat of his approaching body warmed her, set her nerve endings atingle.

"Now, see here. What's this you're on about?" Primly she smoothed her skirt over her knees as if she had no ken of the meaning behind his words. Pretending to be unaware of the smoldering intensity of his eyes resting on her, touching her with an intimacy she'd never before felt.

It was a mating dance as old as time itself.

Advance.

Retreat.

Banter.

Respond.

Callie felt her heart race in anticipation. She was drunk with the smell of him, the feel of him. She lowered her gaze to her hands, which were clenched tightly in her lap like a prudish spinster's.

Except she wasn't a prudish spinster. She was a woman about to be mated with the man who'd ridden into her life and stolen her heart.

"Don't play coy with me, Callie. We both know where this is leading."

"My goodness. The baby." Callie tried to rise. Rafe stopped her effortlessly, his warm naked chest a most erotic barrier.

"Didn't you already settle him for the night?"

"Yes, but..."

She could feel his breath, like scalding steam against her neck, as he nuzzled her hair out of the way. His mustache tickled her sensitive nerve endings, softly tantalizing, followed by the rasp of newly grown chin whiskers. Callie's head lolled back. Her eyelids flickered and closed of their own volition. It felt too good, what Rafe was doing. Much too good. The most incredible sensations were being sparked to life, like a series of candles being lighted one at a time, the flame passed from wick to wick until the whole was ablaze with light. With heat. That's what he was doing to her insides. Lord a'mighty. What might happen if he actually touched her? Kissed her even?

Opening her eyes, Callie realized she was about to find out. For his mouth hovered an inch or so above hers, in teasing mode. She found herself straining upward to reach it. Arching her back, she brought her bosom in direct contact with his unclothed torso. Her reaction was immediate. Through the fine lawn fabric of her blouse, her nipples hardened

She heard Rafe suck in his breath. Then slowly, agonizingly, he rubbed his chest back and forth against hers. Callie stifled a groan of pleasure as his lips fastened over hers. This time she needed no second urging to part her lips. To allow entrance to the divine explorations wrought by his tongue, skimming her teeth, sweeping the inside of her mouth. Tentatively her own tongue met his. He teased it into an exploration similar to his own.

Callie's hands fluttered in her lap, then rose. Her fingers quested upwards over the tensile strength of his forearms, his upper arms. His shoulders.

Without breaking the kiss, he whipped off his shirt.

Callie responded to the blatant invitation with a greedy exploration of her own, allowing herself the unfettered pleasures to be had by alternately stroking and kneading the smooth expanse of taut muscle and warm, fragrant skin.

The kiss ended, each of them gasping in ragged lungfuls of air, their chests rising and falling in unison.

With a deliberate, bold move, Rafe grasped the front of her blouse with both hands and pulled. The buttons held. The fabric didn't, all but disintegrating in his hands. Callie felt herself trembling in anticipation as he next attacked her undergarment, subjecting it to the same rough treatment.

His touch gentled as her breasts tumbled free. His hand shook as he first smoothed a strand of hair back from her face, then cupped her breasts. Lifting them in the callused hollow of his palms, he held them as gently and reverently as the most fragile glass ornament.

The pads of his thumbs grazed the taut, pouting nipples. Callie flinched from the sensation which seemed directly linked to her womb. Puddles of heat lapped at her insides. Gooseflesh prickled the back of her legs clear down to her knees.

"You have beautiful breasts. So white. So soft."

Callie wanted to tell him she found him beautiful as well, but the words refused to form in her throat. Instead, she rested back on her elbows, back arched, offering herself to him.

The heels of his hands slid from the rounded outer contours of her breasts, under her arms, over her shoulders and up her throat. With a groan, he buried his fingers in her hair.

He arched over her, his body taut as a newly strung bow as he forced her down in the hay and stretched himself atop her. He caught her hand in his and carried it down to the man part of him, closing her fingers over his throbbing, turgid length.

Even through his trousers Callie could feel the awesome size and strength of him. Tentatively at first she slid her hand in a back and forth motion and felt his sharply indrawn breath.

"Is that... Did I...?"

Teeth gritted, he shook his head. "It just feels so damn good." He captured her mouth again and gave a low groan in the back of his throat, which Callie took as encouragement to continue her actions.

Somehow her skirts had got pushed up between them, followed by the cool trace of Rafe's fingers on her sensitive inner thigh, coaxing her legs apart. Callie shivered with impatience as he took his time reaching that secret core that needed his caress the most. Even with the barrier of fabric between herself and his touch the ricochet of sensations was intense and pleasurable. She squirmed against the pressure of his hand, unable to believe she was doing this.

Abruptly Rafe's movements stilled. Forcibly he removed her hands from their stroking exploration.

"This is no good," he said. "I'm not making love our first time in a barn."

## CHAPTER 22

Callie caught her breath in stunned silence. Was this Rafe's way of rejecting her? Telling her he didn't want her after all? Or could he be offering her a last-minute reprieve? The chance to change her mind and still retreat with some semblance of dignity?

Blast it all, she had no wish to retreat. But how in tarnation did she set about telling him that?

He watched her, eyes wary, heavy-lidded with desire, and in that moment Callie knew it was as difficult for Rafe to accept her trust as it was for her to offer it. Maybe more. And with that realization came the knowledge that telling him was not the way. She had to show him.

Decision made, she stood and extended her hand to him.

"You're right," she said, her voice quavering with uncertainty and fear. "Not when there's a perfectly good bed inside." Never had she left herself so vulnerable as at this moment, but for the love of mankind, she couldn't pull away.

The intense blaze in Rafe's eyes, shimmering with undisguised emotion, radiated enough heat to melt her insides clear through to the core. The way he looked as he slowly stood and clasped her hand in his was enough to ease her most deep-seated uncertainties. She felt her own hurts pale alongside his and the way she knew he must be feeling.

Without another word they made their way from the barn to the cabin. Inside, the lamp burned low on the high-boy, lighting their way into the bedroom.

"Leave it," Rafe said, huskily, when she moved to extinguish the light. "I want to see you."

Callie felt herself flush to the roots of her hair. She wasn't accustomed to such plain talk, and now they were inside she felt awkward, unsure of herself and of what was expected.

Her hand trembled as she busied herself turning down the coverlet, taking particular pains to see that the edges were lined up perfectly even on either side.

"Callie. What the devil are you doing?" She straightened and felt Rafe's hands on her shoulders pulling her back to rest against him. His chin grazed the top of her head and her spine found the hard supportive wall of his chest. She closed her eyes and basked in the warmth, the contentment she found in his arms. Never before had a man's arms offered such a haven.

"I expect you're nervous." Slowly, gently, Rafe spun her around to face him. Taking her hand, he place it over his heart. His skin was warm and supple. Through her fingertips she could feel the rapid-fire heartbeat beneath his ribs. "Surprise you to find out you're not the only one?"

Callie's gaze fastened on his, saw the reflected truth of his words. With a sigh she laid her head against him, drawing what she needed from his strength. From his warmth. Her hand still covered his heart, but she found it impossible to remain still. He felt so good. He smelled so good. Angling her head slightly, she brushed her nose against the musky skin of his chest and felt the thicket of hair tickle the tip of her nose.

It seemed only natural that her lips would follow. Trail a pathway of kisses across his chest, through the downy thatch of hair covering his breastbone, up the smooth column of his throat, then back down the flat planes of his stomach. She felt his fingers thread through her hair, holding tight. She heard, or thought she heard, him groan her name as she dipped her tongue into the shadowy cleft of his belly button.

His skin tasted wonderful, slightly salty, but she was denied further tastes as he scooped her into his arms and plunked her down in the middle of the bed. She felt the shifting of the mattress as he joined her.

"You're wearing all together too many clothes," he said. "We need to even things up a little here."

As he stripped away her torn blouse and chemise, Callie was aware of the lamp's feeble illumination revealing the creamy skin of her breasts and shadowing the valley between them with its faint sprinkling of freckles. She felt doubly vulnerable and exposed, but when she tried to shield herself with her arms, Rafe gently drew her arms back one at a time.

"You're much too pretty to hide."

"Truly?" No one had ever told her she was pretty before. Bert had always made her feel that her woman's body was an object of shame. Wholly inadequate. More times than not, he didn't finish the act, leaving her feeling that the shortcomings were all her fault.

"Truly." The fire of his kiss chased away lingering doubts and stoked the steadily growing embers of desire. And, recalling what had happened once before in Rafe's arms, the exquisite sensations that had shattered her insides clear down to the soles of her feet, Callie felt her shyness evaporate as if by magic.

Fumbling fingers became adept as she unfastened her shoes and peeled off her stockings. When Rafe knelt behind her, the back of her neck prickled at the brush of his fingers as he lifted the curtain of hair to one side. She felt the whisper of his breath half a second before his lips touched the suddenly sensitive skin that stretched from shoulder blade to shoulder blade.

How could he possibly touch her there, Callie wondered, and have her feel him everywhere else as well? As moist, greedy lips followed the graceful curving back of her neck, her eyes closed. Moving became much too much effort. All she could do was feel. She was awash with sensation. It spilled over her, filling her. Her woman's core yearned for his knowing touch, and her insides tightened in anticipation. Her nipples beaded into hard, tight buds of need, and in a sudden bold move she reached for his hands, drawing them around her waist and up to cup her breasts.

Locked securely in his arms like that, molded against him while his lips nuzzled the sensitive cord at the side of her neck, Callie thought this must be what heaven felt like. Nothing could possibly surpass this moment, the flood of glorious feelings she experienced in this man's arms.

She soon discovered she was wrong. For somehow between kisses and murmured endearments they managed to wriggle free of the rest of their clothes and slip beneath the coverlet. And in that moment, when her tortured, fever-pitched, needful flesh met every lean inch of Rafe's hard masculinity, Callie felt as if the heavens surely sang a refrain especially for her.

"How can this feel so good?" she whispered.

"Sweetlips, we haven't even got started yet," he promised, brushing a kiss across her sensitive nipples. The resultant sensation in her loins was immediate and she clamped her legs together in an effort to ease the ache.

"Relax," Rafe murmured as his fingers found their way from her knee, up the inside of her thigh. then continued to burrow through the thatch of curls guarding her most intimate secret.

She was damp, Callie realized with a start as his fingers found their mark. Slick and hot as a rain-soaked summer night with wanting him. His fingers felt cool against her soft inner lips as he coaxed and teased them into granting him admittance.

"Easy," Rafe whispered against her forehead as he positioned himself between her legs. "Wait for me."

His initial probing felt like an invasion, his entrance stretching intimate parts gone long unstretched. She felt her muscles tense and tried to relax as he withdrew fully, then repeated the motion, sliding more easily in and out of the passageway made slick and damp for their coupling.

Callie lay still beneath him, accustoming herself to the feel of him, absorbing the intimacy of their joining, the way he now fit her perfectly. Abruptly he stopped.

Callie's eyes flew open. "Why did you stop?"

"It's allowed for you to at least act like you're enjoying it, too."

Callie caught her lower lip with her teeth. "I didn't know that."

Rafe rocked against her. Instinctively Callie rocked back. "Feel that?"

She nodded vigorously.

"Me too." He lifted her legs to his waist. "How about that?"

Callie's mouth formed a round O of surprise. Leaning down, Rafe kissed it away. And got down to the very real business of making her his.

With skilled determination he brought her again and again to the brink of fulfillment, only to back off, to slow his pace, to rebuild the sweet tension to the point that Callie dug her nails into his back, urging him on, insisting he lift them both to that precious pinnacle of the ultimate fulfillment.

With an instinct as old as the first woman and man, Callie felt his practiced control starting to slip. It was her turn to hold the power. She locked her ankles behind him, her movements meeting and matching his, thrust for thrust, giving and taking until, with a final triumphant gasp, she tumbled forward into that timeless chasm of total release. Alone.

She saw the sweat bead Rafe's brow as his movements ground to a halt and he lay there atop her, shuddering from head to toe. Somehow, she knew this was different from Bert, the times he'd taken her only to lose interest.

Callie stared at the shadows on the ceiling and bit her bottom lip till she tasted blood. Lord, she must have done something powerful wrong to make Rafe stop just like that. Maybe she'd been enjoying it too much. Maybe respectable ladies didn't act this way with their husbands.

She felt him withdraw, hot and hard and throbbing, before he rolled to his side. The sense of loss was so powerful she choked back a sob. One lone tear snuck out from behind her eyelid, and she dashed it away with the back of her hand. Not quick enough. Rafe caught her hand and kissed the tear away.

Speaking was an effort, but she forced herself. "I know you don't love me. But I always thought men could... You know... That that kind of stuff didn't matter."

Rafe pushed himself to one elbow. "You got it all wrong, Callie. I do care about you. A lot."

"Then why...?"

"I care too much to be leaving you all swollen and misshapen with my unwanted child growing in your belly."

"Oh." Somehow she didn't take much solace from his words. She hadn't given a thought to possible consequences of their lovemaking. But he had. And wanted to have a clear conscience when he left her. She reflected on his first wife dying and all, and felt a small bit comforted that he wanted to spare her.

"Seems kind of a shame," she murmured as he pulled her to his side and pillowed her head in the groove of his shoulder. She could feel him against her, still hot and hard as a branding iron. Gently she ran her fingers across his chest, wishing she had the means to bring him the same kind of pleasure he'd just given her.

"What's that?" Rafe leaned back and closed his eyes as her exploration grew bolder. He jumped when she touched that part of him, then let out his breath in a hiss as she closed her fingers around its swollen length.

"I was just thinking, surely there's something we could do that would be satisfying for you. Something almost as good as..." As she spoke she stroked him in slow, gentle motion, from velvet tip to hair-roughened root.

"You don't have to worry yourself about that."

"Maybe I want to." With a boldness that surprised her she raised herself up so she could meet his gaze eye to eye. "I mean, I'm never going to get married again. Once you leave, the opportunity for learning about this stuff goes with you."

Unconsciously she traced the sensual contours of his lips as she spoke, until with a stifled groan he pulled her finger deep inside of his mouth. The sensation was startling and she tried to withdraw her finger, only to feel him pull it back inside the hot center of his mouth. Back and forth, pulling and sucking, the sensation didn't stop at her finger but seeped pleasurably through her arm and deep inside her. She could feel herself growing damp again. Wanting him again. All of him.

With the gentle strength that she so admired, he eased her away from him and onto her back. He raised himself above her, his weight supported on his arms, one on either side of her. It was a pose that with any other man she would have found threatening. "Are you sure?"

Callie nodded, reminding herself that if she was vulnerable, so was Rafe. Being with her like this made him more vulnerable than if he'd just satisfied himself with a quick rut and left her. And in that moment she knew she'd do anything for him. Anything at all.

Rafe tongued the valley between her breasts, anointing it with dew-like moisture. Then he knelt over her and gently cupped each breast, pushing them together. Her nipples crested, eager for his touch and, careful not to disappoint, he slowly circled them with the pads of each thumb.

Callie caught her breath at the spiral of new sensation, even as she thought, this was supposed to be for him. She quivered at his touch as he first blew on her nipples, then laved them with his tongue, suckling them singly and together.

Shocked, she felt him ease his swollen member into the tight sheath he'd formed between her breasts, then withdraw before plunging back again. The dampness of his kisses had readied the way and, as his pace increased, his breath rising and falling in short sharp bursts, she felt the pleasurable tension rebuilding at the juncture of her legs.

She looked up at him, his eyes closed, one damp lock of hair falling across his forehead, and felt the mounting crest of his pleasure spill through her, seconds before he gave a raspy cry, and the dampness of his seed mingled with the sheen of perspiration dewing her chest.

It was a few minutes before their breathing returned to normal.

"Is it always like that?" Callie gloried in the sense of completion, the feel of Rafe sprawled over her, their sweat-dampened bodies locked from hip to breast.

"Nah. Usually it's much better."

Callie stiffened, then relaxed as Rafe chuckled. Lazily he raised one hand to her face and smoothed away a damp-ened tangle of her hair.

He nuzzled her neck, her ear, then whispered low, "Once in a lifetime is more than most folks ever get to feel this way."

If he could tease, then so could she. "You mean," Callie said in mock-thoughtful tones, "it won't be this way with any other man I bed except you? Are you sure?"

"Just don't take it into your head to go finding out."

Callie warmed to the possessive purr in his words. One look from him like that and she felt her body spring back to life. Rafe rolled to his side, then reached to cup one breast in his sun-browned hand. Such a contrast. Her milk-white skin. The soft pliable flesh next to the lean hardness of the callused palm massaging her, kneading her nipple into a pinpoint of desire and shooting a message of resurging need up and down her limbs.

She sensed a difference in the way he kissed her this time. An openness, a sharing, a giving and receiving of trust that she hadn't been aware of earlier. He'd kissed her with passion, with lust even, but this union of their mouths and tongues spoke of far more than just physical sensation. If there was such a thing as a higher plane, a meeting of soul and minds and not just bodies, then she'd reached it now, Callie thought as she sealed her love, tangling her fingers in Rafe's hair and wishing with all her heart that this special magic between them could last forever.

Reluctantly she allowed him to end the kiss. She'd asked for this, this one brief interlude of intimacy, and she knew it was something she'd never forget. But how could she think that such an experience would leave her unchanged? That, having once felt the forces of heaven in Rafe's arms, she could simply pick up the threads of her life after he left and carry on as if she'd never known how it felt to hold the man she loved.

He kissed her throat, her shoulder, her elbow, the palm of her hand, the indentation of her waist. Her stomach. Her legs. Yet when she felt him start to kiss her there, that innermost secret center, she tried to make him stop.

"Let me love you," Rafe said. "Everywhere." And because she asked for nothing more than his love, and could refuse him even less, she opened herself to him and his special gift to her. She allowed him to show her the sun and the moon. Knowing always there would follow the darkness of his leaving.

## CHAPTER 23

G entle movement gradually nudged the filmy gauze of sleep clouding Callie's brain. Rolling to one side, she encountered an immovable wall of warm, unclothed human flesh. As she pushed herself to her elbow a chill breath of air seeped beneath the bed linens and reminded her that she, too, was naked. She tugged the covers up near her chin and focused on Rafe asleep next to her, one arm circled around baby Luke atop his chest, wee fuzzy black head tucked comfortably beneath Rafe's chin.

Callie blinked herself awake and edged away from her two bedmates. Memories of last night flooded her consciousness, confusing images heaped atop each other. Was it mostly dreams? Or had everything happened the way she remembered?

She slid from the bed and groped about on the floor for her undergarments, which she donned in record haste. From the hook on the back of the door she snagged a plain dress of dreary homespun and pulled it over her head, her gaze never leaving Rafe and the baby, asleep together.

As long as she lived she'd never forget the picture the

two of them made cuddled up in her bed. That special memory, at least, was no dream.

The sky was gray and overcast, the morning air fresh and piney smelling as she let herself out of the cabin and headed for the well. Perhaps the bracing splash of cold water on her face would help her sort out and make some sense of last night. She appreciated things that made sense.

She cupped her hands together and filled them with water, which she sluiced over her face, recoiling from the stinging sensation on her skin. Chill droplets dribbled down her neck and splattered the front of her gown, but she knew an entire bucketful over her head wouldn't chase away the reality of those hours before dawn when finally she and Rafe, exhausted in every sense of the word, fell asleep in each other's arms.

And would she even want it to? Rafe's gift to her, his sharing of intimacy, his giving and taking in the act of love, had the effect of a healing balm. He'd made her a whole woman. He'd rescued her from the persecution of abuse and taught her the ways a man could be gentle with a woman, loving and giving, even if he didn't love her in the true sense of the word.

His physical act of love had given her back a part of herself she didn't even know was missing. With or without Rafe, she had the power to be a woman capable of giving and perhaps one day receiving love.

Now she, in turn, must do something for him.

Something to help heal the loss of his brother and make him forget this crippling vendetta against the Denzells. No good would come from hatred. From killing. Who knew that better than she?

Callie turned to the cabin, then realized she couldn't go back in there. Not yet. Instead, she sank to the ground, her back braced against the stone side of the well, knees bent, her elbows resting atop them. What a weird and wonderful feeling, to love another with an all-consuming fervor. In actual fact, it simplified life. For when another's needs and wants became of the utmost priority, all else paled to insignificance.

Her newfound elation popped like a soap bubble. Had Rafe made her whole, only to take a chunk of her with him when he left? To leave her feeling lost and bereft and incomplete without him? What of her vow the day Bert died? To never again find herself beholden to any man?

It still held, she told herself with new conviction. What had happened between her and Rafe was a pleasant diversion, nothing more. She would thank him kindly for the experience and send him on his way.

She was not incomplete without him, only more fully complete for having known him. So there!

She had just started back across the yard when she heard a rider approaching from the south. It had to be Denzell. No one else rode their horse into such a lather. What did he want now? Maybe Rafe was right when he predicted they hadn't seen the last of her neighbors.

"Morning, Callie." Denzell reined to a stop.

"Mr. Denzell."

"Spotted a trespasser yonder, early this morning. Not the first time he's been seen. Me and the boys want to make sure it's the last. Fella's one of them renegade Injuns from the reservations north of here. Riding a good-looking palomino. Probably stolen. You seen him?"

"I haven't seen anyone of that description."

"What about your hand? 'Scuse me," he corrected himself sneeringly, "I mean your husband. Think he might have an idea where that redskin took off to? The two of them being friends and all."

"How 'bout I come with you? I'm a damn good tracker, if I say so myself. "

Callie swung abruptly in the direction of Rafe's voice.

Her pulse clamored at the sight of him as he crossed the yard, shirtless, carrying little Luke in one arm. So much for remaining unaffected.

Joining her, he draped his free arm around her shoulders and slanted her a truly intimate smile, the meaning of which Denzell would have to be blind, deaf, and dumb to mistake.

Denzell was none of those things. A smirk twisted his features as his gaze slid from her to Rafe to the baby. "My, my. Quite the little family you got yourself, Callie. Bert would be pleased."

"Leave Bert out of this," she said from between clenched teeth. "He's dead."

"I know that. I was there, remember?" Undaunted, Denzell continued to goad her. "Some of the townsfolk thought maybe the two of you didn't have a 'real' marriage. 'Specially after Barnaby... Oh. But that's privileged, isn't it? Client-lawyer secrecy and all that."

"I didn't marry Callie for her land," Rafe said. "More folks who know that the better, far as I'm concerned."

Denzell seemed to deflate at Rafe's words, hunching low in his saddle. Pushing the brim of his hat up slightly, he addressed Rafe. Callie could have turned invisible for all the notice he paid her. "I'm trailing a redskin. Damn savage needs to be taught a lesson about keeping himself on the reservation where he belongs."

Rafe passed the baby to Callie. "I'm right behind you. I'll just saddle up."

"I'd put on a shirt, if I was you," Denzell said, wheeling his horse about. "Got claw marks all over your back, like you bedded down with a mountain lion."

Rafe passed Callie a broad, knowing wink. She, in turn, blushed to the tips of her toes. "Hear that, honey? I told you to go easy. Pretty soon the whole town'll be abuzz with talk about us."

Denzell's mount reared as he dug his spurs in unnecessarily hard and rode off in a trail of dust. Rafe saddled up and made tracks after Denzell so quickly Callie decided he must have a fair share of experience leaving a lady's bed in haste the next morning. Probably for the best. This way she was spared any of the awkward conversation she'd been dreading. She shifted Luke to her other hip and trudged back to the cabin.

"Your uncle," she told the baby as she deftly powdered his tiny bottom, "he's a hard one to figure out. Lord knows what kind of upbringing you'll get with him looking out for you." Was it her imagination, or was little Luke hanging on her every word, his deep-set blue eyes years beyond his chubby infant's face?

"Oh, what am I talking to you for, anyway? You're one of them. You'll grow up to be a man whose sole purpose in life is to turn the head of every sweet young thing you meet, leaving her high and dry, just like you menfolk always do."

Luke chose that particular moment to dampen the front of Callie's dress in his own distinctive way.

"You minx," she said, as she reached for a fresh diaper. "Did I say high and dry? Guess I meant high and wet." She leaned down and blew a wet noisy kiss on his soft belly. "A body would think you understood every word I just said."

Later that morning she was frying potatoes and eggs she wasn't even hungry for when her neck prickled with the unmistakable sensation of being watched. Glancing to the open doorway she saw Rafe's Indian brother-in-law.

"Smells good."

Callie's movements faltered momentarily. "There's plenty for two. Won't you come in?"

Her visitor entered the cabin on silent moccasined feet and pulled a chair out from the table. Callie dished up a plate and set it in front of him.

"I imagine you're the one Denzell and his boys are hot on the trail for," Callie said, casual-like.

He dug into his food with relish. "Rafe will lead them northeast. Keep them out all day."

"Meanwhile you'll go where? West?"

He shrugged. "Maybe. Any coffee?"

Callie brought him a cup, hiding her surprise at the way he used a knife and fork as comfortably as anyone she knew.

He looked up at her, nodded his thanks, and continued eating. Callie sat and picked at her own breakfast. She spread her toast with jam, then set it aside uneaten as she mustered up her courage. "What was she like?"

He gave her a quizzical look. "Who?"

"The woman Rafe loved. His wife."

"My sister." He frowned thoughtfully, then gestured with his hands, indicating the stature of someone petite.

"Small. She was small? Childlike?"

"Spoiled. Bad temper." He shook his head. "She and Rafe. They fight. She yell. Sometimes throw things."

"Oh." Callie sat back, the picture he painted a far cry from the patient, loving wife she had imagined fawning over Rafe, tending to his every need.

Wounded Bear pointed his fork at her. "You. Different. Strong." He swelled his chest. "Inside."

Callie didn't know how to take such a remark from someone she'd only just met. She supposed he meant it as a compliment. At least he didn't seem to resent her taking his sister's place in Rafe's life. Abruptly she reined in her thoughts. She wasn't taking anyone's place. No more than Rafe was part of her life. Like Wounded Bear today, Rafe was merely passing through. She'd do well to remember that.

Wounded Bear offered his finger to Luke, who grasped it and held on. Wounded Bear grinned at the youngster, who flapped and kicked free of his blankets. "This one, too. Strong." His grin faded. "He needs to be. His job is big."

Absently Callie watched Luke's face wrinkle as he studied Wounded Bear. Did he recognize that someone new was here? A strange voice? Whenever she thought about Rafe's reason for being here her heart grew heavy. "Rafe is real bent on avenging his brother's death."

Wounded Bear nodded sagely. "Bad men. Bad hearts. They beat Luke like a dog. Then left him to die."

"Why would they do that?"

"Why do men kill other men?"

Callie had no answer for that. "Your sister. Rafe loved her very much."

"Rafe holds the blame close to his heart. It was not his fault. Still, the guilt was easier to live with than the truth."

"The truth," Callie echoed. Interesting observation, the human penchant to choose guilt over truth.

"Rafe lost his temper. Instead of being gentle, he left. Nishu called after him." He shook his head. "The baby came early. By the time Rafe returned, it was too late."

The facts shone at her with the clarity of glass. Rafe's brother and Rafe's wife had both died when he wasn't there. No wonder he'd directed all his anger, guilt, and rage toward the Denzells, instead of just accepting the truth. *We're all human. Sometimes we make bad choices. Sometimes things go awry without any help from anyone.*

Callie knew firsthand about things going wrong. "Why are you telling me this?"

"To help you understand."

"You think there are things I need to understand?" Wounded Bear slanted her a sideways look and Callie shied from the knowing in his eyes. He had a way of seeing, of looking right through a body's outside face, directly inside, to uncover their deepest, most private thoughts. The whites of his eyes glowed brightly against his dark pupils and bronze skin. "My white brother will be more hurt when he learns of the secret you carry."

"I don't know what you're prattling on about."

"In his heart, my brother knows Luke was wrongly accused. You have the truth."

Callie's hands curled around her knife and fork, white-knuckled. "You're not making one lick of sense."

Wounded Bear's eyes were as black as coal, filled with knowledge. "Not until his brother's spirit is laid to rest will my white brother be able to see past the darkness of his losses, to look once more into his heart and see the good there. See the good here."

Abruptly Wounded Bear stood and, before she could think of a suitable response, he left as silently as he'd entered.

The impact of his words hung in the silence. For the life of her Callie couldn't see what possible good it would do to tell Rafe the truth about what had happened the day Bert died.

Callie was engrossed in making candles when she heard Rafe return. Frankly, she was relieved to hear him ride up. It had been dark for a good hour or more, and she didn't cotton to him being out in the wilds with the men who, in the words of Wounded Bear, had beaten Rafe's brother like a dog and left him to die.

He seemed to be spending a long time in the barn.

Perhaps he was as uncomfortable as she was, yet sooner or later they were going to have to face each other. She forced herself to concentrate on measuring the right amounts of tallow, camphor, beeswax, and alum. She had the candle mixture melted and poured, with wicks in place, by the time Rafe finally came inside.

He looked dead tired, shadows under his eyes and the beginnings of beard growth darkening his jaw. She wondered if the strain of the day or the lack of sleep last night was most responsible for his exhaustion.

"How does chicken and dumplings sound?" she asked brightly.

He slumped down at the table, took off his hat and ran his hands through his hair. "I'm not hungry."

"I heated some water earlier. There's enough left for a bath."

"Quit fussing, Callie."

"Wounded Bear stopped in right after you left this morning."

Rafe nodded briefly. She could tell by his glazed-over eyes that he wasn't really seeing her. Probably wasn't listening to her chatter, either.

"I fed him a hot meal."

"You're good at that."

Callie flinched. Surely he didn't mean the words the way they sounded. He was tired. It had to be a terrible strain, riding all day with men you knew had killed your brother.

Abruptly she put paid to her thoughts. What was she

doing, making excuses? There was no excuse for rudeness. She'd spent her entire life excusing the menfolk around her. Their drinking and bad manners and raising of fists. She wasn't about to do it any more.

Quickly she cleaned up her candlemaking. The sooner she excused herself from Rafe's moodiness the happier she'd be.

"I don't believe there'll be any more trouble from Denzell," Rafe said finally.

"He say that to you?"

"Not in so many words."

"How could you do it?"

"Do what?"

"Spend the day riding with him and his boys. Nothing to stop them from killing you same as they did Luke."

"I have something Luke didn't. An insurance policy."

"What's that supposed to mean?"

"I've got something Denzell wants. Anything happens to me, he'll be one sorry cowpoke. I made sure he knows it.

"I also told him I know about the gold dust in the creek. And that I mean to claim the gold for my brother's son." He spun Luke's basket around to face him. "That way, at least, Luke didn't die for nothing."

"You think that's why the Denzells killed Luke? Because he knew about the gold?"

"He must have witnessed Bert's killing. They felt safe pinning it on Luke, except they couldn't bring him into town for trial and risk having the truth come out. Instead, they beat him and left him for dead out in the wilds. As far as the law's concerned, my brother's still a wanted man."

As Rafe spoke he reached into his pocket and drew out a gold watch with a long gold chain, He dangled the timepiece in front of the baby's face, swinging it back and forth like a pendulum.

"See this, Luke? This belonged to your pa. And one day it'll be yours. Got your pa's name on it and everything."

Callie froze, her gaze riveted on the watch in Rafe's hand. Last time she'd seen that watch it had been lying near the body of her dead husband.

## CHAPTER 24

When Callie's vocal cords finally came unparalyzed, her voice was shrill. "Where'd you get that?"

Rafe shot her a long look. "What's it to you?"

Callie made a valiant attempt at recovery. "No-nothing. I just never saw you with it before, that's all. That your insurance protection?"

"This? Nah." He stood and slid the watch into his pocket. "I got Denzell convinced Wounded Bear is long gone. Which leaves the way clear for me and him to see what we can learn about the gold claim."

"Like what?"

"Like whether or not there's enough gold to get killed over."

Rafe had been gone five interminably long days. Long days and longer nights, where Callie alternated between missing him and dreading his return. Whatever he and Wounded Bear discovered would determine if he returned, only to ride from her life once and for all, taking little Luke with him.

How empty the ranch would be. Lately she'd been

permitting herself the luxury of a few small daydreams. Fantasies where Rafe returned and stated he'd be sticking around indefinitely. Maybe forever.

Daydreams were a safe refuge. No one ever got hurt in a place where one could block out unpleasant past events and look to a future where all would be happy ever after.

These dreams, along with her most heavily guarded secret, she confided to Luke as she bathed him, changed him, fed him, and cuddled him. She spoke aloud, certain he understood, if not her words at least the tone in her voice. Sagely he observed her through dark blue eyes. She gave him a hug. How quickly and effortlessly he'd insinuated himself into her life. Just like Rafe.

"I'll miss you both," she said, as she laid him gently across her shoulder.

Luke gave an answering gurgle of agreement, and Callie hugged him close. She could feel the steady flutter of his small heart, and her own seemed to swell in response. He was so tiny and defenseless. Dependent upon others for his every need. And he trusted her. That realization did funny things to Callie's insides. Trust. A basic human emotion, one that was foreign to her but instinctive in a newborn.

The scent of baby powder wafted up to tickle her nostrils. Closing her eyes, she recalled another stimulating scent. Musky male skin, leather, and the good clean outdoors. The smell of Rafe. The feel of Rafe. The need to trust him, to know there was someone out there on her side. That she wasn't alone. Her sense of him was so keen her heart seemed to skip a beat and then speed up, as if he were really there with her, and at first she wasn't sure if she'd imagined the sound of horses, a sound she'd been uncon- sciously listening for, for days. But the sound grew closer, too clear to be her imagination, and with Luke in her arms she made her way to the window and watched Rafe and Wounded Bear dismount outside the barn.

A heated discussion ensued, complete with gesturing and raised voices, at least from Rafe, who tossed his reins to Wounded Bear and turned in the direction of the cabin.

Callie caught her breath as his gaze met hers. She dropped the panel of printed gingham back into place over the window, knowing even before Rafe entered the cabin that she wasn't going to like what he was coming in to say.

Frustration was evident in every weary step he took, and his eyes passed over her without really settling. The tight set of his lips and the tense line of his shoulders told her something big was afoot. Callie could feel it as he slumped at the table, took off his hat, and ran his fingers through his hair.

Callie pressed her lips together, afraid of saying the wrong thing. More afraid of saying nothing. Of the silence. For months after Bert's death she'd taken refuge in silence, finding the peaceful solitude a welcome relief. Rafe's silence wasn't like that. It had the characteristics of a coiled serpent. Cunning. Stealthy. Waiting to strike.

Finally she couldn't take it a second longer. "What happened?"

Rafe looked up at her as if seeing her for the first time that day. "Nothing. That's the hell of it. There's not enough gold to kill over. Not even enough to argue over. Which makes me wonder what the hell Luke was up to. What was he hanging around here for? Why was he involved with Denzell?"

"Maybe you're looking at this all wrong," Callie said. "Maybe it was the girl, Luke's mother, that he stuck around for. Maybe they were going to settle down. Get married."

"It doesn't feel right. There's something else. I can just about put my finger on it."

"Sounds to me like you're selling your brother short. People can change."

He stared at her from beneath furrowed brows. "What the hell is that supposed to mean?"

"Nothing. Except that—"

"Except that you'd be happy if I changed. Forgot all about the Denzells and concentrated my energies on growing the largest pumpkin in the state. Is that it?"

"No, of course not."

He shot to his feet and snatched up his hat. "I thought I could sit back and bide my time. Wait for Denzell to mess up good. It was a bad call. One I aim to put an end to here and now."

Callie followed him to the door. "Just what are you cooking up?"

"Nothing you need worry about." He brushed past Wounded Bear, who exchanged a questioning look with Callie. Before she could ask him what had happened while they were away, Rafe had saddled up a fresh horse and ridden down the drive. Callie made her way to the Indian's side. "What the devil happened between you two?"

Wounded Bear's gaze was as direct as ever. "I was about to ask you the same thing."

"He was mumbling some gibberish about how people don't change. He's putting an end to it here and now. None of it made a lick of sense to me."

Wounded Bear nodded. "Knowing Rafe, I'd say his patience has run dry. He has gone after Denzell."

"He's heading away from the Double D ranch."

"Exactly."

Callie shot him an exasperated look.

"He stopped there already and was told Denzell is in town. The card game of which he is so fond."

"Aren't you going with him? Make sure he's all right?"

"It's not my arrow he needs to ally himself with."

Callie wrung her hands. "Then what?"

Wounded Bear looked at her with those coal-black, far-seeing eyes of his. "The answer to that question lies inside of you."

"You think I should go after him? What help can I possibly be?"

"All your life you've looked to others to show you the way. When the way you seek is in here." He laid his hand over his heart. "And no one but yourself can see the truth."

Callie took a deep breath and allowed the wisdom of Wounded Bear's words to wash over her. She had looked to others for guidance instead of into her own heart. Right now her heart was telling her, demanding of her, that she go after Rafe. She hadn't a clue why. All she knew was that it was imperative she be by his side for whatever happened next.

She shot Wounded Bear an imploring glance. "The baby?"

"I will stay."

"Thank you."

He turned away. "I will saddle your horse."

RAFE ALLOWED the anger to wash over him in waves, each one more powerful, more destructive than the last. He'd always prided himself on being a patient man, but his patience had come to an end days ago. He wanted—needed—revenge. He could just about taste it. The power of knowing he held another man's fate in the palm of his hand. Is that the way Denzell had felt? The feeling that triumphed as he issued the order to kill Luke?

The town was strangely silent in the late afternoon. Not a soul stirred on the planked walks outside the shops. Not a horse or carriage disturbed the placid stillness of the dusty street. As Rafe dismounted outside the saloon, the quiet sent a warning prickle down the back of his neck. Where was the piano player? The raucous sounds of people getting drunk and having a lively time? He took a deep breath and pushed open the swinging doors. A game was in progress in the back corner, folks gathered around the table three deep. You could have heard a needle stitching as he made his way across the room.

The crowd slowly parted. Rafe's gaze was fixed on Denzell, who glanced up as if on cue. They could have been the only two in the room. "Don't just stand there, Millar," Denzell said, features impassive. "Pull up a seat."

"Don't mind if I do." Rafe swaggered to the table.

"I'm out." One of the players tossed down his cards and cleared out of Rafe's way.

Rafe claimed the man's abandoned chair, spun it around and straddled it confidently.

Denzell shuffled the cards. "Shall we raise the stakes? Make things a little more interesting?"

"You're reading my mind."

Rafe lost all track of time. Past and future ceased to exist in the here and now. Tension radiated from every comer of the saloon, cold, heavy, and breathless. Once more he cut and Denzell dealt. Rafe felt a trickle of sweat between his shoulder blades as he thumbed his cards. It took just as much skill to cheat at losing at it did to win. Maybe more.

The shift of tension was so subtle Rafe might have missed it. Except he was calling on all his energies, and they alerted him to Callie's presence. What was she doing here? Looking as out of place as she must feel. Pretending that he didn't see her, he leaned back, hat tilted low over his eyes, the front legs of his chair lifted clean off the floor and laid his cards down face up.

"You got me. Cleaned me out of cash."

"Let's see now." Denzell pursed his fat lips. "Must be something you have that would be of value to me. How about your ranch?"

"My wife's ranch, you mean."

"Same difference to me."

The front legs of Rafe's chair hit the floor. "All right," he said. "Deal." He didn't have to look at Callie to sense her reaction to the betrayal. He knew what the ranch meant to her. He also knew it was his only bargaining piece.

The cards were dealt, the hand played out. Denzell's crow of triumph ripped through the room.

"Just a minute." Rafe sat forward when Denzell started to stand. "I got one other thing here to wager that might be of interest."

"What's that?"

Rafe pulled the assayer's report from his inside pocket and waved it back and forth. Denzell sat back down. Hard.

"Where'd you get that?"

"Does it matter?"

"That there's stolen property. And you're the one stole it from me."

"Actually, this is a falsified document," Rafe said. "I have the true assayer's report, tucked away somewheres safe. And it won't take much to expose you for the crook you are."

"Me a crook! I know a bluff when I hear one. Sheriff!"

Denzell raised his voice to be heard over the buzz of sudden conversation in the room. "Sheriff, arrest this man."

The sheriff straightened from where he'd been slouched

near the bar. "I hear you right, Denzell? Arrest him? What for?"

"For the murder of old Bert Lambert!" A shocked gasp tore through the crowd.

"He might call himself by a different name. Growed his whiskers. But I suspected for some time now he's the one was hanging around last year using the name Luke Rafael. And that there watch in his pocket should be all the proof you need."

"You mind, son?" The sheriff approached Rafe and held out his hand. For a second Rafe was tempted to refuse. Reluctantly he handed over the watch. The sheriff gave Rafe a sharp look. "This your watch, son?"

"It belonged to my brother."

"Brother, my eye. I spent more time with the man than anyone else. 'Cept for old Bert, who ain't here to speak for himself. I tell you he's one and the same. Using an alias, is all. The boys'll back me up. They recognized him a long time ago. And this paper is one that he stole from me. Stole it right out of my study."

The sheriff hooked one hand around Rafe's arm. "I think maybe you'd best come along with me. Over to my office so's we can sort this out."

"There's nothing to sort out," Denzell crowed. "The man is a murderer. This time he'll hang."

Rafe saw the shock on Callie's face as she shrank back against the wall while the sheriff escorted him from the saloon. Denzell and his hangers-on trailed after them, intent on taking full advantage of the spectacle.

Rafe stared with loathing at the man across the desk with the tin star pinned to his chest.

"We can either do this the hard way, son," the sheriff said, "or we can do this the painful way."

"Long as we do it your way," Rafe retorted.

"Be a damn sight easier with your cooperation."

"I'm sure it would."

At that instant there was a ruckus outside the jail, where townsfolk were crowded six deep trying to peer in the window.

The door flew open to admit Callie, looking scared but determined.

"Go home, Callie," Rafe said. "This is none of your concern."

"Man's right for once," the sheriff said. "Jail ain't no place for a lady."

"It's no place for an innocent man to be spending time, either." As she spoke, Callie made her way to the desk.

"Now listen up," the sheriff said, starting to rise.

"No. You listen up, and you listen good." Her hand against the sheriff's chest sent him careening back into his seat. "You let my husband go. He's not Luke Rafael. And even if he was, Luke didn't shoot Bert. I did."

# CHAPTER 25

A stunned silence followed her announcement. A silence that was broken by a deep belly laugh from Denzell. On cue, his two sons joined in with high-pitched, nervous laughter.

The sheriff spoke first. "Callie. Mrs. Millar. I understand what you're doing and why. Personally, I find it highly commendable that you want to protect the man you're married to. But you can't stand in the way of the law. And there isn't a judge in the country who'll believe a bitty thing like you up and killed Bert."

"But it's true. I swear." Callie took a deep breath and tangled her fingers together. She hadn't fully realized until this second how much the truth was weighing on her. How good it felt to finally get it off her chest.

"I heard Bert and another man outside arguing. Mostly I heard Bert's voice. By the time I got there the other man—he must have been Luke—was starting to ride away. Bert was drunk. He'd taken out his pistol and was fixing to shoot the other fellow in the back. I screamed at him to stop. Then I grabbed his horse's reins. The shot went wide. Bert seemed to go crazy." She shuddered with the memory. "He turned his horse around and came straight at me, trying to run me down. I was afraid he was going to kill me. I had the rifle with me. I don't remember pulling the trigger. But I did. And when I looked down at the ground Bert was lying there, eyes wide, staring at nothing."

She shifted her eyes to Denzell. "Mr. Denzell came riding up just then. I guess he heard the ruckus, and because he passed Luke riding away he assumed Luke had done the shooting. I let him think that. I remember feeling sort of numb-like. From the shock. By the time I realized what had happened, the stranger—Luke—had got away, and I just kept quiet. If everyone thought he did it, then no one had to know it was me. I know it was wrong," she continued breathlessly, "and if he'd ever been caught I'd have come forward with the truth. But you have to believe me. Rafe had nothing to do with it."

"Denzell here swears they're the same man. And the watch is engraved. Same watch as Denzell found alongside Bert's body. Belonging to one Luke Rafael. Makes sense that Rafe Millar could be an alias."

"He's not the man Bert tried to shoot that day. Denzell's lying."

"You just said the man's back was to you. Riding away, you said."

"That's right."

"So, in fact, Mr. Millar could be that man."

"No!"

The sheriff raised a brow. "No? You never saw Mr. Rafael up close, like Mr. Denzell, yet you claim there's no way on earth they could be the same man. Doesn't sound too convincing for any judge."

Denzell interrupted. "Sheriff. I think it's clear that the

pressures of certain recent events are causing Callie to suffer some sort of delusions. Hell, maybe she even believes she killed old Bert. But I know different. Saw the whole thing with my own two eyes."

The sheriff shrugged and turned to Rafe. "You got anything to add?"

Rafe gave Callie a long, searching look. And in that moment she knew she had no more chance of winning his trust than she did flying to the moon. "No."

"Rafe, tell him the truth."

"I've said all I'm of a mind to say."

Callie turned pleading eyes on the sheriff. "Rafe's got something on Denzell. Likely the same thing his brother had. The real assayer's report. Denzell wants Rafe kept quiet. Same as Luke."

"Quite the imagination you've got there, ma'am. Now why don't you run along and leave me to do the lawmaking here?"

"This your idea of lawmaking? Hauling in an innocent man? Slapping those handcuffs on him? Listening to a liar like Denzell? He was nowhere near the place when Bert attacked me and I shot him."

"Right now Mr. Millar isn't saying anything. I got your word against Mr. Denzell's. Way I see it, you got a whole lot more reason to lie. Now get. Before I charge you with obstructing justice."

"Go back to the ranch, Callie. You're only getting in the way here." It was Rafe's voice. Hollow and emotionless. Callie had done that. Destroyed the fledgling trust between them.

"In the way?" She felt hope crumble to ash inside her. "I'm trying to help you. How can you say I'm in the way?"

"The man's making sense for once," said the sheriff.

"This ain't no place for a woman. Go home."

Head low, shoulders hunched, Callie made her way to the door. There she paused and straightened. Her glance touched each man in turn. She'd never felt more determined in her life and that determination rang out in her words. "I'm leaving for now. But I'll be back. And you all will listen to me. You'll have to."

Callie made it about a dozen steps before her knees buckled and gave out on her. Luckily there was a bench she could sink down onto. Her heart was racing like a locomotive. Her hands were clenched so tightly together she could hardly pry them apart. All these months she'd kept her painful secret, only to have nobody believe her when she finally did tell the truth.

Except maybe Rafe. But the look in his eyes had been anything but encouraging, now that he'd found out he'd married a murderer. A murderer who lied. Not only lied, but let his very own brother take the blame for what she'd done.

Callie cast her glance across the rooftops, as if the answer to her problems was within her grasp, if she only knew how to reach out to it. Her gaze skimmed the clean, white steeple of the church where just a short time ago she and Rafe had made their false promises to love and cherish each other. Maybe this was the Almighty's way of showing his displeasure. Somehow Callie found the strength to pull herself to her feet and make her way to the church.

The interior was still and quiet, a quiet born not of fear or tension but of final peace and fulfillment. Would that she could experience such a feeling, such utter contentment. Then it struck her. She had known such inner peace and tranquility. Had felt it every time she was with Rafe.

At the altar she knelt, bent her head and made the sign of the cross. The candles at the feet of the Virgin Mary flickered slightly, as if from a breeze. She turned her head, but she was alone. Low-voiced, she repeated a prayer too long absent from her lips.

"Bless me, Father, for I have sinned. And it's been a long time since my last confession. I know I swore to love and honor my first husband, Lord. But he was a difficult man, a troubled man. I did my best, although I guess my faith in you kind of faded. It was not your fault, but mine. I never meant to kill Bert. I also never meant to let another man take the blame for it. 'Specially when he wasn't around to defend himself. I guess that's what they mean about two wrongs don't make a right."

She licked her lips and thought for a minute. As a youngster the nuns had indoctrinated her well in the Ten Commandments. She'd probably broken them all lately, but she decided to concentrate on the big ones. "I truly am sorry and I guess now I have to do my penance. And I'll do whatever you ask. Just please don't punish Rafe instead of me. He didn't do anything but offer me his name and his protection. I guess maybe our getting married was a sin, 'cause we didn't love each other and didn't plan for a lasting union. But I love him and all I want is for him to go free. Maybe then he'll find the forgiveness in his heart that he needs to heal himself and make him whole again. Amen."

Callie followed up her confession by reciting several prayers she had memorized in her childhood. Then she put a coin in the offering box and lit a candle. For Rafe's safe delivery. As she left the church, her step felt lighter than it had in a long time. So did her heart.

Callie pondered Rafe's predicament as she made her way homeward. She wanted to believe that prayer alone was enough to ensure justice. But it wouldn't hurt to have a few other tricks up her sleeve, just in case the good Lord was busy on the other side of the world.

Wounded Bear must have heard her coming, for he was already mounted and waiting as she drew near the cabin.

"Wounded Bear," she called as she reached his side, "Rafe's been arrested. Denzell is swearing Rafe's really Luke and that lily-livered sheriff is willing to believe him."

"Denzell is like a cornered snake. One doesn't know where he'll strike next."

"Rafe won't say a thing in his own defense. He's just sitting there taking it."

"Rafe has mastered patience. He knows when to speak and when to hold his tongue."

"Fine for him," Callie muttered. "What about the rest of us?" She eyed Wounded Bear. "Rafe's got something on Denzell. I know he has. Whatever it is, he's playing it close to his chest. But you know what it is, don't you? Maybe something you and Rafe found while you were away prospecting. Something that sent Rafe hot after Denzell."

Wounded Bear's black eyes rested on her in a way that made her fidget uncomfortably, twisting the reins between her thumb and forefinger. "Rafe knows the truth about Bert," she went on. "That I shot him, not Luke. Isn't that what you wanted to hear?"

Wounded Bear continued to observe her in silence. "For all the good it did," she added. "The sheriff didn't believe a word I said. Not with Denzell swearing he'd witnessed the entire shooting. Swearing on a stack of Bibles that he saw Luke kill Bert."

"The important thing is that Rafe knows the truth. And truth brings its own measure of peace, do you not agree?"

Callie chose to ignore the latter part of his comments.

"So Rafe knows. He's still not making much of an effort to stay out of jail."

"Perhaps he feels jail is the safest place for him right now."

Callie paced back and forth inside the cabin, detesting her feeling of helplessness. What good was she to anyone? What use was her life if she couldn't speak the truth and have her peers believe her? If she did naught but sit by helplessly while her husband was falsely accused and thrown into jail.

True, he hadn't married her with any intention of consummating the marriage. But husband and wife they were, and she would not remain idle while meddling so-and-so's decreed what happened to her and hers.

Eventually she got the baby up and dressed him for travel. She'd talk to those people in town who'd known Luke, like little Luke's gran. Make them go see the sheriff. To swear that Rafe and Luke were not the same man. The sheriff would have to listen, then.

With the babe in her arms, she stepped onto the front porch. At first she didn't dare believe it, but as man and mount drew near her heart gave a welcoming leap of gladness. Her prayers had been answered. The Lord did listen.

Rafe dismounted and stood at the foot of the steps. His gaze passed from her horse, all saddled and waiting, up to look at her. He didn't quite meet her eyes. "Going someplace?"

Callie took a long calming breath, not sure if she trusted her voice. She wanted to throw herself into his arms with a glad cry of welcome, but she couldn't forget the look in his eyes when she'd confessed to killing Bert.

"Looks like that won't be necessary."

The deafening silence stretched between them, each, it seemed, as reluctant to speak as the other.

"The sheriff let you go?"

"Yup."

"He knows you're not Luke?"

"He knows."

Callie was dying to ask how, but she held her tongue.

Baby Luke stirred in her arms. Absently she shifted her weight from foot to foot in a sideways rocking motion.

"Sounds like you got Denzell on the run. Exactly what you set out to do. "

"I'm getting close."

"Then you'll be leaving anytime. Soon as you finish what you came here for."

"That was the plan all along." He met her eyes then, and there was an unreadable sadness in them. "Was I going to come back here today and find you and the baby gone?"

"What? Oh, heavens, no," Callie said. "I was coming into town. I planned to round up some witnesses who would swear you weren't Luke. But you didn't need my help after all. You managed just fine on your own."

"I've made a point of it. Managing alone."

"Something I'm still learning."

"It gets easier with time."

"I guess." She bit down hard on her lower lip. Anything to stop herself from crying out how it no longer mattered whether or not she managed on her own. Not compared to what Rafe had taught her. All kinds of things about sharing and partnership.

And trust.

What hurt most of all was that she knew Rafe would never trust her after she'd lied. After she'd let him go on thinking his own brother had murdered Bert.

Rafe slowly climbed the steps to her side, and Callie was certain he could hear the painful thudding of her heart, threatening to burst clear out from behind her ribs.

Baby Luke fussed, as if upset by the feelings spilling out of her. Rafe calmed him with the barest touch to his cheek, then looked at Callie. She wished he wouldn't look at her that way. She saw the uncertainty. Heard it in his voice. "You going in, then?"

"I guess. You?"

Rafe cast his eyes at the ground then back up at her. "I don't think so."

Callie felt something akin to panic squeezing the breath from her lungs. He was leaving. He couldn't stand to be near her, a lying murderess. Callie shut her eyes against the sensation of loss that threatened to swamp her. Right here, Rafe and the baby were everything that mattered, everything she held dear. And she was losing them. Holding on with empty hands to something that was hers only briefly, something that wasn't meant to last. Two people that meant the world to her, but would never be really, truly hers.

Just then a deafening explosion ripped through the air and rocked the porch beneath their feet. As the sound echoed through the valley, it was followed by the unmistakable smell of burning timber.

# CHAPTER 26

Rafe grabbed her, his hands roughly urgent as he half dragged, half carried her and the baby to her waiting horse and practically threw them into the saddle.

"Take Luke. Ride for help." She glanced over her shoulder to thick black smoke pouring overtop the barn roof. "I'll try and stop it from spreading to the house," he added, giving her horse a slap on the rump.

Until that second she hadn't been aware of the wind, but she felt it now and watched in mingled shock and horror as gusts grabbed glowing sparks from the roof of the barn and scattered them through the air in the direction of the cabin. A pathway of hungry flames licked their greedy way from the barn wall through the tinder-dry grasses between the barn and the cabin.

Thank goodness no animals were in the barn. Callie saw Rafe place the ladder against the cabin and begin hauling buckets of water up to wet down the shingles in an effort to stop the fire from spreading. As she rode away, she noticed he seemed to be having no difficulty on the ladder today.

Callie stopped a short distance from the fire. secured the

baby basket atop a wide, flat tree stump, and carefully covered Luke with her cloak. "Sleep tight, little one," she murmured, pressing a soft kiss to his furrowed brow before she ran back toward the fire.

At the well she grabbed two empty buckets, which she filled with water and hauled toward the cabin. Rafe didn't spare her a glance when she passed him the buckets. The heat from the barn was a blistering inferno, the fire choking the air with thick, dark smoke. A few skeletal black beams still stood, although most of the roof and outside walls had caved in.

Rafe stepped nimbly from the ladder. "I thought I told you to go for help."

Callie ripped off her jacket and relieved him of the empty bucket. "This is my ranch. I'm staying."

Another army of gluttonous flames raced from the barn, consuming every blade of dry grass before attacking the cabin. Callie stomped on the monsters, beat frantically at them with her jacket. But for every inch of fire she destroyed, two or three other determined battalions made it past her. In minutes her flowerbeds were reduced to a charred and blackened mess as the cabin became the fire's next victim. Not even their combined efforts, plus those of Wounded Bear, who arrived to help, were enough to save the structure.

She straightened at one point and felt her insides shrivel into a painful tight knot at the sight of her home, its cheery gingham curtains engulfed in flames. When the glass window shattered she felt something inside herself burst into a million fragile, irreparable splinters.

Hope. Dreams. A family. A future. Everything she held dear, snatched from her grasp in the space of a few short minutes.

Callie had no idea how much time passed before the fire finally played itself out. The barn was a mass of smoking charcoal rubble, the cabin not much better. Rafe and Wounded Bear had dug a trench beyond the cabin to stop the fire from racing into the fields, and although the flames had jumped a few spots they were quickly contained.

The injustice of the events set deep inside Callie's bones, numbing any emotion she might have displayed as she stared at the destruction that had been her home.

"I'm sorry, Callie." It was Rafe's voice, behind her.

Quiet. Sympathetic. Exhausted. She whirled, suddenly feeling her emotions rekindle. This had been her home. What did he have to be sorry for?

"Why? It's not as if the fire was your fault."

"I blame myself. I should have seen something like this coming."

"How could you see this coming?"

"The fire was deliberate, Callie. Remember the explosion we heard? It was dynamite."

"What's dynamite?"

"It's made from nitroglycerin. Highly explosive. It must have been stored inside the barn."

"In the barn? You put explosives in my barn?" With an outraged cry she launched herself at him, fists flailing. Effortlessly Rafe caught her wrists and held her at arm's length. Subduing her didn't require much effort. She was bone weary. After a brief struggle she sagged against him, defeat dragging at her limbs.

"Listen to me." His touch gentled as he released her wrists, hauled her against him, and smoothed a sweat-dampened hank of hair back from her forehead. "I didn't put the dynamite there. But I should have known Denzell would stop at nothing to destroy that assayer's report. And me along with it."

"What assayer's report?"

"It's a long story. I'll explain it to you later. Right now we need to get you and Luke Junior into town before dark."

Callie felt safe in his arms. A feeling of security she'd never found anyplace except with Rafe. "What did you have in mind? Drop us on the steps of the church like a couple of homeless orphans?"

Rafe drew back far enough to give her a dark, unfathomable look. "I plan to do what any man in my position would do. Check my family into the hotel, then let the sheriff know what happened."

Before she could tell Rafe she didn't need or want him or his misplaced familial responsibility, a shrill whistle sounded. They both looked to where Wounded Bear was squatting in the burned rubble of the barn.

Rate turned to Callie. "You stay here."

For once she did as she was told, and went to sit with Luke on a nearby stump. He felt so small and defenseless in her arms. So warm and alive. She took a deep breath and thanked the heavens the fire hadn't ended in a far worse tragedy. What were a few burned-down buildings compared to the vitality of human life?

A short time later, the two men returned to her with grim faces.

"Tell me." She knew before she asked that it was bad.

Rafe squatted alongside her and took her hand in both of his. In some far-off region of her heart she was conscious of the solid strength in his hand, the comforting warmth of his touch. She curled her fingers against his and held on tight. "Looks like the Denzell boys. Both of them."

"Inside the barn?"

"Yeah."

"Are you sure?"

"Can't tell for absolute certain. They're too badly burned. But Wounded Bear spotted their horses down near the creek and followed their trail up to the barn. It's a safe bet they started the fire but didn't know about the dynamite. The explosion likely knocked them out, or maybe they got trapped inside and overcome by smoke. Either way…"

Callie shuddered. "What a terrible way to die."

Rafe straightened without releasing her hand. "You ready?" His expression was unreadable. She imagined he spared little pity for the two men who had beaten his brother to death. And in a way, justice had been served here today. She found she could bear the loss of her home if it helped free Rafe from the burden of vengeance darkening his heart. She turned to thank Wounded Bear for his help but he was already out of earshot. "I wanted to thank him."

"You'll see him again." Rafe picked up her cloak where it had fallen behind the stump. "You'll probably be needing this."

At the sight of her cloak in Rafe's hands Callie started to laugh. Once started she couldn't stop. She laughed and laughed hysterically, shaking her head when Rafe moved toward her with a concerned look on his face.

"I'm all right, really. It's just…" She broke into a fresh spate of giggles. "Of all the things to have brought with me today. Look." Reaching out she raised the hem of her cloak and ripped at the stitching. She pulled out a fistful of money. "From Bert's money sock. At least we won't starve."

"I managed to save something of value myself."

"What's that?"

"Mandra's journal and the true assayer's report. I expect Denzell was counting on them being in the barn."

RAFE LAY BACK in the tub, eyes closed, feeling the heat from the warm water gradually seep into his weary, aching muscles, wishing it would blot out the heavy guilt dragging him down every time he thought about the charred remains of what used to be Callie's ranch.

From the first moment they'd met, he'd known Callie's home meant everything to her. The one thing that was well and truly hers. And now it was gone. Wiped out. All because of him.

He cursed himself for his arrogance. He was getting sloppy. Careless enough to believe that Denzell had given up the ghost. He should never have stopped in on Callie in the first place. Without meaning to, he'd turned her life upside down, and it was one more thing he'd regret to his dying day.

He shifted and a groan tore through him. Damn, but he ached. He must have pulled something in his shoulder. Every movement pained as he sat up and opened his eyes.

"Are you hurt?"

"I'm fine." The concern and caring he saw reflected in her gaze was echoed in the gentle tone of her voice. Two emotions he didn't deserve. Not when her home had been destroyed, thanks to him. Inwardly he cursed her, the fates, and the Denzells of the world for their interference in his life. For the position he now found himself in.

"Would you rather I left you alone?"

"Doesn't matter." Deliberately he made his voice gruffer than usual. It wouldn't do to have her get too comfortable with this little marriage arrangement. To leave her thinking there was any hope of their union lasting any longer than it took to get an annulment. He ignored the taunting inner voice that asked him how he expected to have the marriage annulled after it had been consummated.

He thought of his first wife and their volatile outbreaks of temper. The sheer physicality of their relationship whether they were fighting or loving was nothing like the slow steady ebb and flow of emotion, the sometimes uneasy tolerance that Callie displayed toward him.

Of course that had all changed when they got into bed together. In bed, at least, their emotions met and matched, burning with a mutual intensity that was difficult to ignore. Just the thought of Callie's response to his lovemaking was enough to wreak havoc with his control.

"How'd it go with the sheriff?" She leaned forward, crossed her arms over her bent knees, and rested her chin on her arms. There was something so trusting, so wifely, so comfortable about the pose that Rafe felt a strange twisting sensation in the pit of his stomach. He cleared his throat noisily.

"'Bout the way I expected."

"You promised you'd tell me what you've got on Denzell. The dynamite. The assayer's report. All of it."

Might as well tell her and be done with it. Then maybe she'd leave him in peace. "I'm still filling in the blanks, mind you, but as far as I can gather it goes like this. Denzell was in debt. Bert was always broke. Together, they decided to fake a gold rush. After all, there's been gold discovered in California and Idaho. Lots of it. Why not Oregon?

"First they planted gold shavings in the creek that runs through your property. I expect Bert and Denzell struck some kind of partnership agreement and forged an assayer's report. My guess is they were planning to dynamite, to blast traces of gold deep inside the hillside. After which they'd sell individual claims to nonexistent gold mines and sit back laughing while all the suckers busted their backs mining for gold that didn't exist."

"What was your brother's part in all this?"

"With his reputation, Luke would have lent their scheme extra validity."

"Helping Bert and Denzell to clean up," Callie added.

"Luke was no angel, but he was no crook, either. He stumbled across the real assayer's report and probably threatened to blow the whistle on them."

"Which could well be what Luke and Bert were arguing about, the day Bert died."

"So Denzell sends the boys after Luke to make sure he's silenced. Permanently. 'Cause Denzell's got too much time and money invested in the scheme."

"That's why he wants my land so bad. He could stake a claim and then re-sell it."

"Then along I come. Not only do I get my hands on the real assayer's report, stating there's no gold, I also have Mandra's journal, where she duly wrote down everything Luke told her what he knew about the scheme."

"Suddenly we're both in Denzell's way."

"He panics. Claims I'm Luke to get me put behind bars. Anything so I'll lose credibility in the eyes of the townsfolk."

"How'd you convince the sheriff to let you go, anyway?"

"I had him telegraph the sheriff's office down in Tucson. Sheriff there verified I had a twin brother named Luke, plus the fact I was holed up in jail there the day Bert was killed. Which kind of took the wind out of Denzell's sails."

"What were you doing in jail?"

"None of your business." His voice lowered with the memory. "I should have been here with Luke. Now will you kindly leave the room so I can get out of here before I'm all shriveled?"

"Why, Rafe, don't tell me you're going modest on me all of a sudden."

He'd show her modest. Gripping the sides of the tub with both hands he made to haul himself to his feet.

"All right, all right! You finish bathing. I, for one, am starving."

Callie darted around the screen to the main room, where her dinner was waiting, growing cold. She suddenly felt so ravenous, she attacked it anyway. Stuffed trout. Venison. Sweet potatoes. Some sort of trifle. From time to time she glanced over her shoulder, or straight ahead into the looking glass where the backlit screen revealed the shadowy outline of Rafe reclining in the tub, head back, knees bent. He lay so still she wondered if he might have fallen asleep. Not for anything was she going back there again. She didn't know what on earth had come over her. It's just that for a short time they felt like a real family, her and Rafe and the baby.

With her home gone, she needed something real to hang onto. Rafe was very real. She felt a painful tightening low in her abdomen, recalling the night they'd made love. Was it wrong of her to secretly wish that he'd lose control? That he'd rise up out of the tub and come to her, toss her down on the bed and ravish her till dawn?

Yes, it was wrong, Callie told herself firmly. They might be married in the eyes of the law, but not in the eyes of the Lord. Not when in their hearts they were strangers still. She reminded herself that yesterday he'd been set to say his good-byes.

Meal finished, she crawled into the sinfully soft feather bed, closed her eyes, and dreamed of a man whose gentle, loving touch brought pleasure to her body and had given the healing balm of love to her heart and soul.

# CHAPTER 27

It was scandalously late when Callie woke. The sun was high in the sky, streaming through the curtains and flooding the room with warmth. She shifted and stretched, reluctant to leave her warm, comfortable cocoon. Then she rolled over and saw the cradle. It was empty.

In a flash she was on her feet and through the door to Rafe's room. In the slat-backed rocking chair Rafe slept, baby Luke snuggled against him. The picture was reminiscent of the morning she woke to see the two of them asleep in her bed, and the memory filled her with bittersweet longings for the future. These two, who filled the emptiness inside her, made a mockery of her plea for independence. Could a body be both independent and needy at the same time?

Gently she laid a coverlet across Rafe and the baby and returned to her room. What she wouldn't give for a comb. She raked her fingers through her tangled hair, trying to bring some semblance of order to the snarled mess, and had just decided it was hopeless when she heard a gentle knock on her door. She opened the door a crack and peered out.

"Thought you'd be needing these, ma'am. We cleaned them up as best we could." The clerk passed her a skimpy bundle of clothing.

"But how..."

"Your husband brought them down late last night. Asked us to see what we could do." He passed her a second package. "Miss Simon and the town ladies rounded up a few things, too. And for the young'un, as well." He glanced studiously at his feet for a moment then back up at her. "Understand you lost everything, ma'am. Real sorry to hear that."

"Thank you."

Not everything, Callie thought, her eyes automatically flitting to the doorway separating her from Rafe. She hadn't yet lost the only things that were really, truly important. But soon she would. And when the time came, she wasn't sure if she could bear the pain.

After they'd eaten in the hotel dining room, Rafe arranged for the owner's wife to watch Luke while he accompanied Callie shopping. What a difference from the last time she'd come to shop. The proprietress remembered Rafe from his recent purchase of the taffeta which, along with everything else, had been reduced to ash. Grim-lipped, Rafe ordered the rest of the bolt.

Beaming, the shopkeeper fairly hovered over them, applauding Rafe on his excellent taste. She fitted Callie in several new gowns that were already sewn, just needing the final adjustments before they'd be ready to wear.

"Rafe," Callie whispered. "I can't possibly afford this many new clothes. It's more than I've owned in my entire life."

"I've taken care of it," he said tightly, passing her several parcels containing shoes, hats, and underpinnings as he arranged to have the rest of the purchases delivered to the hotel as soon as possible.

"I don't want you 'taking care of it,'" she said once they were back on the street. "I insist on paying my own way. And that's another thing. My money won't last long if I stay in the hotel. I must locate an inexpensive boarding house."

"Callie." Rafe glanced around to ensure they wouldn't be overheard before he continued. "For the here and now, in the eyes of both the law and the church, you're my wife. My responsibility."

To Callie it sounded like he wanted to say, "his burden."

One he was shouldering masterfully, but a burden none-theless.

"This wasn't part of any deal we struck."

"You being burned out of your home?" His lips tight-ened. "Indeed not. And as I hold myself responsible, I deserve the chance to at least try to make it up to you any way I can."

Guilt. The world's greatest motivator.

In her mind, guilt went hand in hand with pity, some-thing she'd seen plenty enough of as a child. Daughter of the town drunk. Pathetic, ragged little urchin. Although she'd been too young to fully understand the slurs and the insults, Callie could still recall the deep-burning shame she felt over something that wasn't her fault. The pitying looks. The loud-enough-to-overhear whispers. The hand-me-down rags. She'd vowed then and there to one day make her own way, dependent on no one save herself. And she'd been doing one fine job of it before Rafe Millar came riding into her life. Damn the man!

"So that's what you're about? Laying waste to your guilt? Well, you needn't bother. I managed fine before you appeared on the scene. And I'll manage very nicely on my own again, thank you very—"

The rest of her sentence was smothered by the sudden urgent pressure of Rafe's mouth on hers. She barely had time to absorb the sensation of his warm lips molding hers, the heady, all-consuming taste and smell of him, before he released her. Keeping one arm securely around her waist, he looked up.

"Well, well. If it isn't Mr. Abbott."

"Mr. Millar. Mrs. Millar." Callie felt herself color as Frank Abbott tipped his hat in greeting. "Sorry to interrupt. I happened to hear tell the sheriff was looking for you. Saw you standing here and thought I'd take a moment to pass the word."

"Thank you for letting me know. I'll swing by there now. Callie, why don't you run along back to the hotel and—"

"Why I wouldn't hear of it," she interrupted sweetly. "You know how it pains me having to leave your side, even for a short time."

"Indeed." Rafe glowered down at her. She met his look with one of her own that clearly said, "Tit for tat." She secured her arm through his, aware of Frank Abbott's smirk as he watched them walk away.

As soon as they were out of sight, Rafe dropped all pretext. "I mean it, Callie. Go back to the hotel and wait for me there."

Callie flung his arm off hers. She wasn't intimidated by his superior size or strength. And she was downright soured on men ordering her around, thinking they knew what was best for her. They could all just go to the devil as far as she was concerned. "Perhaps *you* would care to run along to the hotel and wait while I have words with the sheriff concerning the fire at my ranch."

Rafe tried another tack, lowering his voice to its most persuasive tone. "I'm having a bit of a hard time with the sheriff. I really feel it's best I speak to him in private."

She knew a con when she smelled one. "What kind of a hard time would that be?"

Rafe clasped his hands together and rocked back on his heels. "Denzell has him in his pocket."

Callie blew out an impatient breath. No wonder men presumed women were too daft to understand, they insisted on speaking a coded language all their own. "What exactly do you mean?"

"I mean Denzell pays the sheriff to do whatever he says."

"But surely that's not right."

"No, it's not right. But it happens all too often."

"Well, I don't care." She set her mouth in a stubborn line. "I'm coming with you. After all, 'twas my ranch burned down, you might care to recall."

"How could I forget?" But she felt him weakening and savored the faint stab of victory. Took her long enough to figure out that Rafe Millar was nowhere near as tough as the act he put on. He might have grown up hard and fast, relying solely on his wits to survive, but it hadn't turned him into a bitter, hardened man. The more she knew of him, the more multifaceted he became. And the more she loved him.

"Bad business, folks," the sheriff stated once they were seated across from him. A young, surly-looking deputy leaned against the far wall, arms folded across his chest, eyeing them with hostility. "Stopped by the Double D on my way back from your place. Servants haven't seen Denzell since late yesterday. Apparently he was watching the smoke from the fire, dancing about all gleeful. Till about the time it started to get dark. That's when the boys' horses come back riderless. Hear tell old Denzell lit out of there like the devil himself was at his heels."

"Did you remove the remains from the barn?"

"That's another thing. No bodies there that we could see."

"What?" Rafe straightened abruptly. "You must be mistaken. I saw them."

"Seen the spot where they musta bin," the sheriff said, taking off his glasses and polishing them on the tail of his shirt. "The spot where you said. Lots of bootprints all around. Expect the old man took 'em off and buried 'em. Followed his trail for a spell. Lost him at the creek. Couldn't pick it up on the other side." He shrugged. "Anyway. What's done is done."

"Except for whatever Denzell might be planning next," Rafe said. "What can you do to ensure my wife's safety?"

The sheriff leaned forward, elbows on his desk. "I don't expect he's got no beef with your wife, do you, Millar?"

"No, I suppose he hasn't."

The sheriff rose and made an unsuccessful effort to tuck in his shirt. It pulled right out again over his protruding belly. "Way I see, it's like this. The barn and house is burned down. The men responsible are dead. We got no proof Denzell had anything to do with it. I say we leave things the way they are. Let the man grieve."

Rafe stood so abruptly his chair crashed over behind him.

"What of everything I told you about the phony gold rush scheme?"

"So far as I can see, no crime's been committed."

"What about my brother's murder?"

"All you got there's the say-so of some Injun. Like as not your brother'll show up one day, fit as a fiddle, right as rain.

Happens all the time. Somebody cries foul. Gets a lot of folks' feathers ruffled. Till along comes the foulee, just as fine and slick as they come."

Callie would hate to find herself on the receiving end of the look Rafe gave the sheriff.

"Come on, Callie," he said. "Let's get out of here."

"I don't understand." Outside the sheriff's office Callie half ran to keep up with Rafe. The wooden planks underfoot rang hollowly with every loud, angry step he took. "What just happened back there?"

"What just happened back there is the exact kind of whitewashing of criminals that passes for justice in these parts."

Callie tugged on Rafe's arm in an effort to slow his steps. "Luke's dead, Rafe. Nothing you can do will bring him back. And it appears the Almighty dealt with the Denzell boys in his own way. Can't you just let it be?"

"Your ranch, all your possessions, everything you owned is gone. Can you let that be?"

"Yes."

"What?" He stopped so abruptly she ran right into him. Automatically he reached out and steadied her. She felt herself melt against him, felt the strength and security of his hands on her waist. Her heart rate increased, her breath caught in her throat at the look in his eyes, the way he stroked her gently and didn't release her. She closed her eyes against the conflicting sensations flooding through her. She didn't want it to feel this good, being held by a man.

When she opened her eyes Rafe was gazing down at her, a myriad of emotions chasing across his rugged features. Confusion left her feeling slightly lightheaded. Unguarded. Instinctively she leaned closer to him. With Rafe alongside her, Callie realized, she could let almost anything else be.

"I've still got the land. And the animals. I can rebuild."

"It's not that easy."

"Started out with nothing but the clothes on my back once before. No reason I can't do it again."

"But your home—"

"Truth be told, that cabin was chock full of bad memories. In many ways, it'll be a relief to rebuild. This time I'll have the kitchen face south, the way I always wanted. To let in lots of sunlight. And a porch looking west so I can sit in the evenings and watch the sunset."

"Just like that, you think you can start over?"

Callie's lips curved in a satisfied smile. She'd found the inner strength that came from knowing her own capabilities. And she didn't need to keep the world at arm's length to prove her independence. "I've still got a pretty fair hammer that was a wedding gift. Ought to come in real handy when I start rebuilding." As she spoke she absently smoothed the lapel of his jacket. Curled her fingers around the cloth and hung on as if she meant to never let go. "Truth be told, I could always use a hand. I've seen you swing a hammer. You're not half bad, even if you don't cotton to ladders too good. I wouldn't turn down your help. If you're of a mind to stay awhile, that is."

She watched his eyes widen as he realized what she was suggesting. Watched his breath catch in his throat. Saw the erratic movement of his Adam's apple as he struggled with his answer.

Gently she placed her fingertips against his lips. "Don't say anything right now. Just wait and see if maybe you get a better offer before you decide."

With that, she turned and moved on, a half-step in front of him.

*Damn the woman*, Rafe thought. As if he didn't already feel responsible for what had happened to her home.

Now she had to turn about and be all forgiving sweetness and light. Let him know he had a place here, should he so decide. A place with so many damned strings dangling, it was fair enough to make a man choke just thinking about it. And the biggest, weightiest string of all was something he'd known from the first. That Callie wasn't a leaving kind of woman.

He'd known other women, plenty, happy to just enjoy a man's company for as long as he fixed to stay. They didn't put on a big show, languid sighs, or burdens of anxiety when he fixed on leaving.

Callie was different. Didn't take much to figure how she'd grown up, never having one single thing to call her own. If any man ever got so close to her that she started thinking on him as hers, that man would never find an easy time to leave. Not unless he was of a mind to tear the very heart from inside of her and take it off with him. Callie's heart, so starved and badly used over the years, was a delicate thing indeed.

The hell of it was, Rafe could nearabouts picture it.

Him and Luke Junior out at the ranch, building Callie a new cabin with her damned south-facing kitchen and west-facing porch. Plowing and planting and seeing to the livestock. Watching the boy grow up happy, healthy, and strong, teaching him everything he and Luke had learned the hard way, with no one to show them the ropes.

Yes, sir. He could see it, clear as the sky above. Except for one thing. For as far back as he could remember, he'd never stayed in any one place for longer than a year. And after the first six or so months, staying put had tore him up something fierce.

Nishu, his wife, had seen the war he waged with his wanderlust. And while he'd loved her something fierce, not even their exchange of love had been powerful enough to settle his blood.

Memories stole over him with the stealth of west coast fog. Memories he'd spent years working to forget. Like their last confrontation. He'd been feeling extra restless as Nishu's belly swelled. He was happy about the baby and all, maybe even a bit jealous, when it came right down to it. At any rate, he'd made plans to go hunting with Wounded Bear. Nishu had looked at him with her big, dark, liquid eyes and begged him not to go. Said she wanted him there when the baby was born.

The baby wasn't due yet for another two moons, and he'd said as much. Accused her of trying to manipulate him. Using her condition as another excuse to chain him to her side.

No. He'd gone off hunting. And returned several days later to find his wife and infant son dead. Knowing as their bodies were put into the cold hard ground that he'd killed them, sure as he lived and breathed. That deadly knowledge made settling in one place impossible. 'Specially if the deal included a woman like Callie.

Rafe was startled to feel Callie catch hold of his arm.

"You walked right past the hotel," she said quietly.

He realized she already knew his answer to her offer that he stay and be part of her life here. So sure, in fact, that she half expected him to just walk on down to the livery right this minute, saddle up, and ride off without looking back once.

"Just thinking about some stuff," he said, holding the front door of the hotel open for her.

"Like where you're headed to next?"

"No," he said. "I'm wondering what new surprise Denzell might have up his sleeve."

"You heard the sheriff. He's gone off to grieve someplace after burying his boys."

"Maybe," Rafe said. He knew he sounded as unconvinced as he felt. "But I've come up against his kind before. For some reason, they don't crawl away and lick their wounds the way you or I would."

"What do they do?"

Rafe pursed his lips thoughtfully. "Depends on the man. Oftentimes they do something real stupid. Self-destructive, even."

"You see?" Callie said. "He won't bother coming after us again. He's already tried that. With devastating results."

They were halfway down the hall when Callie saw a door fly open with a thud.

A distraught older woman raced out and barreled straight into them.

"Mr. Millar. Mrs. Millar," she babbled. "I'm so sorry. I don't know how it happened. I must have dozed off for a minute or two. When I woke up, the baby was gone!"

# CHAPTER 28

Callie's purchases tumbled from her arms. She watched numbly as Rafe grabbed the woman, who was sobbing and moaning hysterically, and gave her an impatient shake.

"When?" he barked at the woman. "How long ago?"

Even Callie cringed from the raw emotion in his voice as his anger won out over fear. She felt the rise of those same conflicting reactions herself and took a deep breath. One of them had to hold onto common sense. As Rafe hurled questions at the woman, her moans and wails grew to ear-splitting shrieks.

"Here, let me talk to her," Callie said. "You're frightening the poor thing half to death." But Callie had little more success than Rafe. As the woman subsided into incoherent sniffles and sobs, Callie turned to him. "She's not sure exactly how long ago. She lost track of time."

"It doesn't matter," Rafe said, turning on his heel and marching down the hall. "We know where he is."

Callie trotted to keep up with him. "You're sure it was Denzell?"

"Who else?"

"Why would he take the baby?"

"To ransom him, of course," Rafe said impatiently. "I warned you before, he'll stop at nothing."

"But would he take the baby to his ranch? I mean, isn't that kind of obvious?"

"There's no telling what that madman might do. At least it's someplace to start."

Out in the street, Rafe started in the direction of the livery. Callie tugged his arm, but he gave no indication he even noticed. "Aren't you going to the sheriff first?"

"Haven't you figured out yet that the sheriff is next to useless?"

"He's still the law in these parts."

"I'll make my own laws from here on in."

Inside the livery, Callie grabbed her saddle and followed Rafe to their horses.

He glowered at her. "Just what do you think you're doing?"

"I'm going with you."

"Who says?"

"I do. I have a stake in this, too, you know."

"Callie, the man's dangerous. There's no telling what he might take it into his head to do."

"You can stand here and argue all you want," Callie said, as she pushed past him into the stall and began to saddle her mare. "We're wasting precious riding time."

"Woman, you are cussed stubborn when you put your mind to it," Rafe muttered, as he set about readying his own mount.

"I've been taking lessons from you."

Callie and Rafe had just led their horses outside and mounted when the clerk from the hotel came rushing up.

"Mr. Millar. Mr. Millar. Reverend Bligh needs to see you over at the church right away."

"Tell Reverend Bligh he'll just have to wait. I've got more pressing concerns."

The clerk grabbed the horse's bridle. "He said to tell you Mr. Denzell is with him."

"Hell, boy. Why didn't you say so in the first place?"

Rafe was out of the saddle so fast Callie's vision blurred as she scrambled from her horse. He tossed the young man a coin along with the reins. "See to the horses, will you?"

Rafe stalked ahead of her without a word, up the wooden steps of the church and down the center aisle toward the altar. As before, Callie was conscious of the empty pews and the smell of burning candles, underscored by the ominous echoing silence. No comfort to be had this time in this hushed place of worship. What she really longed to hear right then was the familiar cry of a baby.

At the altar rail Rafe stopped short. He stood, legs planted apart, hands on his hips. "I'm here, Bligh." His voice echoed loudly through the empty church, sounding out of place in a building typically reserved for murmured prayers, Latin incantations, and the muted strains of the organ.

The reverend appeared from the vestry almost immediately. "Thank you for coming, Mr. Millar. Mr. Denzell is most anxious to speak with you."

"Where's the boy?" Rafe barked.

"Boy?" Reverend Bligh's face wrinkled.

"The one I'm fixing to adopt."

"I'm not sure what you mean. Has the boy been misplaced?"

"Damn right. By that fugitive from justice you're harboring in there."

Reverend Bligh tugged at his sleeves. "I believe you're

mistaken, sir. I offer solace to a grieving father, a man who was so overcome with emotion he took it upon himself to bury his own without benefit of the last rites, of a decent Christian burial. Why, just now we were discussing—"

"He'll be lucky if he can still breathe, let alone grieve, by the time I get through with him."

"The church offers safe haven for all her fold." Bligh glanced at Callie. "Please remain here. It's Mr. Millar with whom my grief-stricken parishioner wishes to confer."

Reluctantly Callie nodded. As the vestry door closed behind the two men, she sank to her knees and commenced praying. She knew she'd been asking an awful lot of Him lately, but if He could hear her now, please let Him ensure Luke's safe return.

The plush opulence of the vestry contrasted markedly with the spartan church. Denzell sat back in a wine-colored, velvet-upholstered chair, his stubby feet resting on an embroidered footstool. He was smoking a cigar and staring thoughtfully at the ceiling as he blew a smoke ring.

Rafe reached his side in two easy strides. "What have you done with the boy?"

Denzell shifted slightly and glanced sideways at him. "Is that any way to offer condolences?"

"You're not deserving of the devil's sympathy." He glanced up at the gaudy, oversized crucifix on the wall above Denzell. "May the Lord have mercy on your miserable soul. You sent those boys to their death doing your dirty work. Or did you forget about the dynamite you and Bert stashed inside the barn?"

"My boys undertook that little venture as a surprise for me. Unfortunately, they've never been very capable. A fact which I've drawn to their attention time and again over the years. Still, they had their uses, and I'll miss them. Now, to the business at hand. I believe you have some documentation which belongs to me?"

Even Rafe was shaken by the cool way Denzell dismissed his loss. "Had," he said. "Everything was destroyed in the fire."

"How unfortunate," Denzell said, slowly straightening in his seat. "Because without those papers in hand, you won't be laying eyes on that squalling, red-faced brat."

Rafe reached carelessly into his inside pocket and withdrew a packet of papers. "I still have your considerable gambling debts. Fair trade for one small baby, wouldn't you say?"

Denzell shook his head. "I'm disappointed in you, Millar. Not for one short minute do I believe you left those documents lying around anyplace on Callie's ranch. No, sir. That just doesn't strike me as the way you do business."

Rafe glanced over at Bligh, who was observing the negotiations with undisguised interest. "How can you, a man of the cloth, stand there and be party to this?"

Bligh hugged his Bible to his chest and rolled his eyes skyward. "Our lord is all-forgiving, all-loving. He would no sooner turn his back on one of his flock than he would give me leave to abandon a man in his greatest hour of need."

Rafe snorted loudly.

Denzell heaved himself to his feet. "I'm going out to the Double D." He tapped a rigid forefinger against Rafe's chest. "I'll see you there before nightfall. Bring the assayer's report. And that little twit's journal, as well."

"And if I don't?"

"Fish bait. Consider the brat fish bait."

Rafe stormed from the vestry, past where Callie waited, his face a thundercloud of emotions. She followed him out of the church and watched him clench and unclench his fists at his side, as if struggling to control his temper.

"What did he say? Is Luke all right?"

"Denzell's stashed the boy someplace. I need to find out where."

"Why not just give him the assayer's report if that's what he wants?"

"I told him it was burned in the fire."

Her eyes widened. "That's not true."

"No. But I'll burn it myself before Denzell gets his dirty hands on it."

"Why? What difference is it? He can't use it. Not as long as we're onto his ways."

"Can't he?" Rafe rocked hack on his heels and faced her, a dangerous look about him. "That's where you're mistaken. Maybe not tomorrow. But wait till next year. Or the year after that. There'll be hundreds of new settlers passing through this way. Easy prey for Denzell. And we both know the sheriff won't lift a finger to stop him."

"Aren't you forgetting something? He still needs my land to pull it off."

Rafe turned away, but not before she caught the flash of emotion in his eyes. His voice sounded less than its usual steady tones. "I made the mistake once of underestimating him. I won't do it again. And I don't want to hear a year or two from now how you were found drowned in the creek. Or smothered in your bed. Or 'accidentally' shot while you were out riding the fence line. Believe this, Callie, if you never believe another thing I say. Denzell will stop at nothing to get what he wants."

"Ask yourself who you're really doing this for, Rafe. For me? Or for yourself? Because you're so twisted up inside you can't recognize truth from fiction. Or maybe you're still looking to see justice served for your brother's death. His son could very easily die here. And you'll mourn. I know you'll mourn. But then relief will set in. 'Cause you won't have the responsibility or the bother of another person in your life. Someone loving you who might expect you to love them back."

"You don't understand," Rafe called after her. His voice broke, the words a shattered whisper. "I can't spare the risk of loving. Everyone I love dies on me."

Callie didn't hear the tail end of Rafe's sentence. And she didn't much care. When he wasn't looking she ducked into the livery and saddled her horse. She left by the rear exit and made her way from town, taking back roads and alleys so she wouldn't risk running into Rafe.

Her detour had taken longer than she thought, but finally the Double D ranch came into view. She reined in abruptly at the sight of half a dozen riders approaching from the ranch. Denzell's servants?

They passed without sparing her a second glance, speaking among themselves in Spanish. She caught the word *loco* several times.

"Excuse me." She stopped the last rider, a large dark-haired woman she recognized as the cook. "I'm looking for Mr. Denzell."

The woman waved one hammy fist toward the ranch house. "There."

"Is he alone?"

"Alone?" The woman frowned. "Much alone." She pointed to her temple. "His mind is gone. "

Taking a deep breath Callie urged her mare forward in the direction of the empty ranch house. What was Denzell up to that he had dismissed his entire staff? The wind sent a handful of leaves skittering across the road in front of her, and she felt the hair prickle against the back of her neck. Was she being warned away? Denzell was inside, likely observing her approach and plotting his next move. What if he had harmed Luke? What if she was too late?

Her hands trembled as she adjusted her grip on the reins. She couldn't be too late. But it seemed her horse slowed its pace, as if sensing her reluctance to enter the courtyard. She glanced about with trepidation as she dismounted and hitched her horse to the rail. If, as the cook had said, Denzell had truly lost his mind, would she even be able to get him to listen? She thought of Luke, so helpless and small, and knew she had to try.

The hand-carved double front doors stood ajar, and she stepped forward hesitantly, into the tiled front entranceway. She approached the staircase to the second floor with the thought of searching the house room by room till she found the baby, but was stopped by the sight of Denzell halfway up the stairs, his gun trained straight at her.

"Well, well, well." Slowly he descended the steps until he stood two from the bottom, the barrel of his Colt revolver resting against her temple. "Look what the wind blew in."

"Put the gun down." Callie managed to speak with far more confidence than she felt. "I'm here to make you an offer. The best one you'll get, I might add."

"I think I'll be leaving my gun right where it is for the time being."

Callie was glad he couldn't see the way her knees were knocking together beneath her skirt. She could feel a single drop of perspiration start at her hairline and slowly wend its way down her temple to her cheekbone.

"I find it somewhat distracting," she said evenly.

"Maybe I like you when you're distracted, gal. Kinda found it insulting, you up and marrying your hired hand after I offered you all this." His free hand sliced the air next to her ear, and Callie shivered.

Luke, she reminded herself. Think of Luke.

"That's sort of my offer to you," Callie said. "I know you want my land. And you can have it. Lock, stock, and barrel. I've got no use for it anymore. Too many memories."

"Funny," Denzell sneered. "A short while ago you wouldn't even consider the overpriced parcel of cash I was willing to shell over. Now you're offering it to me as a gift?"

"That's it," Callie said. "A gift. From me to you. All I want in exchange is for you to return the baby safe and sound." She felt the gun barrel waver as Denzell drew a deep breath.

"Land's not worth a plugged nickel to me. Not as long as Millar hangs onto that assayer's report."

"I'll get that too," Callie said quietly. "I know where he stashed it. It's not too far away. Just give me the baby and—"

"You think I'm a fool? Once I hand over that brat I've seen the last of you."

She eyed him sideways, careful not to move. She'd never been so frightened in all her life. She thought she'd mastered her fears, 'specially of dying. But she found suddenly she had an awful lot to live for. "I swear. An even trade. I'll sign over the land and hand you the assayer's report myself."

"Where's the report, Callie?"

She licked her dry lips. "It's—"

"Don't lie to me, gal. I can always tell when a woman lies to me."

She focused all her energies toward the icy cold gun barrel against her temple, aware that Denzell's grip was anything but steady. She weighed the risk of a sudden plunge to the floor, the effort required to dislodge the gun from his hand on her way down. It was risky. But no riskier than her position at this very second.

Praying for courage she took a breath and raised her arm at the same time she dropped. Her ears rang with the sound of the gun discharging, and she felt a hot tearing pain in her shoulder. She hit the floor and instinctively rolled for cover.

From behind her came a shout. Rafe's voice. Followed by the volley of more shots. She tucked her head under her arms as a surprised look spread across Denzell's face, just before he toppled face first down the last two steps.

Rafe found her cowering behind the entryway bench. Gently he positioned her so he could examine her shoulder. Her head ached from the sound of gunshots as she swam through the cloudy maze of pain and confusion to ask, "Did you find him, Rafe? Did you find the baby?"

"He's not in the house." Rafe spoke slowly, gathering her close against him. "Does it hurt real bad?"

"Not too bad," Callie said, burrowing against the familiar security of Rafe's broad chest. She was shaking so much she would have fallen over on her own. Beyond them lay the inert form of Denzell, a puddle of blood forming around him on the floor. "Is he dead?"

"I'm afraid so."

She pulled back and stared at him, awash in fresh waves of despair, gripped by a sense of loss worse than death. "That means we might never find Luke."

# CHAPTER 29

Rafe's throat tightened as he stroked the back of Callie's head and tangled his fingers in the softness of her hair, savoring the warmth of her skin and the ragged sound of her breathing. Here she was shot and bleeding, and all her thoughts centered on the well-being of someone else. Did a less selfish, more loving woman exist?

He took out his handkerchief and knife, cut away at Callie's sleeve, and wadded his handkerchief against the wound to staunch the flow of blood. "Hold that firm," he said, placing her hand over the hanky and pressing it into place with his. "We'd better get you to town. Get that seen to before you lose much more blood."

"But what about Luke?"

His arms tightened as he helped her to her feet. She'd been prepared to sacrifice everything. Herself. Her ranch. The only thing she'd ever cared about, to ensure the safety of one small baby. A baby that wasn't even hers. "We'll find him. I promise. If we have to tear apart every room in every house in every town in the entire state, we'll find him."

"I'm happy to say that won't be necessary."

They both turned. Rafe spoke first. "Abbott. What are you doing here?"

"Came by to help you mop up."

"Since when does a con man care about mopping up?"

Abbott grinned. "Good cover, don't you think? Even had you fooled. And you're no easy man to fool."

"Who are you, Mr. Abbott?" Callie asked.

He smiled modestly. "Actually, I work for Pinkerton."

"You're a detective?"

"Yes, ma'am." He indicated Denzell's body. "Been watching this one for quite some time. He pulled that same gold rush swindle in Idaho about ten years ago. Just before he pulled up stakes and landed here. Yes, sir. We knew it wouldn't be long now. 'Specially since he'd run out of money."

Rafe felt a grudging respect for the man in front of him. "I don't suppose you were watching where he took the youngster after he stole him from the hotel."

"Matter of fact, I was. The boy's just fine."

"Why didn't you stop him?" Callie wanted to launch herself at Abbott. Slap him hard for the worry he'd put her through. Both of them. As if he read her thoughts, she felt Rafe's grip tighten, holding her still.

"Didn't want to tip my hand too soon. Besides, I was waiting for a few of my colleagues to join me." He indicated two gentlemen who were busy wrapping Denzell's body in a sheet.

"Where's the baby?"

"Denzell left him in the care of his mistress. She has a cottage on the edge of town. I'll stop by there, break the news about Denzell, and bring the boy around to the hotel while you take Mrs. Millar over to the doc's office and get that gunshot wound looked at."

"What about the sheriff?"

"Ah, yes. The sheriff. I think we can happily say he'll sign whatever needs signing, including his resignation." Abbott gave Rafe a long look. "That'll leave the sheriff's job up for grabs. Myself, I've got a hunch who the townsfolk might be looking at to maybe take it on."

"Who's that?"

Abbott pointed a finger at him. "You got yourself a fair following in the short time you've been here."

Rafe managed to laugh. "I've never stayed in one place longer than six months, not since I wasn't much bigger than Luke Junior."

Abbott shrugged. "You're a family man now. Things like that have a way of changing a man's perspective. The boy deserves the stability of being raised all of a piece in the same place."

"I've been thinking along those lines myself," Rafe said, with a long look at Callie.

She felt her heart give a wild leap of hope. She'd offered to have him stay. Maybe he'd changed his mind. But his next words dashed her hopes to rubble.

"How about it, Callie? I know Luke isn't kin to you, but you must care some for him. After all, you were willing to hand over your ranch to Denzell in exchange for the boy's safe return. And Abbott's right. Luke needs a stable home. I know you'd do right by him."

With an immense effort Callie pushed herself away from Rafe. "In a pig's eye," she spat out, as she whirled around. She must have moved too quickly. The room started spinning. She saw spots in front of her eyes. Then nothing.

Rafe and Abbott both grabbed for Callie when she started to go down. Abbott was closer. He dipped one hand under her knees, the other under her shoulders, and raised her in his arms.

"What the hell came over her?" Rafe asked, looking down at Callie's ashen features. The way Abbott held her, arms and legs sprawled limply, head lolled back, she looked like a broken rag doll.

"For one, she's been shot. For two, she's been insulted. If she hadn't lost so much blood, I expect she would have taken a right good swing at you."

Rafe frowned. "I thought she was genuinely attached to the boy."

Abbott let out a snort. "For someone who fancies himself a ladies' man you sure don't know beans about women, mister. You expect this gal to sit tight here and raise your boy while you gallivant off looking for adventure. Sure, and you'd drop back every year or two to see how they're doing. Just often enough that she doesn't have a chance to forget you, to get on with the business of her own life. If I was her, I'd have told you to go straight to hell."

Rafe felt something deep inside him come alive. "That's my wife you're holding," he said gruffly.

"So it is." Abbott passed Callie to Rafe as if she weighed no more than Luke Junior. "Maybe you'll come to your senses and realize that you got something here most men spend their entire lives looking for and never find. Now get her up to the doc's, quick as you can. I'll take care of Denzell and fetch the boy for you."

~

CALLIE OPENED her eyes to an unfamiliar room. She felt a dull throb ripple through her arm, and when she tried to move it she couldn't. Her throat and lips felt parched. She tried to speak, but nothing came out except a hoarse, frog-like croak.

She heard movement and followed it with her eyes.

Rafe stood at the window, Luke cradled in his arms. It appeared he was talking to the boy, his voice so low she couldn't hear the words. When she shifted on the bed, Rafe came to her side immediately.

"You're awake. How you feeling?"

"Thirsty." It hurt to talk.

Everything ached.

"Here." He laid the baby alongside her, and Luke gave a soft coo, the sweetest sound Callie had ever heard. She felt her eyes fill with tears. The baby gazed studiously up at her and she could have sworn his lips curved in a gummy, contented smile. Rafe meanwhile slid his arm behind her to raise her head up some while he held a tin cup to her lips. More of the water dribbled down her chin than her throat, but she didn't care. Having Rafe care for her was something she wanted to savor for as long as she could. Then she remembered what he'd last said to her, and she sighed sadly and closed her eyes. Gently Rafe lowered her head back to the pillow.

"The baby's fine. Just like Abbott said. Except that he missed you."

She opened one eye. Then both. Rafe looked more uncomfortable than she'd ever seen him. "He did not."

"Did too." Rafe perched next to her on the bed and smoothed the tangle of hair back from her face. She felt the way his hand shook unsteadily against her clammy skin. "He refused to settle down till I brought him around here so he could see with his own two eyes that you were on the mend."

It seemed to Callie that Rafe was having difficulty saying good-bye. "I feel like I was run over by a stagecoach," she said.

"Doc got the bullet out of your shoulder and sewed you up good as new. He said it was a lucky thing you passed out, 'cause it would have smarted something fierce if you'd been awake."

"It's because of Bert, isn't it?"

Rafe frowned. "What's because of Bert?"

"I'm the one who killed him. That's why you won't stay, isn't it? I don't exactly have a good track record with husbands."

Rafe let loose with a deep, gut-wrenching sigh. "I never met Bert, but from all accounts his dying wasn't much of a loss. I think they ought to give you a medal. Maybe I'll see to it if I get elected sheriff."

"What do you mean, if you get elected sheriff?"

"I was a blind, stubborn fool, Callie. And much as I hate to admit it, it took Frank Abbott to point that out to me."

"Frank Abbott. What did he do?"

"Mostly he forced me to admit how I felt today when I saw you'd been hit. I wanted it to be me that died, not you. Because I couldn't imagine living without you. That scared me so much I did what I always did in the past. I said the one thing guaranteed to piss you off good at me. That way I could walk away, telling myself it was for the best."

"So why are you still here?"

"I heard you offering to trade your ranch for this here little one, and I knew that meant you loved him. Up to that point I didn't think you cared much about anything except your ranch." He paused. "Love changes a body. Everyone I ever loved has died on me, Callie. My folks. Nishu. Luke. I never wanted to feel that again.

"And there you were, all laid out bleeding, still with the gumption to tell me where to go. I loved you more right then than I ever loved another living soul. I'm a flawed human being, Callie, not much of a prize, but I swear to our Maker, I love you. And I'm fixing to stay, if you'll have me. I gotta warn you, though. It's a package deal. Me and the little fella here. And I can't promise I won't get the urge to up and bolt, six months from now. But I kind of have the feeling you might help me through that if it happens."

Callie blinked as the full impact of his words slowly penetrated her pain-fogged mind. "Are you really going to run for sheriff?"

"I'm the first one to complain about these small town sheriffs and the lousy job they do at lawmaking. I guess maybe I'm ready to give it a shot. There's more, I'm afraid."

"More?" She sagged back against the mattress. How much more could there possibly be?

"You remember how I was buying up Denzell's debts? Seems I'm holding the note to his ranch. He's got no other living kin, which means I'm stuck with it."

Thinking seemed to require a supreme effort. "Would we have to live there?"

"Not if you don't want to."

"I want to build on my land."

"The two spreads are adjacent. Together we'll be one of the biggest land barons in the state."

She gave a painful laugh. "Something neither of us cares a plugged nickel about. We need to do something with the ranch house, though. Something good."

"You got anything in mind?"

"I don't know. It's hard to think. Maybe a home for kids

with no folks. A place you and Luke could have gone after your folks died."

He was silent so long she wondered if she had somehow said the wrong thing.

"How do you know about that?" he asked finally. "I know I never told you."

"You talked a lot when you had that malaria attack. Bits and pieces. I just kind of put them together."

"What else did I say?"

Callie laughed for real this time, then winced when it hurt her shoulder. "Be warned. I know all your secrets."

"All of them?"

"Every last one." Grabbing his shirtfront with her good arm she pulled him close. "And you know mine. The secret that's right here." She pressed her hand to her heart. "I've never loved anyone before. And I don't expect I'll get it right all the time. But if you'll be patient, between you and Luke Junior, I'm willing to bet I can learn."

He leaned down and spoke against her lips. "Soon as we get these bandages off you, we can get down to the practicing part."

He sealed his words with a kiss. A promise of a future rich with the rewards of their love. And as they deepened the kiss, pledging their promise of a long and happy life together, the next generation watched contentedly, gurgling his own expression of approval.

Thanks for reading *Callie's Honor*. You might not know how important reader reviews are, but they mean a lot.

Review wherever you purchased *Callie's Honor* or on Goodreads or BookBub.

Just a short sentence saying you enjoyed the book goes a long way with new readers and puts a smile on this author's face.

Keep reading for a preview of *Anora's Pride.*

Dear Reader,

The American West in the last half of the nineteenth century offers my heroines a chance to assert their independence and also introduce them to a hero who is their match in every way. My characters have their own ideas of right and wrong, good versus evil, and deal with it on their terms. It wasn't called the Wild West for nothing. Life was about conquest, survival and persistence,

I love writing a historical genre where the reader, by the simple act of picking up the book, instantly suspends disbelief. She easily forgets about her world and her woes in a tale where no one needs to empty the dishwasher or take out the trash, and adventure lies around every corner.

As an author, it's fun to carry her away to a time and place where anything could, and often did, happen. The customs of the day and the manner of dress might be different from today's world, but people are still people. They laugh, love, hurt and heal. Celebrate and mourn. They live life large. And in the untamed wildness of the settling of the west anything can happen.

Read on for a preview of *Anora's Pride*.

Sincerely,
Kathleen

~

## CHAPTER I

The train was late.

Anora tapped her foot, aware that a larger crowd than usual had turned out to meet the 12:10 out of St. Louis. She noticed the Reverend Fish on hand, standing alongside the mayor of Boulder Springs. Neither of them had greeted the noon train before.

Penny skidded to a stop alongside Anora. Breathless from her run from the schoolhouse, between gasps she asked, "Am I too late?"

Anora smiled at her friend's unexpected arrival. "You're supposed to be at the school, aren't you?"

"I know," Penny said in a loud whisper, tugging at her bonnet brim as if she were trying to hide. "I just couldn't resist running down to get a peek at the new marshal."

"What new marshal?"

"Lord, girl, where you been? The whole town's been talking about nothing else for weeks."

Just then the scream of the steam whistle was followed by the sight of the gleaming black locomotive gliding into the station. Anora automatically straightened her bonnet and pasted a smile on her face as she stood alongside her rickety wooden wheelbarrow full of cheesecloth-wrapped sandwiches and boxed lunches.

"I declare!" Penny grabbed her friend's arm and squeezed hard. "That must be him. I heard he was tall, dark, and very, very handsome. Not that you'd care. Being married and all. But as a single gal I—"

Anora shook off Penny's arm as the first flurry of customers approached. As she passed out sandwiches and collected coins, she tried unsuccessfully to tune out Penny's magpie chatter.

"The mayor's shaking his hand. So's the reverend."

" 'Lo, Anora. I'll take six, today."

"Hi, Butch." Anora scooped six sandwiches from the wheelbarrow and exchanged them for precious money.

"Who's that?" Penny asked with an interested gleam in her eye as the young man hopped nimbly back on board.

"Butch." Anora checked the station tower clock. Five minutes, tops, to sell the rest of her lunches.

"What's he do?"

"Rides the train. Sells peanuts and drinks and my sandwiches to the passengers."

"Look!" Penny exclaimed.

Anora followed her friend's gaze to where a dark-haired man, dressed top-to-toe in black city clothes, stood head and shoulders above most of the people mingling around the station. His gaze was riveted on her in a way that made her skin flush.

At that second a woman dressed in an eye-catching red and black gown launched herself at the stranger, who scooped her up in his arms, swung her around, then set her back on her feet before he bent down to plant a lingering kiss on her painted lips.

Anora shifted her gaze. How dare the stranger watch her at the same time he kissed another woman?

"Gotta go!" Penny said. The train whistle sounded two short blasts, setting off a final brief flurry of activity, and Anora stared down at half a dozen unsold sandwiches.

Maybe she could sell the rest in town. As she grasped the handles of her wheelbarrow and turned it around, she passed the dark-haired man, who didn't take any notice. He was busy talking to the stunning woman hanging on his arm. Richelle, the bordello queen whom Anora knew by reputation alone, was obviously no stranger to the new marshal.

Jesse found his interest piqued by the young woman who trudged past him and Ricki as if they were invisible. "Who's that, Ricki?"

"Where?"

"Little gal with the lunch wagon."

Ricki pinched Jesse playfully on the arm. "Nice try, Casanova, except for you're barking up the wrong tree this time. Anora King lives over yonder with her husband."

"Married, is she?"

"Wife to one sorry excuse for a man. And I've seen some real gems in my day."

Jesse frowned. "She doesn't look married." He'd caught the way the young woman had lowered her eyes as he kissed Ricki. A maidenly gesture if ever he'd seen one.

"Can't be much of a marriage," Ricki said blithely. "Given that Ben King's lame and spends most of his nights in the Maverick."

Jesse turned to meet her gaze. "That a fact?"

"As the town's new marshal, you'll no doubt be meeting Ben King in person real soon."

"How long have the Kings lived in Boulder Springs?"

"Not long. Three, four months, maybe. Showed up after old Dan King drank hisself to death, claiming to be his kin.

Moved into his shack on the edge of town." Ricki shuddered. "I gotta hand it to the gal. Word is she's one hard worker. Got to be, I guess, saddled with a shiftless husband."

Jesse laid an affectionate arm across Ricki's shoulders. "Have I told you yet how stunning you look?"

Ricki managed a fretful pout. "Not yet. And I had this frock made special."

"You're more beautiful now than the day I first laid eyes on you."

Ricki tapped his chest with her folded fan. "Twenty years ago. And even if you're too polite to remind me of time passing by, I do own a looking glass."

Jesse laughed. "Twenty years. Has it really been that long?"

"You were the randiest fifteen-year-old boy I ever met. Even if your ma was my best friend." Her voice dropped. "She never found out about us, did she?"

Jesse shook his head. "She died without suspecting a thing."

Ricki blew out a breath. "That's good. Now, I've made arrangements for you to stay in the boardinghouse closest to your office, like you asked. Fetch your bag like a good boy and I'll walk down there with you."

"Yes'm," Jesse said with a mock salute. "While we walk you can fill me in about this gang of outlaws that's stirring folks up in these parts."

"Don't you expect the mayor'd be the one doing that?"

"I'm willing to bet your sources are a sight more reliable than anyone else's in town."

"I declare, Jesse Quantrill, you've gotten more cunning as you've grown."

"Got to, if a body wants to stay alive."

When Anora glanced over her shoulder, she saw the new marshal and that woman locked in conversation, their heads near about touching. Observing the way he bent attentively over Richelle, Anora felt a momentary twinge of envy. Imagine having a man look at you as if you actually had something to say worth listening to, hanging on your every word that way. Even Ben, who at one time had minded what she said, went his own way now that they were established in Boulder Springs. She knew he was drinking more than was good for him, even if the liquor did help dull the pain of his childhood injury. She just had to get enough money to send him to those special doctors.

The door to the general store stood open and she stepped inside, out of the noonday sun. The blinds were half-drawn to help keep the interior cool. The store was crowded the way it tended to be after the train came through, on account of Lettie was also the town's postmistress. And just about the sweetest woman Anora had ever met.

Anora made her way through the cluttered shop, careful not to knock anything with her basket. The smell of freshly ground coffee and cinnamon wafted through the crowd as she approached the counter to purchase some rice and tea.

"Did you see him?" Lettie asked with a bawdy wink.

"See who?" Anora peered inside her money pouch, pretending she had no idea who Lettie meant.

"The new marshal. Jesse Quantrill. Came all the way from Philadelphia. Retired, he was, with a spotless reputation. This here town won't know what hit it."

"I wonder what prompted him out of retirement," she said innocently.

"Sweetcheeks, that ain't no secret. Him and Richelle are old, old friends."

"I guess she won't be worried about him closing her down then," Anora said.

Lettie shot her a sharp look, and Anora squirmed beneath that knowing gaze. "That don't sound like the gutsy young woman who marched in here, cocky as you please. The one who convinced me and Sam to let her have supplies on credit so's she could make up lunch packets for the train passengers. Didn't I hear you say a woman has a right and a responsibility to provide for herself the best way she knows how?"

Anora flushed. Lettie was right. Could it be she was jealous of the attention she'd seen the new marshal pay to Richelle?

"Richelle's just doing the same. Woman has a heart of gold under all that rouge and kohl she wears." Deftly Lettie weighed out a scoop of rice and a handful of tea leaves, each of which she wrapped in brown paper and tied with string.

"You're right," Anora said quickly. "How much do I owe you?"

"You got any sandwiches left?" Lettie asked.

"Six," Anora admitted.

Lettie held out her hand. "Let me have them."

"Lettie, you don't have to." Anora reached into her basket and passed over the foodstuffs reluctantly.

"Anyone says I do? More than likely some old boy will wander in later and buy them. If not, I'll just feed them to Sam for dinner tonight. It's too hot to cook, anyway."

Anora dug into her money pouch. "I want to pay some on my account." She passed Lettie a handful of coins, most of the money she'd taken in today.

Lettie looked Anora square in the eye. "Ben was in

earlier. Bought some tobacco and some beef jerky and some other stuff. Put it on your account."

Anora's heart grew heavy. Some days Ben acted as if money grew on trees here in Boulder Springs, running up her tab with Lettie faster than she could pay it off.

She returned Lettie's level look. "That's fine. I told you before. Whatever he needs, just put it on my account."

"I heard you," Lettie grumbled, picking up a rag and rubbing at an imaginary speck of grit on her spotless counter. After a surreptitious glance over her shoulder to where Sam was busy with several customers, she leaned toward Anora. "We both know who brings in the money. And who spends it. Just you say the word and—"

"I won't hear of it," Anora said briskly. "A man has needs."

Lettie compressed her lips into a thin line, her look implying she thought she knew exactly what Ben needed, and it wasn't stocked in her store. "Mollycoddling ain't never turned no boy into a man." Her look softened on Anora, and she changed the subject. "Penny down to the station checking out his nibs?"

Anora smiled as she gathered up her purchases. "Yes, she was there."

Lettie shook her head. "I declare. That girl is just itching to get herself hitched. You might consider having a friendly word with her."

Anora fumbled the rice. "Me? Have a talk with her? What about?"

"Marriage. You know. Woman to woman."

Anora blanched, wondering what her new friends would say if they were to learn the truth. "Why, I wouldn't know what to say."

"Honey," drawled a whiskey-smooth female voice from

behind her. "You're the first woman I ever heard make such a claim. Ask any woman about being married and usually you can't shut her up."

Anora spun around, purchases clutched to her chest, belatedly aware the store had grown unusually silent with the arrival of the infamous Richelle, new marshal in tow.

Seemingly unaware of the stir she was causing, Richelle addressed Lettie.

"Lettie, this here is Jesse Quantrill. The man who'll be putting a little law and order back into these parts."

" 'Bout time someone did," Lettie said. Raising her voice, she called, "Sam, get your sorry hide over here and say how-d'you-do to the new marshal."

As Lettie's husband Sam approached, Anora tried unsuccessfully to sidle unnoticed past the gathering crowd. "Mrs. King," Richelle said. "Don't go yet. Jesse was just saying he was a tad peckish. I expect one of your famous sandwiches'd hit the spot."

Anora's tongue stuck to the roof of her mouth. She tried to point to Lettie, but the packet of tea slid from her grasp. When she bent down to pick it up, the marshal beat her to it and her head bumped into his as he straightened.

"Sorry," Anora stammered, aware her face was redder than Richelle's gown.

"No harm done," Jesse said, passing her the tea. His lean brown fingers brushed her open palm in a way that set a couple of dozen butterflies batting about her insides. Lord, what a smile the man had. And his eyes. He had a way of looking clear through a body, leaving Anora with the uncomfortable feeling that in a few intense seconds he'd unearthed every one of her carefully guarded secrets and ferreted out a few new ones besides.

As Jesse's eyes remained on Anora she felt a wave of heat

creep up her neck. Beneath her bonnet her ears were burning.

"Marshal Quantrill, meet Mrs. King," Richelle said pointedly.

"A pleasure," he said, clasping her hand, tea and all in both his hands. "Ricki tells me you live on the outskirts of town. Any problems out your way with Rosco and his boys?"

"No, sir."

"You let me know if that changes, you understand? 'Cause I hear tell they've rustled cattle from several of your neighbors."

"Don't have much in the way of livestock at Three Boulders," Anora said. "So I guess they won't be coming around bothering us none."

"Never can tell what a group like that will do," he said, releasing her hand and turning his attention to Lettie and Sam. Packages clutched tight, Anora pushed her way through the crowded store, feeling a deep abiding sense of having narrowly escaped. Escaped from what, she hadn't the faintest idea.

Get your copy of *Anora's Pride* today or keep reading to see more books by Kathleen.

Mail Order Olivia

Mail Order Rachel

Mail Order Martina

A Bride for Shane

A Bride for Riley

A Bride for Weston

Mail Order Noelle

Chelsea's Choice

## Sweet Contemporary Romance

Blue Sky Island

One Cinderella Spring

One Stolen Summer

One Fantasy Fall

One Wondrous Winter

## Sweet Christmas Romance Novellas

Holly's Wish

No Groom at the Inn

## Steamy Historical Romance

Taboo

Unmasked

## Steamy Contemporary Romance
## SECRET SEDUCTIONS

Her Untamed Cowboy - Book 1

Her Undercover Cowboy - Book 2

Her Unwilling Cowboy - Book 3

Who Needs a Cowboy! - Book 4

Intimate Strangers

**Women's Fiction**

Fabulous at Fifty

**Romantic Suspense**

Final Heat

Afterburn

For a complete book list visit KathleenLawless.com

To be the first to hear about Kathleen's new releases, special fan pricing sales, and also receive a free book, sign up for her VIP Reader Newsletter at http://eepurl.com/bVosbI

# ABOUT THE AUTHOR

USA Today Bestselling Author, Kathleen Lawless, blames a misspent youth watching Rawhide, Maverick and Bonanza for her fascination with cowboys, which doesn't stop her from creating a wide variety of interests and occupations for her many alpha male heroes.

With well over 40 published novels to her credit, she enjoys pushing the boundaries of traditional romance into historical romance, contemporary romance, romantic suspense and women's fiction. and stories for young adults.

She makes her home in the Pacific Northwest and loves to hear from her readers.

Sign up for Kathleen's VIP Reader Newsletter to receive updates, special giveaways and fan-priced offers. http:// eepurl.com/bVosb1

Website: KathleenLawless.com
Twitter: twitter.com/kathleenlawless
Facebook: facebook.com/kathleenlawlessnovels
Instagram: instagram.com/kathleenlawless